Evil
Within

ELAINA COLASANTE

DEDICATION

This book is dedicated to my father, John Colasante. Dad, you were taken away from me far too soon. I love you and miss you more than you could possibly know.

ACKNOWLEDGMENTS

I want to thank Paul Cassidy for taking the time to assist with whatever needed to be done. Your famous line to me is, "Just point me in the direction I'm supposed to go in…" There are no words to express my undying gratitude to you for all that you have done and continue to do to support me in all my endeavors! Paul Cassidy is responsible for the awesome photo of me and he collaborated with me on the cover for my novel. A big thank you!

A heartfelt thanks to my dear and loyal friend who morphed into my editor. Together we discovered a deeper appreciation for the power of words…I consider myself extremely blessed to have your support and dedication. Thank you for believing in me and my abilities.

To contact Paul Cassidy

pbc.create@gmail.com

Tracy,

It was a pleasure
meeting you and I would
love to get to know you better!
Thank you for supporting me!

Evil
Within

❦

Blessings,
Elaina Colasanti
2014

PROLOGUE

THE RAIN POUNDED AGAINST THE WINDOWS as the wind thrashed out into the eeriness of the night. There was a menacing darkness as the storm raged, showing no signs of relenting. She leaned against the window and felt the cold air from the outside seep through the glass and into every pore of her body. Staring out the window, she watched the storm build. Grey clouds drifted over the ocean while the waves smashed savagely against the rocks, showing no mercy.

She jumped back as the storm picked up force while thunder and lightning seared through the heavy darkness. She tripped over the front leg of the antique mahogany chair by the edge of the window, gripping the arm with both hands.

Any other time she would have found this "little trip" amusing, and laugh at herself, but now all it did was bring about a fresh flow of tears. Not fully trusting her coordination, she took baby steps to where bursts of ruby orange flames crackled in the fireplace on the opposite side of the tiny room.

As the warmth caressed her body, she gazed into the roaring embers and saw flashes of her life gradually emerge and play out like a theatrical production. When the visions faded, she turned and walked back to the chair by the window to sit. Suddenly, a cold chill swept through her body. Leaning forward, she reached for the cozy striped blanket draped on the edge of the bed. She sat back as she pulled the warmth into her body and snuggled. A heavy sigh escaped her throat as she closed her eyes and allowed her mind to wander. Murphy's Law--whatever could happen, would happen--usually did to her, and whatever came down always crashed right into her.

She thought back to the day when out of sheer desperation she went to her church and banged on the convent door. An elderly nun, wearing the ancient habit of days long gone by, flung open the door. Her face was heavily creased with deep unforgiving lines, and was

1

sunburned from far too many hours in the sun—doing just what, the young woman didn't want to know. The nun stood no more than 5'2", and the young woman was reminded of her deceased grandmother and silently vowed, wouldn't ask.

When the sister spoke, the young woman detected an Irish accent. "Good morning, young lady. What can I do for you today?"

"I was wondering if you could spare a few moments for me."

"Well now, I think I can do that for such a sweet looking thing. Come in, come in."

"Thank you, Sister."

"Please call me Sister Mary. And you are...?"

"Charlie."

Sister Mary stared at Charlie, waiting for her to finish.

When it was apparent that Charlie wasn't going to offer her last name, Sister Mary shrugged her tiny shoulders and smiled.

"All right, Charlie, let us go into the sitting room where we can have some privacy."

Charlie followed Sister Mary down the narrow corridor that was filled with religious paintings of Jesus and Mary, and thought how she looked and waddled like a penguin. Sister Mary turned left, and motioned for Charlie to follow.

"Have a seat, my dear, and make yourself comfortable." Charlie settled on a deep red wingback chair, stretching her lean legs out in front of her. Sister Mary quietly closed the door. Sister Mary's steps were slow and deliberate, buying her some time to steal a few quick sidelong glances at her mysterious visitor.

She sat opposite Charlie on a faded orange couch that was so worn, even her tiny frame sank down just inches from the faded linoleum floor. Once settled, Sister Mary waited...then waited some more.

She didn't know why, but this young woman intrigued her. She was quite the beauty, Sister Mary thought, but sad—yes, very, very sad.

Fidgeting in her chair, Charlie noticed the sparsely furnished room for the first time since entering. The only other piece of furniture was an old wooden desk that looked like it had seen better days. There was a rusty steel chair behind it, and when Charlie looked up, she noticed cracks that ran rampant over the white plaster walls of the room. There were no paintings or ornamentations adorning the walls, and she assessed that the atmosphere could be improved with a little elbow grease and paint. Not knowing where to begin Charlie looked down, clenching and unclenching her fists in her lap.

Noticing her discomfort, Sister Mary said, in her most soothing voice, "Now, Charlie, I find it's always best to start at the beginning. Don't worry about rambling, because sooner or later you'll get to the point."

Charlie slowly lifted her head and met Sister Mary's gaze. Her green eyes sparkled like rare emeralds and Charlie felt all the tension ease from the muscles and joints in her body.

"Well, okay. You see, it all started the day I met my husband, Darrell Farake..."

CHAPTER 1

SUNLIGHT STREAMED THROUGH THE BAY window, highlighting the red undertones in her chestnut hair. Slowly, she emerged from her slumber, her dark, thick lashes fluttering open. She let out a long yawn. Arching her back, she stretched, working out the kinks in her body. She had fallen asleep in the chair by the window, and remembered having vivid dreams throughout the night. She got up and glanced out the window, shielding her eyes from the intensity of the sunlight that engulfed the tiny room. A small smile formed at the corners of her mouth. It was a new day filled with hope and promise. Jumping up, she haphazardly threw the warm blanket off to the side and ran to the simple but elegantly appointed bathroom, and took a quick shower.

She couldn't wait to go and sit by the beach and soak up the glorious sun. Feeling refreshed, she put on her new swimsuit, grabbed the beach towel and book she had packed, and headed for the door.

The storm from the previous night left the air smelling fresh and crisp. She smiled as she watched some sandpipers and seagulls scurry along the shore line, searching for their breakfast. A warm breeze caressed her body, whisking her long curls into an alluring dance around her face as she laid her things down on the sand. Oh, how she loved Narragansett Beach. She had been coming here since she was a child, and after all these years, still felt the same exhilaration. The grey stone wall wrapped itself around the outer edge of the coastline, protecting the spectacular homes from any harm. This was a distinguished landmark, known not only to native Rhode Islanders, but to thousands of tourists as well. People traveled hundreds of miles to come and sit on the famous stone wall. It was a showplace during the summer months, where thousands would flock to show off their sleek bodies, or their new Harleys. Growing up, it was her ritual that she and her friends would go to Iggy's and get what they knew were the best clam cakes and chowder around. They would bring them to the stone wall, sit, and while dangling their feet over the edge, watch all the tanned and buffed bodies stroll by. She couldn't forget the drooling and laughing.

Smiling at the fond memories, she ran to the water and let out a shriek when the frigid liquid made contact with her luminous skin. A fierce wave rushed towards her, knocking her off balance and hurling her into the icy water.

DOWN THE SHORE, A TALL MAN WITH GOLDEN blond hair went unnoticed by her. He had been out for his morning walk and just happened to glance in the direction of the tiny cottage on the beach when a glorious creature emerged from the door. He stood there motionless, holding his breath.

His piercing blue eyes slowly detected every inch of her body, starting with her breasts, then lowered to her curvy hips, and finally, her shapely thighs. My God, she was exquisite. She was the most beautiful woman he had ever seen in his life, and in his sixty years he'd seen a lot of beautiful women. Yet none could match the fire and sultriness of this one. He liked that she had some meat on her, too. Too many women walked around like they were living skeletons. In his opinion, that was definitely not sexy.

He closed his eyes and listened to the wind swirl off the water. When he opened them, he took in all the different shapes and sizes of the fluffy white clouds floating in the sky, and smiled. His smile turned into a wide grin as he saw the waves pull the woman under, and he laughed when she came up shrieking and giggling with the innocence of a child. He felt something shift deep inside him. Whatever it was, he hadn't felt it for a very long time.

She glanced his way and saw him watching her. God, he felt like an idiot! Forcing his legs to move he slowly started walking towards her. With each step in her direction, he contemplated turning around, but knew he would look foolish if he did, so instead he confidently strode towards this extraordinary woman.

⧯⋙⋘⧯

CHARLIE SURFACED FROM THE WATER, STUMBLING and laughing. She swept the mass of tangled hair from her face. When she was safely on solid ground, she glanced down the beach and saw a man who looked like a mighty warrior watching her.

He was tall and muscular, with blond hair that glistened as the sun danced down upon it. She couldn't make out the color of his eyes, because he was still too far away, but assumed they were some shade of blue to blend with the light hair and fair skin.

With avid curiosity, she openly watched him stride towards her, noting that every movement he made was smooth and elegant. Her heart started to pound wildly, and every hair on her arms stood up straight as as he approached her. The vision she saw coming closer took her breath away. As she worked to restore her labored breathing she contemplated turning and running. She determined such a retreat would be infantile, and did the next best thing. She froze, grounded to the spot where she stood, and simply waited.

⧯⋙⋘⧯

THE CLOSER HE GOT TO HER, THE MORE radiant she became. Droplets of water glistened over her olive complexion, and her bathing suit fit like a second skin--well molded to the contours of her voluptuous body. His heart pounded in his chest and his throat constricted when his eyes met her huge, sparkling chocolate eyes.

Usually he was fluent in his speech, but now, so entranced, when he attempted to open his mouth and say something breezy to her, he found he couldn't. He noticed a gleam of mischievousness in those eyes. A smile tugged at the corners of her alluring mouth and he fought to control the panic that welled up inside him.

She sauntered right up to him, stood there, and dazzled him with a flash of her pearly smile. He was more than warm now, he was on fire as desire surged through him. He wanted her, and he didn't know who the bloody hell she was! Her eyes were soft, her face flushed from the heat of the sun. Then she seductively, and in the huskiest, most sensual voice he had ever heard, said, "Hi, beautiful day, isn't it?"

He just stood there gaping at her. His mouth was bone dry, and his vocal cords were M.I.A.. When she tilted her head to one side and smiled at him, he thought he would swallow his tongue. He opened his mouth, then closed it again.

She looked at him now, her eyes wide and bewildered. "Are you alright?"

"Hmm? Uh, yes, I'm fine thank you, and me?"

Her rich, deep laughter exploded into the breezy air. Robert noticed her biting the inside of her cheek. This maneuver told him she was trying to keep a straight face.

"I don't mean to pry, but did you by any chance have a few cocktails this morning?"

He was totally mortified, and felt like a jackass! He wanted to bury his head in the sand and suffocate himself! His mind raced to say something that would save face, but when he spoke, nothing remotely close to charming or clever emerged .

"No. No! I don't drink in the mornings, only the evenings! I mean....."

Completely losing it now, she replied, "Oh, well now, that's comforting to know."

He had crashed and burned, and knew it was time to leave before he swallowed both his feet!

She gazed into his captivating blue eyes and noted the palpable strain between them.

"Well, I guess I'd better get going. It was a pleasure meeting you."

He didn't want her to leave--not yet, anyway. Intrigued by this woman, he desperately searched for something to say to make her stay.

"What's your name?"

"Excuse me?"

"Your name, silly...we haven't been properly introduced. I'm Robert."

She extended her hand, and when her skin made contact with his, he felt like he would explode right there on the sand. He didn't realize that he had tightened his hold on her as he spoke.

"Yes, that's it, Robert Fordes."

"Well, Mr. Fordes, it's a pleasure to meet you."

Amusement glittered in her dark eyes as a small chuckle escaped her throat. He quizzically arched a blond eyebrow. "Ah, Robert?"

"Yes, Charlie?"

"You can let go of my hand now."

"Oh, God, I'm sorry, I wasn't thinking... I didn't realize...."

"It's okay. Really."

He was by far the most handsome man she had ever seen and in her fifty-three years she had seen many, but this one far surpassed all her expectations.

Robert nodded, clearly distracted, and looked off into space, his eyes narrowed in deep thought.

He noticed that she shifted her weight. He knew it was time to end the uncomfortable situation. "Well, I guess I should be going now."

"Right. Of course. Take care, Robert."

"I will. Goodbye."

"Bye."

She turned and headed for her towel. He stood there, frozen, his legs heavy weights sinking deep into the sand as he watched her bend over, pick up her things, and head for the cottage. She never glanced back, and within moments, the beautiful vision was nothing but a mere memory in his mind's eye.

CHAPTER 2

ONCE IN THE SAFETY OF THE TINY COTTAGE, she exhaled. She hadn't realized she was holding her breath. Her legs were weak, and her heart pounded fiercely. She walked to the window that faced the beach and looked out to see if Robert was still there. She saw him turn and head back down the shoreline, kicking the sand with his bare feet, his shoulders sagging.

My God, what the hell was that, she thought? Never before had she had such a strange encounter. The man was clearly perplexed about something. It showed in his eyes. Those eyes-they were magnificent. Charlie waited until Robert was out of sight before heading back out again. This time, when she placed the towel on the glimmering sand, she plopped down on it. She closed her eyes and replayed the morning's events in her mind, trying to make sense of it all. Images of Robert Fordes played out in her mind's eye--his elegant stride, head held high, and that body--lean and muscular, not an ounce of fat anywhere. His face, now that's what really got her attention. He looked to be in his late forties, early fifties, but she couldn't be sure. Looks were deceiving, sometimes. There were deep lines etched around his eyes and forehead, but they weren't laugh lines. The creases curved downward on that glorious face from years of frowning, not smiling. Well, Mr. Fordes, it was definitely interesting meeting you.

She rolled onto her stomach, placed her head in the palms of her hands, and wondered if she would ever see him again. Did he live nearby? Was he married? What did he do for work? She reprimanded herself to stop being foolish--she would never see him again. It was for the best, anyway. Her wounds were still open and raw, and she knew it would take time for them to fully heal.

That was one of the reasons why she had driven to the state line and sought solace at the church. It was a blessing that she had met

Sister Mary and was able to communicate her fears to her. She needed to get everything off her chest. She needed a confidante who would not pass judgment, or, more importantly, know her, and Sister Mary fit the bill. Suddenly, fatigue engulfed her entire body. Before she even realized what was happening, she fell into a deep sleep. The last thought that registered in her consciousness was that she needed to release the demons once and for all.

CHAPTER 3

HIS NAME WAS DARRELL FARAKE. HE MOVED to the United States from Syria five years earlier. How she loved him with every fiber of her being. He was tall, dark, and handsome with a thick mustache that adorned his top lip. His hair was thick with unruly curls, and when he smiled, one saw straight white teeth. His milk chocolate eyes would sparkle when happy, and turn to cold, calculating ice when angered. They dated for over a year, but it wasn't until after they were married that the bizarre episodes, aloofness, and cheating, started.

She awoke one night, crying, and clutched her hand to her heart as she sprang up in bed. It was empty next to her. Darrell wasn't home-- again. Something was wrong, she knew it. Her heart felt a sharp knife plunge into it and twist. Heavy beads of sweat trickled down her brows, her breath expelled in small spurts. It wasn't a feeling anyone could put into words. A woman just knows. Her husband was cheating on her, and they had been married less than five months.

After that horrifying evening, everything quickly unraveled between them. She felt helpless, and didn't know what to do. When she couldn't take the isolation and loneliness any longer, she confronted him. He was good with his words. He gave her dozens of reasonable excuses for his actions, but that's all they were—excuses, not the truth. He tried to justify his actions with them, but refused to take responsibility for the irreparable damage they had caused.

She kept pushing him for answers...there was no stopping her now. She was hysterical, and had lost any and all sense of composure.

Screaming like a mad woman, she demanded, "I want to know why, damn it! TELL ME WHY!"

Not accustomed to having a woman demand answers or raise her voice to him, he snapped. In his country, if a woman showed disrespect to her husband, he would simply beat her according to

11

what he felt was her level of disrespect.

Unfortunately for him, now was not the right time to teach her how a wife should properly behave towards her husband. Yes, for now, he would simply try to explain to her... make her understand the way it was to be between them. Then later, when the moment was right, he would teach her the art of the submission and respect due a husband..

"All right, you want the truth? I'll tell you the truth! In my country it is customary for a man to have more than one wife, or to even date other women while married!"

The weight of his revelation was a punch first in the gut, then right smack between her eyes--or at least that's what it felt like. The pain was unbearable as she fought to gain control of herself. When she was finally able to speak, her words came rushing out.

"What do you mean, 'date other women or have more than one wife?' You never mentioned any of this to me while we were dating! You're crazy if you think I'm going to stand idly by and allow you to court or wed another woman! Bigamy isn't allowed in this country, you idiot!"

Her brain clicked into overdrive. Questions.... she had asked so many questions while they were dating, but he always avoided answering them! She remembered now that every time she asked or inquired about his religion or homeland he would answer her with yet another question, and then change the subject altogether. How could she have been so stupid? She had made a drastic decision, and knew she couldn't turn back now. In her mind, she had deliberated over her situation, and finally concluded that she deserved more. She refused to be one of those women who "settled." She deserved a husband who would be faithful and honest with her. It occurred to her that she really knew nothing about her husband. She was married to a total stranger! Charlie recalled how weariness overcame her as she looked him directly in his eyes and said, "I can't handle this charade any longer, Darrell."

Darrell, not knowing if he had heard his wife correctly, lowered his voice so that it took on a menacing quality, and asked, "What did you just say to me?"

Charlie felt her frustration rise to new heights at the icy tone of his voice. She curled her hands into fists. The pain... there was pain everywhere, her head, legs, arms...

"The charade, Darrell... the fucking charade I've been living! I thought I married a man who loved me, who was going to build and share a life with me! Obviously, that's not the case. I want a divorce. It's over between us."

Darrell's thoughts ran rampant, he couldn't believe what he was hearing! Women weren't allowed to leave, let alone divorce, their husbands! A woman was only allowed a divorce if the husband clapped his hands together three times and said, "I divorce thee, I divorce thee, I divorce thee!" No wonder this idiotic country had so many problems! Women were allowed to speak! Inhaling deeply, he fought to gain control over the dangerous emotions that flowed through him. He had been highly educated in his country on every form of law in the United States. He took every course he could, and knew if he wanted, he could take the bar exam here and pass with flying colors. He knew she could file for divorce on grounds of adultery and there would be nothing he could do to stop her...for now, that is.

Darrell's bored expression pushed her over the edge. There was no grief or sorrow in his eyes, just a cold aloofness.

"GET OUT, DO YOU HEAR ME! I never want to see you again! If you fight me on anything, or come within one inch of me, I'll kill you, do you understand?"

Like a thief in the night, he had come and stolen her heart, and then had carelessly tossed it aside. Locking eyes with him, she snapped. She bashed him hard across his jaw, then lifted her right leg, and with all her might, kicked into his groin.

Spewing profanities at her, he crumpled down onto the floor like a dead weight. She ran to the front door and flung it open. Her eyes were glazed and her face was chalk white.

With slow, precise movements, he got up from the floor, his steely gaze unwavering. Not saying a word, he strode out the door and never looked back. If he had, Charlie would have seen the sickening smile spread across his face.

He wouldn't contest the divorce. No, he would let the almighty US legal system take care of everything. He had other things in store for her. No one threatened him-especially a woman.

He'd let her have her way for now, but silently vowed he'd make her pay when she least expected it.

As he opened his car door, his thoughts raced full speed ahead to the next step he would take…

❦

SHE CLOSED THE DOOR AND COLLAPSED ONTO the cold wooden floor. Deep sobs escaped from the depths of her soul. As she rocked back and forth, her tears and screams of rage echoed throughout the silent house. She remained rooted in that fetal position, too weak to move, and prayed for death to come and claim her.

Death didn't come, but much needed sleep did. Her last thoughts before drifting off into a restless slumber, were of her lost dreams, hopes, and aspirations for a full life with Darrell, now they dissipated like vapors in an ocean breeze.

She would never be able to give her heart to, or trust, another man again.

❦

SUNLIGHT STREAMED IN THROUGH THE windows, filling the family room with comforting warmth. Finches chirped melodic tunes as they made their nests in the oak trees that surrounded the beautiful Victorian home.

Aching and stiff, Charlie raised her head off the floor and sighed, the terror of her confrontation with Darrell still weighed heavily on her heart.. She massaged her swollen knuckles and was grateful for the few hours of sleep she had had… a brief respite from feeling the pain and anger that now surged to life with a force all their own.

She stood up, testing the strength of her legs, and hesitantly made her way to the kitchen for some desperately needed coffee. There was a deafening stillness in the house now, and it gave her an eerie feeling as she passed through the family room. She glanced at the clock on the far wall, and saw it was nine-thirty.

Walking to the edge of the kitchen counter, she picked up the phone, and dialed her lawyer's office.

"Good morning, Mr. Luca's office. How may I help you?"

The sweet soothing voice of Giorgio Luca's secretary, Jennie, brought a sad smile to her lips.

"Good morning to you, too, Jennie."

"Good morning, Charlie. What can I do for you today?"

"I need to speak to Giorgio, please. Is he in?"

"Yes, he is. Hold on, and I'll buzz you through."

"Thanks."

While she waited, she unconsciously gripped the phone cord, and wound it around her fingers. She gripped it with such fierceness that her knuckles turned white. She didn't realize what she was doing until the base of the phone lifted off the counter.

Unraveling the cord, she sighed and gulped down the threat of a fresh wave of tears. Finally, she heard the voice she had been waiting for, and let out a sigh.

"Charlie! How are you?"

"I've been better, my friend. I need you to do something for me right away, if you have the time."

"Oh, my God... what's wrong, Charlie? You sound terrible."

Her voice cracked a hair when she replied, "I need you to file divorce papers for me. I want you to file under adultery, and I want it done today if possible."

"Oh, Christ, Charlie, I'm so sorry. That bastard! As soon as we hang up I'll file, set the paperwork in motion to freeze all accounts for you, and offer him nothing but the friggin' clothes on his back. What else do you want me to do?"

"Nothing, I'll handle the rest."

"Charlie, I know this is a stupid thing to ask, but are you alright? I mean, do you want to talk about it?"

"No! I don't. I..."

Not wanting to push her, Giorgio said, "I'll need you to swing by the office in an hour or so, so you can the sign the necessary paperwork. I'll be in family court all afternoon, so I'll file while I'm there. Then I'll call the bastard's lawyer and set up a meeting for tomorrow. I'll call you with the details."

"Thanks, Giorgio."

Just as she was about to hang up, she heard his deep voice again.

"Charlie?"

"Yes?"

"Please take care of yourself, and if you need anything...

anything at all, all you have to do is ask. Understood?"

"Understood. I'll wait to hear from you... and thanks again." With that said, she placed the receiver down on its cradle. A suppressed sea of emotion overcame her, and she finally opened the floodgates to an ocean of tears.

CHAPTER 4

THE SOUND OF CHILDREN'S GIGGLES ROUSED her from her troubled memories. She had fallen asleep and dreamt of the past yet again. She rolled onto her back and let out a screech. Her mouth was gritty, and she knew from the throbbing pain down her backside that her skin was burnt to a crisp.

"Crap."

She didn't know how long she had been asleep, so she shielded her eyes with her hands as she located the sun's position. By her calculations, she figured it was late afternoon. Once the residual drowsiness subsided from her body, she got up, gathered her belongings, and went back to the tiny cottage.

She was leaving Narragansett in the morning, and needed to pack the few things she had brought with her.

Whenever the demons came to haunt her, she would go away somewhere, anywhere, to fight them off again. They didn't haunt her as frequently as they had in the past, but every now and then they surfaced as a constant reminder that they would always be there, ready and waiting, when she least expected them.

She had never sought professional help or felt comfortable speaking to anyone about the tragedies she had lived through. Sister Mary was the first, and would probably be the last. Her friends constantly worried about her, fearful that one day she would crack and just lose it.

During and after her divorce she uttered not a word to anyone. If people pushed, she simply left. She dealt with things in her own way, regardless of the many protests from those in her small inner circle.

She pushed the dark thoughts aside as she finished packing, then hopped in the shower, hoping it would ease the throbbing pain that ran through her back side.

Absolutely famished, she decided to try a little Italian restaurant she had spotted down the street. Spurred by her hunger, she put purpose in her steps. She was glad she had chosen to walk. It was a beautiful night. There had been no stars the previous evening, but tonight the sky teemed with thousands of tiny lights that twinkled and danced in the twilight.

She often dined alone these days and was accustomed to the stares and sidelong glances she received from people. The restaurant was quaint with no frills in the décor. The furnishings were simple and modest, but the exquisite quality of the food compensated for such a modest ambience.. She prided herself in knowing that, although Rhode Island was the smallest state in the Union, and one could drive from one end to the other in an hour's time, it was known by millions to have some of the best restaurants in the world. Her meal tonight was superb, and she was glad she had ventured out.

When Charlie returned to the tiny cottage, she went in briefly to deposit her handbag. She wanted to take a stroll by the ocean and enjoy the moonlight. Since she was a child, she had always loved Rhode Island's beaches. Though the state was small, it had endless points of interest, to offer, making it a highly sought after tourist attraction.

With the stars lighting her way, she made a few decisions. First, she was putting her home on the market. It wasn't a home, anyway, just a house, a house filled with nothing but tainted memories and sleepless nights. There were too many reminders of things that were supposed to have been, but never would be.

A small crest of peace washed through her as she realized that it was here in Narragansett, by the ocean, where she now belonged.

The second decision she made was to follow her friend Nadine's advice and start a new venture. It was time to begin a new enterprise. The only problem was that Nadine had neglected to reveal just what this bold endeavor was to be. Nadine had only declared that Charlie needed to have some excitement in her life, and as her dearest friend, she knew the perfect business venture to provide just that.

Nadine was well known for her hair-brained schemes, which more often than not landed both of them in some pretty precarious situations. Whatever the new venture was, Charlie knew she'd be the brains and brass behind it.

CHAPTER 5

NADINE'S VIVID BLUES EYES SPARKLED WITH mischief as she leaned on the kitchen table, clutching her mug of coffee. Charlie was no stranger to that "look," and held her breath as she anxiously waited to hear her best friend's latest scheme.

As far as appearances went, they were total opposites. Nadine was 5'11", with blue eyes that gleamed like diamonds against her creamy complexion. Her blond hair was short and styled to frame her face, accenting her high cheek bones.

A common denominator for them was their unique beauty, but as far as brain power went, Charlie raked her confidante over the coals. Nadine at best was a nitwit, a loving, kind one, but a nitwit nonetheless.

A smile tugged at the corners of Charlie's mouth as the nickname she appropriately gave Nadine flowed through her thoughts-- Amazon Woman. It fit her to a tee.

Nadine flashed one of her blinding smiles at Charlie as she lifted her Snoopy mug to her mouth and took a huge gulp. The steamy liquid ran down her chin and onto her white cotton blouse.

"Shit."

Jumping from her chair, Nadine ran to the sink and grabbed a towel to blot the stain.

"See, Charlie, this is why I never wear white!"

"Mmm."

"What do you mean 'Mmm'? What's that supposed to mean?"

Stifling a laugh, Charlie asked, "Did you eat this morning?"

"Why?"

"Because I can see one of your fits coming on which tells me that you haven't had your usual four course breakfast, that's why."

Nadine ate from the time she got up straight through until she went to bed.

Charlie, on the other hand, forgot to eat.

"Well, it just so happens that I haven't."

"I'll tell you what. Let's go get a big breakfast and you can fill me in on this latest venture you'd like me to embark upon with you, okay?"

Thrilled at the prospect of having a big breakfast, Nadine forgot about the stain on her blouse, and bolted for the door, yelling behind her, "Let's go!"

They got into Nadine's shiny red convertible.

"It's a beautiful day, Nad! Put the top down!"

The wind tossed their hair freely about while the sun beat down on their faces. They were quiet for most of the ride, which didn't bother them; they were used to each other's moods and ways.

They rode together in amicable silence, each lost in their own thoughts, until Nadine turned onto a side street and slammed on the brakes, bringing the car to a complete stop. Charlie hurtled into the dashboard, and Nadine, into the steering column.

"Cripes! Nadine, what's wrong with you?"

Nadine jerked the car to the right, brushing both tires along the cement curb, and shut the car off.

"Well, there goes another set of hubcaps, Nadine. How many have you gone through now?"

"Shut up, Charlie, and listen, okay?"

"Uh oh, I have an uneasy feeling right now, Nad. This can only mean one thing."

"Which is...?" Nadine asked, with just a touch of sarcasm.

"Trouble, I smell trouble. Out with it, and now! I'm not waiting any longer!"

"Okay, okay."

Charlie, held her breath, and waited.

"The new venture is that you and I become Private Investigators! We'll fight crime together and actually get paid to get into mischief and spy on people--which is what we basically do now, only we don't get paid for doing it! So what do you think, great idea, right?"

"Oh, my God," was all Charlie could muster.

She turned in her seat, mouth agape. In the past, Nadine had told Charlie that her life was pathetic—she needed to get out more. So to kill time, they did spy on people, and did get into their share of mischief. But to do it for a living was another story altogether.

"Um, Nad, don't we need training and licenses and guns for this occupation?"

"Yes, we do, but look!"

Charlie's gaze followed Nadine's finger, which pointed off to the right behind them.

"Charlie! It's a detective agency! This is definitely a sign from above. I know it--I just know it!" Nadine firmly believed that everything that happened in her life, whether good or bad, was a sign from above.

Before she could reply, Nadine started the car and backed it up once again, grinding both tires alongside the cement curb. Putting the car in drive, she pulled into the parking lot, and slid between two vehicles, almost sideswiping one of them.

"Nadine, I'll need a frigging can opener to get out! Back out and find another space. Where did you learn how to drive, anyway?"

"Oh, stop complaining, will you? You should be thanking me."

"Mmm."

"Charlie, you know I love you like a sister, but I really hate it when you do that."

"Do what?"

"Mmm! It drives me crazy."

"Nad?"

"Yeah?"

"I think you are crazy. I think some of the wires in your brain have shorted out."

"You know something, Charlie, it's time for some hard love right now!"

Charlie leaned her head back against the seat, closed her eyes, and sighed. She knew all too well what was coming now. Whenever Nadine told her it was "hard love time," a long story with no point usually followed.

"Look. I'm going to give it to you straight, okay? You've been through hell. I won't deny that, but look what's happened to you, damn it! There's no more fire or sense of adventure left in you! You don't trust anyone, you don't go out, and you've written off all your friends except for me. You don't even see your family anymore!"

"What family, Nad?"

"Okay, forget about that... for now."

Before Nadine could go on, Charlie raised her hand to stop her, and interjected, "I don't see my family because they are dysfunctional idiots!"

Rolling her eyes, Nadine continued, "I'm going to give you a piece of your own advice right now, Charlie. Life's the balls-we just have to find 'em to grab 'em!"

A wide grin spread across Charlie's face as tears streamed down her cheeks. Turning her head to look at her friend, she nodded. Her voice was hoarse with emotion when she finally replied, "I said that, huh?"

"Yes, you did, my friend. Charlie, you used to be so full of life and laughter. I desperately want to see that again."

She couldn't believe it, but this was the first time Nadine actually made a point, and it was a good one.

Sighing, Charlie said, "Well?"

"Well, what?"

"Are you going to move this car to another space so I can open my door and actually be able to get out of the car, or what?"

"Why do you do that?"

"Do what?"

"Ramble on and on.... All you had to say was move the frigging car so I can get out, instead of all this 'actually be able to' crap?"

"Oh! Is that what I really sound like?"

"Yes, Miss Britannica, in actuality, when you ramble on like that, you do!"

"Touché! Now start this friggin' thing up and move it!"

It took Nadine forever to back the car out; she said she wasn't good at judging spaces. Once they were safely at the end of the lot, they got out of the car.

"Nadine, do me a favor, please?"

"Sure, what?"

"When we get inside, promise me that no matter how

nervous you get you won't do the high wire thing, or I'm running for dear life, got it?"

"Got it!"

As they approached the side door, Nadine's thoughts ran rampant. She couldn't help but feel guilty for what she was doing. She kept telling herself that it was for Charlie's own good. The only problem was whether Charlie would see it the same way. Nadine loved her friend very much and felt the need to push her into something...

anything! She hoped that if Charlie had a new job, it would soften the blow for when she told her she was leaving. She had received a phone call from her former workplace last week and was offered a new job in New York.

She would be a fool to refuse. The problem was she felt guilty because she was deceiving her best friend by prolonging this farce. Nadine knew she had no intention of becoming a Private Investigator, but before she left, she had to make sure that her beloved friend had something new and exciting to occupy her time and mind.

Nadine just hoped that Charlie would see her deception as a gesture of love.

CHAPTER 6

THEY ENTERED THROUGH A SIDE DOOR AND into an extremely sterile environment filled with chrome and glass. Leaning close to Charlie, Nadine whispered, "Charlie, it smells like disinfectant in here."

Charlie, more interested in her surroundings, mumbled, "Maybe they're overly concerned with hygiene."

Stopping in mid stride, Charlie faced Nadine and asked the million dollar question.

"So what do you propose we do now?"

"I don't know, follow the yellow brick road, and see where it leads us."

"Great. You go first; I'll follow."

Face turning red, Nadine blurted out, "Why me?"

Charlie, purely for theatrical purposes, slowly swiped her hand across her right cheek, then her left.

"Because this was your idea, not mine, remember?"

"Okay, okay... sorry about the spray."

Charlie silently nodded as Nadine hesitantly made her way down the curved hallway. Charlie followed close behind, all the while biting the inside of her left cheek, hoping it would help hold in the laughter that threatened to explode. There were closed doors on each side of the corridor, and curiosity got the better of Charlie. She opened one of the doors on her right, sneaked in, and quietly closed it.

Just as she was about to flip on the light switch to see what was inside, she heard a male voice.

"HI. CAN I HELP YOU, MISS?" CHARLIE froze inside the

23

darkened room. Where had she heard that voice before? She knew it sounded familiar to her, but couldn't place it, or the face that went with it. Nadine cleared her throat.

"Yes, I'd like to speak to the owner, please."

"I'm the owner. What can I do for you?"

"My friend and I would like some information on your agency."

The tall man arched a questioning eyebrow at Nadine as a small smile tugged at the corners of his mouth.

"You said you and your friend?"

"Yes, me and my friend."

Charlie stood in the room, rooted. She couldn't move.

Then it hit her like a fierce wave crashing into her gut--that voice-- she recognized it now, and the face that went with it! How could she have forgotten that deep, raspy voice, those magnetic blue eyes and hard lean body?

It was Robert, the same Robert she had met on the beach--she was sure of it now! My God, she felt like an idiot. She was standing in the dark, and Nadine didn't realize she was no longer standing behind her!

He blinked in confusion, "And your friend is....."

Nadine abruptly turned to include Charlie in on the conversation, and finding the hallway behind her empty, gasped. Feeling like a total idiot, Nadine said, "She was here just a moment ago. Where the heck could she have gone?"

Letting out a breezy laugh, he asked, "Does this happen often?"

Not really paying attention, Nadine managed to mumble, "What?" Where in God's name could she have gone?

Nadine's mind raced, and she felt like she was getting dizzy. Robert brought her back to the present by asking her, "Losing your friend."

"Oh...no, it doesn't happen often. Maybe she went to the ladies' room. Do you have one?"

As his smile grew wider and wider, Robert silently counted to ten, while desperately trying not to lose it in front of this woman.

"Yes, but you haven't gotten that far yet, so unless she has the ability to make herself invisible and went by you undetected, I can safely assume she's not in there."

"I am so sorry, Mr.... ah... Mr..."

"Fordes, Robert Fordes... and you are?"

"Nadine--that is--Nadine Collasponato."

Finally losing it, Robert roared, and couldn't stop laughing for a few moments. Once he collected himself, he said, "Wow, that is a mouthful!"

Feeling like a total loser, Nadine inhaled sharply, and said, "I'm sorry for wasting your time, Mr. Fordes."

"Please, call me Robert. And it's okay, things happen."

Talking more to herself than Robert, Nadine murmured, "I just don't understand... it's not like Charlie to just take off."

Robert opened his mouth then closed it again. Why did that name ring a bell? In the dark recesses of his brain he knew he had heard it recently, but couldn't remember when or where. Charlie...Charlie?

"I understand. I'll tell you what, when you do find her, feel free to come back, and I'll be happy to speak to the both of you."

"Thank you, Robert."

"If you don't mind, Nadine, I'd like to give you a piece of advice."

"No, not at all, what is it?"

Not able to hold in the laughter again, Robert gave a hearty bellow and said, "Make sure your friend Charlie walks in front of you next time, that way you won't lose her!"

She liked this man, and laughed at his advice. He turned an embarrassing situation into a humorous one. It didn't go unnoticed by her that his laughter didn't reach his eyes. Sure, they sparkled, but there was an underlying sadness there, and her heart went out to him.

"Would it be okay if Charlie and I came back tomorrow, Robert?"

"Of course, it is."

"What's better for you: morning or afternoon?"

"Probably the morning. By the afternoon I'm usually running around like a chicken without a head, if you know what I mean."

Nadine laughed. She liked his quick wit; not to mention his extremely good looks! She had a very good feeling about Mr. Fordes.

Robert's beeper went off and he excused himself.

"I'm afraid business calls, Nadine."

"No problem, and thanks again, Robert."

Nadine watched as he turned and hurried down the hallway. She pivoted, heading back the way she came, exiting out the side door to search for Charlie in the parking lot.

When she found her, she was going to wring that silky neck of hers!

❧❧❧

THERE WAS NO WAY IN HELL SHE WAS COMING back tomorrow. She paused at the door, listened, but heard nothing. Quietly, she turned the brass knob and eased the door open. Hesitantly, she stuck her head out, and glanced down the hallway. The last thing she needed was for Robert to come back and find her sneaking out of the darkened room. She closed the door behind her, ran down the corridor and out the side door. Charlie could see frustration written across Nadine's face as she paced around in small circles, calling out her name.

She ran up behind her and clasped her hand over her mouth. Nadine jerked around, faced flushed, and pushed Charlie's hand away.

"What the hell happened to you? I looked like a complete fool in there! I turned around, and presto, you were gone! Well, at least you're here now!"

Dragging Charlie by the hand, Nadine was oblivious to the panic on Charlie's face as she kept talking.

"Come on, let's go back in and see if Mr. Fordes can fit us in."

Not answering, Charlie tugged hard on Nadine's hand and started pulling her back towards where the car was parked. Finally, Nadine noticed Charlie's appearance--her breath was coming out in small spurts, her face was chalk white, and she was trembling.

"My God, Charlie, are you alright?"

Feeling like an idiot, Charlie whispered through clenched teeth, "Please, just open the door and let's get out of here."

Nadine, not wanting to argue with her, quickly unlocked the doors, and they both got in. Charlie laid her head back against the seat and closed her eyes.

"Don't ask anything Nadine, not yet. Let's go get some breakfast and then I'll fill you in, okay?"

"Sure, Charlie, no problem."

Nadine was worried for her friend. The last time she saw her look like this was when she went through her divorce. Nadine had tried talking to her but she wouldn't say a word. She hated to see Charlie suffer, and hoped this time she would open up and talk to her.

As she drove out of the parking lot, neither of them noticed Robert standing by the window in his office, frozen like a Greek statue, mouth open. watching them.

ROBERT WAS SITTING BEHIND HIS DESK WITH the phone cradled in the crook of his shoulder. He was half listening to the voice on the other end drone on endlessly about dates and times, when he glanced out the window and saw a woman dragging Nadine to a car parked at the end of the lot. Convinced he was hallucinating, he jumped up from his chair to get a better look. It was her--it had to be!

He slammed down the receiver with no explanation or goodbye to the person on the other end, and froze. My God! Nadine's friend Charlie was the same extraordinary woman he had met on the beach! Stunned, he stood there, crossed his arms over his chest, leaned a shoulder against the window watching Charlie drag Nadine to the car.

He felt himself weakening and stiffened his back as a fierce chill plunged through his body. He was losing control. His heart was pounding hard against his chest and he couldn't breathe. It felt like all the air was being sucked out of his lungs.

After the car pulled out of the lot, he retreated from the window and sank heavily into a mahogany chair. He lowered his head into the palms of his hands, closed his eyes and visualized her. He saw her standing on the shore line in front of him, her fiery brown hair slicked back from her face, the generous curves of her body, and those magnificent onyx eyes. My God, she was luminous! He didn't want to lose the vision, so he kept his eyes closed as he raised his head and leaned it back against the warmth of the leather.

The conjured memory became an erotic movie that slowly started to play out in his mind. His hands sifted through her mass of fiery curls as he placed light sensual kisses along her ear and neck. He moved his mouth to hers and kissed her deeply as his hands slowly glided down her bare skin. As he slipped his arms around her waist, a tremendous current of desire surged through him. He eased her down onto the sand and stretched himself out over her. He could feel the heat from her body mingling with his. His hands caressed her throat, shoulders, and breasts....he pressed his hot mouth on hers as excitement built within him.

He raised his head and stared down at her. "Charlie," he moaned. He fought to control the storm that flowed through his body. He wanted to be the one to give her pleasure, no one else.

His body trembled violently in the chair, snapping him back to reality. Anger and frustration replaced the warmth and desire that consumed him only moments ago.

Slamming both fists on his wooden desk, he rose and stormed out of his office. Without a word to anyone, he left the building, got into his car, and headed to his home by the ocean.

He needed a cold shower.

CHAPTER 7

NADINE SILENTLY WATCHED CHARLIE FINISH her breakfast. The color had returned to her face, her breathing was even, and the trembling was gone.

"Feeling better?"

"Much, I think I just needed to eat."

The early morning traffic had passed and left the diner quiet, with only a handful of patrons seated at the counter. Trying to lighten the mood, Nadine gave a weak laugh and said, "You really had me worried there for a minute. I thought you were kidnapped by some religious cult who wanted to make you their leader."

Charlie smiled, knowing what Nadine was trying to do. She reached over the table, grabbed her hand, and tightly squeezed. "You know, I was bursting at the seams with pride as I listened to the way you handled Mr. Fordes. You did great, Nad. You've come a long way."

"Thanks to you, Charlie-you know you're my mentor."

Nadine waited a few beats before she plunged into the issue at hand. "So, ah... do you think you can tell me what happened now?"

"Yes."

Charlie leaned back in the booth and Nadine noticed a faraway look that crept into her eyes...then her voice took on an echoing quality-like she was there, but not really. "I met Robert Fordes while I was staying at the cottage in Narragansett."

Nadine jumped forward in the booth and asked louder than she should have, "What?! How?"

"I was in the water and a wave crashed into me, knocking me under. When I surfaced and regained my balance, I glanced down the shoreline, and there he was, watching me."

"Did you speak to him?"

"Yes, we spoke."

Nadine was chomping at the bit now with excitement for her friend. "And?"

Smiling for the first time that morning, Charlie said, "I introduced myself, and he was...."

"Was what? You're killing me!"

"Well, it's hard to put into words, but he was tongue tied.

His words didn't come out the way he wanted them to, and he was embarrassed."

"My God, what the hell did you do to the poor guy to make him trip over his own tongue!"

"Nothing, that's just it, Nad. I stood there, smiled, and said 'Nice to meet you.' Then he said something like, 'thank you, nice meeting me, too.'"

Nadine was dumbfounded. Her mouth dropped open as she gaped at Charlie across the table. "Charlie, you heard him this morning--he didn't sound like the type of man who has any problem communicating with people."

"I know, and to make matters worse, I asked him if he by any chance had consumed any cocktails that morning."

Nadine, roaring now, doubled over and held her side with her hands. "You asked him what? No, no, forget that. Just tell me what he said to you."

"He said no, that he only drank in the evenings, and I told him that was comforting to know."

Nadine, overly enthusiastic for her friend, squealed, "OH, MY GOD! You're attracted to him, and that's why you disappeared this morning, isn't it?"

Whispering fiercely, Charlie said, "Lower your voice! The whole diner doesn't need to hear this broadcast!" Glancing around to make sure no one was looking, Charlie continued. "Nadine, I didn't intentionally disappear! As we were walking down the corridor, curiosity got the better of me, so I opened a door to one of the rooms and went in. Just as I was about to flip the light switch on I heard his voice and froze! When I realized it was him, I couldn't come out, because I'd look like a schmuck!"

Rolling her eyes, Nadine said, "Oh, so you let me look like the idiot who had an imaginary friend with her! Thanks."

"Hey, I already told you that you handled the situation superbly! I couldn't have done it better myself!"

"Yeah, right. So what are we going to tell Mr. Fordes tomorrow?"

"I don't know. I'm not sure that I can go back, Nad."

"Charlie, you're not backing out on me! Now level with me and tell me the real reason why you're afraid to go back."

A touch of sarcasm layered her voice when she asked, "Who said I was afraid?"

"Charlie, I know how and what makes you tick, so don't try to bullshit me, okay? Since you're not afraid, answer me this question, then."

When Nadine didn't continue, Charlie, now frustrated, asked, "okay what is it?"

"Were you attracted to Robert?"

Charlie didn't answer immediately. She thought of lying, but knew her friend would see right through her. Hesitantly, she answered, "Yes, I was, and I'll admit it scared the bloody hell out of me."

This was better than Nadine could have hoped for! Her friend was attracted to Robert! This was definitely a sign for her! A sign that she was doing the right thing for her friend! All she needed to do was keep coaxing her along. Nadine felt like exploding, but now was not the time. She was killing two birds with one stone for her friend--not only would Charlie have a new job, but a new love interest as well! It was about time.

"Hello, Earth to Nad!"

"Sorry, you were saying?"

"I'm not going there, Nadine. I'm not ready. Something did stir inside my body but to go to this man for a job feeling the way I do will only cause problems and heartache. I don't need or want either."

"I agree that you've had your share of heartache, Charlie, but you're still going with me tomorrow."

"Oh, Nadine, please don't tell me that if I don't go through with this you're not going to, either!"

"That's it, exactly! We're a team, you and I, so either we go together or we don't go at all. End of discussion. Now, let's get going. I have a million and one things I have to do today."

CHAPTER 8

EXCITEMENT AND APPREHENSION--THE TWO emotions were entwined as Charlie stood by the kitchen counter waiting for the coffee to finish brewing. She called the real estate broker and made an appointment for the following afternoon.

Her eyes scanned the interior of the big cozy kitchen. She had taken many pains in decorating it herself, and hadn't stopped until it was exactly what she had envisioned. She was more than pleased with the results. Big picture windows flowed along the entire back of the house with flower boxes filled with all her favorite blooms. The stucco walls were a buttery yellow, which provided the room with an illusion of constant sunshine. The counters were Italian marble, all her appliances stainless steel, and a long window seat lined with large colorful pillows framed the picture windows. A sad smile formed as she thought back to how she and Darrell would cuddle there, stare up at the moon and stars, and talk for hours.

Snapping back to the present, she poured her coffee and sat at the oak table by the windows. She forced herself not to be depressed. It was time she moved on with her life now, and she knew she couldn't do it in this house. She never allowed herself to think about her divorce, but the way it ended still cut deep.

As if having no control, her mind wandered back to the courthouse, located in downtown Providence, on the final day of her trial.

GIORGIO HAD DONE AN EXCELLENT JOB OF proving

all of Darrell's illegal doings and adulterous affairs, most shockingly the affair with her seventeen years old niece, but this unfortunately didn't sway the judge from ruling in Darrell's favor. Charlie recalled herself sitting next to the judge on the witness stand, answering the many irrelevant and demeaning questions the judge asked her. She knew she had to be careful and not lose her temper because this particular female judge had been labeled a woman hater throughout the courts. Her many facial expressions were those of a person slightly demented, and Charlie wondered how she had managed she stay on the bench for so long.

As she answered one inappropriate question after another, she smelled a rat, and a mighty big one. Something wasn't right, and warning flags waved inside her brain. She wasn't the bad guy here-Darrell was! Every time a question was posed to her, the judge would stop her in mid-sentence and demand she "Just answer yes or no"-when a mere yes or no wasn't possible!

It took every ounce of self-restraint she had not to jump over the stand and grab the judge's throat when she caught her winking at Darrell's lawyer. That was the last straw. She was openly showing favoritism towards Darrell's lawyer, and if that wasn't bad enough, she refused to allow any of Charlie's witnesses to testify! She said she had heard more than enough. Well, after eight fucking days of testimony, Charlie certainly hoped so, but all the testimony came from Darrell's side, not hers.

When a break in the proceedings finally came, she and Giorgio went into one of the private rooms and closed the door. She was on the verge of losing it, and said as much. She spoke through clenched teeth as she faced off with her friend. "What the bloody hell is going on in there, Giorgio!" She sat heavily in one of the straight back steel chairs and seethed.

Giorgio sat across from her and took her hand in his, looking very nervous. "Charlie, I found out something, and I don't think-or rather, I know-you're not going to like it."

At the sound of his voice, Charlie fidgeted in her chair as she smoothed the lapel of her jacket. Her pants felt too tight, and she was finding it hard to breathe. Not knowing how things could possibly get any worse, she stared blankly past him, waiting for him to continue.

Giorgio didn't know how to tell her. This type of situation

happened quite a bit in Rhode Island's courthouses, but it had never happened to him. His firm had power and clout, not to mention some of the best lawyers the state had to offer. Now he was one of "them"-"them" being the lawyer and client who couldn't, and wouldn't, win. Giorgio had to tread with extreme caution from this point on. He had appeared many times before this particular judge and knew if he exposed what he found out, she would make his life a living hell. Not knowing how to begin, Giorgio got right to the point.

Better to give it to her right between the eyes instead of trying to pussyfoot around the issue.

"Charlie, it seems your husband has an endless flow of resources. These 'resources' seem to have somehow funneled their way into this courtroom." He stopped so she could digest what she just heard. From the blank look on her face, he knew "it" hadn't clicked yet as to what was going on. Slowly, he continued, his eyes never wavering from hers.

"It seems your husband's background, and what I mean by background is that his being of Syrian descent has also aided in his defense, since the judge happens to be Armenian. I'm not one hundred percent sure of this, but it's just one more piece of the puzzle that I've managed to put into place here.

Confusion was etched across Charlie's taunt features, her face losing all its color as she listened, convinced she had heard her attorney wrong. Charlie was about to say something, but Giorgio raised his hand, stopping her. "I know this is difficult, Charlie. I, too, am in a very grueling situation."

Charlie felt like she was going to be sick, and swallowed hard. Everything was going black. The words that were said... the words that were heard. Slowly, it was coming together...all of it.

Jumping up from her chair, she frantically paced around the small room. Charlie turned around, face ashen. "So the bastard bought her off... that son of a bitch! I assume that when you said his 'resources,' you meant his money! What the hell kind of judge is she? Why hasn't anyone investigated her, for
 Christ's sake?"

Before he could reply, Charlie started pacing again, and continued to speak as if Giorgio wasn't there. "So this judge not only hates women, but also accepts bribes! That bitch!"

Her eyes were mere slits, her heart beating hard when she walked to the wall and gave it a hard bash with her fist.

"Shit!"

Giorgio got up and grabbed her by the shoulders. Looking her square in the eyes, he told her the rest. "We can't win, Charlie...not in this courtroom, anyway. Look, let's sit down and discuss our options."

Charlie allowed him to lead her back to the chair, and wearily sat down. Tears threatened to flow as she bit down hard on her lower lip. Giorgio's heart broke for her, but he needed her to be in control before they went back into the lion's den. "Charlie, we have an air tight case that we can bring to the Superior Court."

She let out a bitter laugh, and when she spoke, her tone was thick with sarcasm. "Why, Giorgio? Are the judges in the Rhode Island Superior Court immune to bribery? Don't bother wasting my time or yours, let alone the thousands it will cost me. Now I know why this damned state has the reputation it does!"

Nodding in agreement, Giorgio sighed, relieved. Thank God she was thinking clearly. "Charlie, I feel like I've let you down. I'm sorry...so very sorry."

Charlie couldn't hold in the tears anymore. She lowered her head and silently sobbed while her body rocked back and forth in the steel chair. Giorgio let her be; he knew she needed to release all the frustrations she had been keeping pent up inside of her. It was better that she get it all out here in the privacy of this room rather than in the company of the enemies.

When Charlie raised her head to look at him, her eyes were red and puffy. She spoke with conviction when she said, "Giorgio, I don't ever want to hear you say that you let me down. Do you understand? Like you said, we have an air tight case. You proved everything and more that we needed to win. It's not your fault that that bitch is not only prejudiced, but crooked! She'll get hers in the end, along with my ex-husband. I'm a firm believer that what goes around, comes around."

Pride swelled deep inside him. She was a fighter and knew when to back off... he just hoped this wouldn't haunt her for many years to come. She was in shock right now, but once the shock wore off, she would go through a series of other harsh emotions... and those emotions would always rally to reel her back in to remember... and to feel.

He stood by and waited patiently while she fixed her smeared mascara and lipstick. When she was finished, he tightly grasped her hand and helped her up. Not letting go, he said, "Let's go get this over with. What do you say?"

She wanted to answer him, but found her mouth to be as dry as the Sahara desert. She had no saliva, so she did the next best thing. She raised her head high, and mustered the bravest smile she could, then placed her free hand on the brass knob and turned.

She pulled the door open and led her lawyer out into the courtroom where she knew she would lose everything to the devil himself.

❧

SHE HADN'T REALIZED SHE WAS CRYING. Her tears threatened to fill the half empty mug she held in her hand. She got up from the table and walked to the kitchen sink, putting the cold water on full blast. She splashed the cool liquid over her face again and again, and when that didn't help, she got some ice cubes out of the freezer and laid them on her red, puffy eyes.

Nadine was due to pick her up any minute now. She didn't want her friend to see her like this. She had to forget the past...just had to. Her life depended on it. She applied fresh make-up and studied her face in the mirror hanging on the side wall. The puffiness was slowly subsiding, but her eyes still were a murky red color.

She placed her mug in the sink as a horn blasted from outside. She put her sunglasses on and headed for the front door.

Her last thought, before locking the door behind her, was fear need test her, but it need not stop her.

CHAPTER 9

THEY WALKED INTO ROBERT'S OFFICE, AND HIS gaze riveted on her the minute she entered. The vision he saw coming towards him once again snatched his breath away. The black-on-black suit she wore molded perfectly to the curves of her body. Her hair was pulled back from her face, which had minimal makeup on it. She didn't need it anyway, he told himself.

He strode to where the two women stood, and extended his hand to Nadine's, his eyes never wavering from Charlies. When he extended his hand out for her to take, and their skin touched, his body felt the same intense feeling as the first time they met. His eyes bored into hers, searching and questioning.

"The fates must be smiling down on me today. I never thought I'd see you again. How are you, Charlie?"

She blushed at the compliment, and was transfixed by the soothing quality of his voice. "I'm fine, thank you, and you?"

Nadine, feeling like the invisible woman, found a seat on one of the leather chairs by the edge of the desk. Her mouth hung open, her eyes wide saucers as she watched the two incredibly attractive people interact with each other. Her mind raced with saucy thoughts. This was better than a movie. He was still holding her hand! Any closer and they'd be locking lips, which wouldn't be a bad thing, because Charlie could definitely use some extracurricular activity in her boring, monotonous life right now.

"I'm fine, thanks."

Hating to break the contact with her, Robert reluctantly pulled away and strode to the back of his desk, where he sat in his chair while Charlie made herself comfortable in the vacant one by the desk.

Swallowing hard, he glanced from one beauty to the other. They were both stunning women, but in Robert's mind, Charlie was the exception. Nadine was indeed sultry, but much too thin for his taste.

Robert's insides erupted every time he gazed at Charlie's dark exotic beauty.

He cleared his throat, trying to keep his tone nonchalant as he directed his question to Nadine. "So, what can I do for you ladies?"

"Well, Robert, Charlie and I would like to become Private Investigators, and we thought you could more or less take us under your wing and train us."

A wide smile formed across his face as he let out a chuckle. "Sorry, but did I just hear you right? You both want to become PI's?"

Nadine glanced over at Charlie and grinned at what she saw. Fire flashed in her friend's eyes and her back became erect as she slid to the edge of her seat, ready to do battle.

Her tone was on the icy side when she asked, "Yes, you did, and I'd like to know why you find it so amusing, Mr. Fordes?"

The hairs on his arms sprang to attention. He knew he had hit a sore spot and had to tread carefully now. He noticed the changes in her demeanor immediately. Anger flashed in her onyx eyes, her body stiffened, and she looked like she was ready to pounce on him.

"Charlie, I apologize, I wasn't demeaning either your intelligence or your abilities. Do either of you have any background in this particular field?"

Charlie curtly replied, "No."

Fidgeting in his seat, he glanced from one to the other. What in God's name was he supposed to do now? It seemed the fates weren't being so kind to him after all. An eerie silence filled the room. It remained for what seemed an eternity until Charlie finally broke it asking, "Tell me, Mr. Fordes, do you employ any women agents?"

"No, I don't."

"May I ask why?" His mind raced, trying to come up with the right answer. "I really couldn't say, Charlie, but just think, if you go through with this, you'll be the first." He knew that what he was going to ask her next would really irritate her, but he couldn't help himself. "Think you can handle it?"

He regretted asking the question as soon as the words left his lips, and silently cursed himself. You idiot! Of course she's going to say she can handle it!

Nadine was elated for her friend when the "old" Charlie surfaced. Her take-control demeanor, the don't-give-me-any- of-your-shit attitude was back, and Nadine had to fight the urge to leap up from her seat and do a jig! This was exactly what her friend needed: a formidable opponent, a challenge-- and whether Charlie realized it or not, Robert Fordes was it!

They were going to drive each other crazy and push the envelope to the limit, but Nadine knew it was what they both desperately needed. "I know I can handle it- the question is: can you handle ... me?" Her tone was icy and sarcastic. He had to think twice before answering that one, not to mention that she threw him for a loop with the "me" part. She threw a double edged sword straight at him, and it hit him square between the eyes.

Stuttering slightly, he replied, "I think I'll plead the fifth on that, if you don't mind?"

Amusement flickered in her eyes, and relief flowed through him.

Nadine gave a small chuckle and finally spoke. "So does this mean we're hired, Robert?"

His gut told him to say no-too dangerous...way too dangerous. The upside would be he would get to know Charlie better, but what if she didn't have what it took? It would ruin everything. Panic stricken, he sat there, weighing out the situation, while the two women stared at him, waiting.

Okay, just say no. Give them any reason. "You're hired on a temporary basis." *My God, did I just say what I thought I said?*

Clearing his throat, he plunged on, not sure where he was going. "Charlie brought up a good point. I don't have any female investigators, and I think it will be an asset to my firm if I had some." *Okay, this is sounding good, keep going with the flow.* "Women sometimes have a way of finding out things that men can't.

Ladies, I need to know your intentions here. Is this attraction to become detectives, a lifelong career, meaning you both are willing to dedicate many, many hours of study and intense training? Or does the idea sound romantic to you both and you are acting on a whim here?"

Seeing the flicker in Charlie's eyes, he quickly added, "And I don't mean that in a sexist way..." Shit, he was stumbling again. "I meant to say that women's senses are keener, more acute than most men's, if you know what I mean."

Both women simply sat on the edges of their seats, staring blankly at him. Why did he have the feeling they were playing him? When neither said anything, he continued, "After you both have completed the training and are sure that this is something you'd like to stay with, I'll help you apply for your licenses."

He couldn't bring himself to look into those piercing onyx beams; he was fearful of what he might see. So he played it safe and kept his gaze on Nadine. "Do either of you have any other questions?"

They both glanced at each other and shook their heads no. "Okay, I'd like you both here at eight o'clock tomorrow morning, wearing sweat suits and sneakers. Oh, and ladies, no makeup or jewelry, please. I'd also like some information from you both."

He opened his side drawer and took out two standard forms for them to fill out. After they wrote their information down and handed it to him, Robert stood, and walked around from the back of his desk. They each rose and shook Robert's hand and thanked him.

When Charlie extended her hand for him to shake, his gaze locked on hers. He looked questioningly into her eyes for anything, anything at all, but all he saw was a cool, detached look. There was no emotion, just a blank slate as she shook his hand.

He couldn't believe that she said nothing more; she merely turned and walked out the door with not so much as a backward glance. Robert opened his mouth to say something, but thought better of it and closed it.

Nadine shrugged helplessly and tried to make up for her friend's abrupt departure. "I'm sure she has a lot on her mind, Robert. I don't think she realized what she just did."

"It's fine, Nadine. I'll see you tomorrow."

Nadine took a few steps, stopped, then turned around to face Robert. "Thank you for giving us a chance Robert, you won't be sorry."

He watched Nadine turn and leave his office, and strained to hear the whispers coming from the hallway. When he heard no more, he walked to the back of his desk and glanced out the window that faced the parking lot. He leaned his shoulder against the cool glass and waited for them to appear. When they emerged from the side door, he watched them walk to a shiny red convertible.

As Charlie closed her door, the expression on her face was still cool and detached, and he wondered what had happened to make her so adept at turning her emotions on and off so quickly.

CHAPTER 10

THEY RODE IN AMICABLE SILENCE, EACH LOST in their own thoughts. Nadine reflected about the drastic decision she had made, and knew it wasn't going to go over well with her friend. Three months ago, she was laid off from her job as a nurse at Rhode Island Hospital, due to severe cutbacks, and was told they would contact her if any other positions opened up.

She loved what she did, and was well respected by her peers, which made the phone call she got that much more exciting. Her favorite doctor, Fred Tierney, called and told her he was relocating to Saint Francis Hospital in New York, taking over as Chief of Staff, and asked if she be would be interested in relocating there and working in his group! She didn't have to think twice about his offer, because the man was gorgeous...and single!

Nadine harbored a clandestine crush on Dr. Tierney, and was thrilled at the opportunity to not only work in his group, but also secure a fat raise and a better position. Nadine knew, after seeing Charlie and Robert together, that she had made the right decision. But now she was getting nervous, because she had to tell her friend the truth.

Charlie took a quick side glance at her friend and knew something was brewing. "What are you thinking, Nad?"

"Nothing, really. Why?"

"You're quiet."

They pulled into Charlie's driveway and both got out of the car. "You're coming in?"

Nadine stood on her side of the car and answered hesitantly, "Yes... there's something I need to tell you, Charlie."

"Oh, no! What's wrong, Nadine?"

Not able to look her dear friend in the eye, Nadine focused her attention on the pavement of the driveway when she said, "Let's go inside and have a glass of wine and talk."

Charlie was clearly perplexed as she unlocked the front door. Nadine silently followed her through the family room and into the kitchen, where they both plopped their handbags onto the oak table. Charlie went to the refrigerator and took out a bottle of white wine. As she placed it on the counter, she stole a quick glance at her friend, who sat on one of the high back stools by the kitchen counter.

Charlie opened one of the drawers to look for the wine opener and noticed Nadine staring down into her lap, clenching and unclenching her hands.

Charlie was nervous now, but vowed to stay silent. After opening the wine, she poured two glasses and handed one to her friend. Charlie was white now, and her hands shook as she raised the glass to her lips. She watched Nadine over the rim of her glass, and felt a blow coming. "Come on, Nad, let's sit by the windows and get comfortable."

They sat on the padded window seat, facing each other, and stretched out their legs in front of them. Charlie was anxious now, and knew it showed on her face. Nadine was looking around the room, pretending to be interested in the paintings and copper pots that adorned the walls. Charlie knew she was stalling for time, and decided to put an end to it.

"Okay, Nad, out with it. I can't handle you this quiet! Whatever it is, just tell me, I won't break or crack, I promise!"

Nadine looked at Charlie and gave her the smallest of smiles. "Charlie, I made a decision recently and I don't think you're going to like it very much."

"Okay. How recent are we talking here?"

"Recent."

"Okay." Charlie, filled with apprehension, leaned forward, gripping the stem of her wine glass. "Go ahead."

Nadine didn't know how to tell her. She choked when she said, "I'm leaving."

Charlie didn't think she heard right, so she repeated what she thought she had just heard.

"Leaving?"

Nadine was uncomfortable now, and fidgeted on the window seat, keeping her gaze firmly fixed on her lap. She felt her friend's unwavering glare and snapped her head up. Nadine knew it was now or never, so she inhaled deeply and told her best friend about the phone call from Dr. Tierney and the wonderful opportunity he had offered her. She gave her friend all the little details, including her "crush" on the hot doctor.

"I see," Charlie said, her voice a mere whisper. "I guess it wouldn't matter at this point if I asked how long you've known this, and why you didn't tell me sooner."

She knew she was going to cry, but hoped she could hold off until her friend left. Nadine couldn't speak, so she stared into her friend's eyes, feeling the pain she knew she was feeling.

Trying to make light of the heavy situation, Charlie said, "I'm so happy for you, Nad, really I am. You deserve the job and the man!"

Relief spread through Nadine. "Charlie, this is a great opportunity for me! Saint Francis Hospital is known for being one of the best heart centers in this country! It puts more emphasis on the diagnosis, treatment, and prevention of heart disease than any other hospital!"

Charlie had never seen her friend so happy or animated. She knew now that Nadine was right about what she said. Everything that happened in life was a sign from above. Charlie took this as a sign that it was not meant to be for her to become a Private Investigator.

Sighing, she said, "I guess it's best we back out, then." Nadine jumped from her seat, her wine splashing over the rim of her glass, landing on the padded cushion, and yelled, "NO!, Charlie, you have to go through with it! You just have to!"

Stunned by her friend's intense reaction, Charlie asked, "Why! Why are you so insistent that I follow through with this, Nad?"

Nadine didn't want to get into a long discussion about what Charlie had been through. She knew the wounds were still raw, and tried to find a simple explanation. "It's just a feeling I have. I can't explain it. Please, promise me you'll go tomorrow. If you don't like it, then quit, but at least give it a chance."

"Nad, I finally believe that everything that happens in our life is divinely sent to us! I take this as a very strong sign that I'm not supposed to do this!"

Nadine kneeled down in front of Charlie, grasped her hand, and tightly squeezed it. "I know you don't understand right now, but I'm asking you to trust me on this one." Nadine's gut told her not to tell her friend the real reasons why she was pushing her. "I've always trusted you in the past, and I'm asking the same from you now. Why does this have to be a sign that you DON'T do it? Did it ever occur to you that the sign here is for you to DO it?"

Charlie, for the moment, was too stunned to speak. To her annoyance, tears filled her eyes; tears of fear-fear of going into the unknown without her best friend by her side-and also helplessness. The tears trickled warmly down her flushed cheeks as a sigh escaped from her throat. When she finally found the courage to speak, her voice was the merest whisper. "Okay, Nad, for some strange, ungodly reason, I'll trust you. Why... I don't know, but I will."

Their arms locked around each other in a tight embrace, and for reasons known to each of them, they cried long and hard. When they could cry no more, Nadine broke the silence, and said she had to go. "I have so much I have to do. I'm sorry I'm leaving you now, Charlie."

Gripping her friend in a tight bear hug, Charlie whispered into her very best friend's ear, "Don't you dare apologize. You deserve all the wonderful things that are coming your way. I never want to hear you say 'I'm sorry'. Embrace all your new beginnings like an innocent child, and enjoy yourself. I'll always be close to you, because I'm forever in your heart, my friend. Don't you ever forget that."

Nadine pulled back, and Charlie saw tears once again spilling down her friend's pale face. "You're in my heart, too, Charlie."

Mustering all the courage she could, Charlie laughed as she said, "I know you are. Now get the hell out of here, before I throw you out!"

With their arms tightly wound around each other, they walked to Nadine's car. After she backed out of the driveway, Charlie silently went back into the house and closed the door. Going to the kitchen she picked up her glass of unfinished wine. She stood staring out the large bow window as large droplets of tears flowed down her crestfallen face.

Pain. When you cared deeply for someone, it was inevitable that at some point they would cause you to feel it.

CHAPTER 11

HER EYELASHES SLOWLY FLUTTERED OPEN AS she rolled onto her back in the king-sized bed. Her mind was groggy as she glanced at the alarm clock on her night stand. It was six a.m., and every muscle in her body felt like it had jet lag. She had tossed and turned all night and was exhausted.

She got out of bed and stumbled to the kitchen to make her much needed coffee. As she waited for the strong java to finish brewing, she combed her fingers through her mass of curly hair.

She had gotten her clothes ready the previous evening and had laid them out on the bed in the guest bedroom. She didn't want to be late and give a bad impression on her first day, so the previous night she had torn through her vast wardrobe for three hours to find exactly the right thing to wear. Most people would have found a sweat suit and sneakers an easy choice, but for her it was a major dilemma. She was used to wearing leather and boots, not sweat suits and sneakers.

She made a mental note to do some shopping the following day. After finishing her coffee, she jumped in the shower and let the water run ice cold over her aching muscles and joints. She slicked her thick hair back from her face and got dressed.

As she went to put on some makeup, she remembered the added note Robert had given the day before: no makeup or jewelry. Everyone, or at least she hoped everyone, knew that lipstick certainly did not count as makeup. It was a necessity, like wearing underwear. You'd feel naked if you didn't have it on. To play it safe she chose a light color that accented the flush in her skin tone. She was grateful for the great skincare line she used, Elaina Marie Beauty. It was organic and the owner was the developer of the line, and Charlie loved the way her skin glowed. Since she started using Elaina Marie Skin care, Charlie no longer had to wear foundation so the no makeup rule was no biggie for her!

As she headed back down the stairs to the kitchen, a small smile tugged at the corners of her mouth. It turned into a full grin as she opened the refrigerator door and inspected the interior's contents. She was going to make her first brown bag lunch since high school. God, she was pathetic; getting excited over making a bag lunch!

She made two tuna fish sandwiches, grabbed two bags of chips, a banana, and an apple. She found her thermos and filled it with ice water. "There, that should hold me over until dinner." Having second thoughts, she snatched some carrots and grapes and threw them in, just in case she needed a quick snack, she told herself.

Subconsciously, she knew all the food was to help ease the tension that flowed throughout her body. She always ate more than she should when she was nervous, and today certainly qualified. She gathered everything up off the counter and headed for the door.

She was going to brave it alone, without Nadine. She would be OK; she could handle it, couldn't she?

⤙∕⤚

IT WAS A BRIGHT, WARM DAY WITH A CLEAR blue sky. There was a gentle breeze blowing, with the slightest aroma of pine in the air. As she drove through the thick morning traffic on 95, she pondered exactly what her training would entail.

She didn't realize her hands were sweating profusely until the car jerked sharply to the right. Shuddering, she grasped the wheel and fought to straighten the car out. She arrived safely at the agency and pulled into the lot. She found a space towards the back and parked.

She killed the engine, dug into the bottom of her purse searching for her Elaina Marie Body Elixir Spray, retrieved it and doused herself with the sweet smelling fragrance. She threw the bottle back in her handbag, leaned over, and opened the glove compartment to grab the wad of napkins she kept stashed there.

Water was oozing out from under both her arms, and she felt like she needed another shower. Not realizing it, she started mumbling to herself. "Shit! It figures I wore grey today! My God, you can see water stains under my arms!"

She was nervous, and felt each pound of her heart crash up

46

against the inside of her chest. Her breath was coming out in spurts, her hands were shaking, and she was sweating profusely. Without thinking, she shoved her hand, which tightly gripped a stack of napkins, down the front of her sweat shirt, and proceeded to wipe vigorously.

Then she felt it: heat, hot and thick, with a sinking feeling that followed right behind. It was the feeling she got when she'd been caught doing something perfectly normal in her mind, but when viewed by another person, didn't look normal at all.

She slowly glanced to her left and was mortified to see Robert bent over at the waist, peering in the window of her car with the widest, smuggest grin locked on his face.

CHAPTER 12

AS HE GOT OUT OF HIS CAR, HE SAW HER PULL into the lot. His wave went unnoticed by her as she whizzed by him, frowning deeply. She looked troubled about something, and he silently hoped nothing bad had happened.

He also noticed that she was alone. God, he hoped nothing had happened to Nadine. His gut instinct told him to mind his own business and just head for his office and wait for her there.

Once again, he ignored the warning lights that flashed in his head, and made a beeline straight for her car, but stopped dead in his tracks when he saw her frantically searching in her handbag for something. She pulled out a lovely cobalt bottle, liberally spraying herself with the fragrance, making him wince.

A smile tugged across his mouth as he watched her open her glove compartment and grab a handful of napkins. He was definitely intrigued now, and couldn't believe his eyes when she shoved her hand down the front of her sweat shirt, mumbling to herself the whole time.

He leaned over and peered in her window to get a better look, just to make sure he was really seeing what he thought he was seeing. His eyes gleamed wickedly as he watched her little plight.

She was very nervous, and obviously sweating quite a bit. With her hand still down the front of her shirt, she suddenly froze. She wanted to die, and she wanted to die now! She sat there, frozen, gazing into those beautiful blue eyes with her hand down the front of her shirt! Letting out a groan, she mumbled to herself, "My God, it looks like I'm playing with myself!"

As nonchalantly as she could, she slowly lifted her hand out from under her shirt and gave a feeble smile. Her body cringed as his laughter permeated the glass. Dragging her gaze from his, she took the car key out of the ignition, and opened her car door.

She grabbed her purse and lunch from the seat, got out of the car, and slammed the door with such force that the car rocked.

❧❧

HE KNEW HE SHOULD KEEP HIS BIG MOUTH shut. He should say nothing and head for the door, but the temptation was too huge for him to pass up. "Hi! Having a little trouble this morning? You know I'd be happy to help out." *Why the hell did I just say that?*

How was she ever going to get through this? She hoped he would be polite enough to just keep his big mouth shut, knowing how humiliated she was, but no, he had to dig, didn't he!

He knew he had made a huge mistake when he saw fire flash in her onyx beams. Her tone was heavy with sarcasm when she asked, "Do you always sneak up on people and leer into their windows? Are you that depraved?"

He couldn't help himself; he started laughing and grinning at her. She looked so dammed sexy standing in front of him, fighting for composure, face flushed, breath labored, with water stains under her arms.

"Robert, get that jackass grin off your face or I swear, I'll wipe it off for you, do you hear me!"

He swallowed another gush of laughter that threatened to explode and tried to look serious when he asked, "I'm intrigued by why you had your hand down the front of your shirt. Care to enlighten me?"

Nothing. She stood hardly a foot away from him, her feet firmly planted on the ground, glaring at him.

"Charlie, aren't you going to answer my question?"

Fury rose and her temper snapped, "WHAT QUESTION, ROBERT?"

What in God's name am I doing? I don't think she's enjoying this banter we're having. "Why you had your hand down your shirt?"

"You're a smart guy; why don't you use your imagination!"

"Charlie, if I use my imagination, I might get into trouble." *That was good.*

"Don't flatter yourself!"

Well, maybe not that good.

It was too late before he saw it. She had somehow managed to close the car door on the back of her oversized sweatshirt. What a shame, he thought, that she felt the need to hide those luscious curves. She started to storm away from the car, but with not more than two steps taken she was instantly jerked back, her body slamming into the side of the car, and landing right smack on her beautiful behind.

Her purse sprang free from her grasp, all the contents flying up and out like a colorful fireworks display, landing haphazardly on the pavement, not to mention her sweat shirt yanked up to her neck, exposing a very tight, revealing sports bra.

He leaned down to see if she was okay, inhaled a good dose of the fragrance she wore, and decided this wasn't the right time to tell her that she overdid it with the spritzing.

Bringing his mouth close to her ear, he whispered, "Are you accident prone? Because from what I've seen this morning, you look like one waiting to happen."

She turned away, her face red with anger now. Flustered she freed herself, then snatched up her belongings now splayed out on the pavement, throwing them haphazardly into her purse. She was going to kill him if it was the last thing she did!

Still kneeling on the ground next to her, he couldn't resist the urge to badger her. "Just so you know, Charlie, you closed the door on the back of this lovely and most becoming oversized sweatshirt that you have on. I guess this explains the little tumble you took, what do you think?"

Just as he was wondering if he'd gone too far, she swung around on the ground and slapped him hard across his face. The force of her slap took him off guard and he fell backwards onto the pavement.

"I guess I deserved that."

She said nothing to him as she continued to gather the remainder of her items. When she had everything back in her purse, she slowly got up from the ground, with Robert holding onto her arm. She tugged free from his grasp, and unlocked her door.

When he finally looked at her face, he saw tears streaming down her flushed cheeks, and noticed that she was having trouble getting air into her lungs. He felt like such a jerk! At sixty you'd think he'd have a little more finesse, but no, not him! "Oh, my God, I'm so sorry, Charlie! PLEASE, I didn't mean it, I was just joking!"

Dear God, what have I done?

CHAPTER 13

SHE NEVER LOOKED AT HIM; SHE COULDN'T. Ripping her door open, she threw her purse and lunch onto the vacant seat, slid behind the wheel, and started the car. She backed out of the space, leaving him in agony, apologizing over and over, his words lost in the wind.

She was too enraged to think, and had no sense of where she was going. Her knuckles turned white as her grip tightened on the wheel. Tears flowed warmly down her flushed cheeks as her thoughts careened one into the other.

The first thing she was going to do was kill Nadine. She was going to wrap her fingers around that skinny neck of hers and squeeze until she turned blue, or passed out, whichever came first!

Charlie turned right onto the road that would lead her home, and remembered that the real estate agent was supposed to come by that morning and put a For Sale sign up on the front lawn.

Frustration and embarrassment surged through her again, making her forget about the sales agent. She couldn't believe the gall that jackass had! How dare he treat her like that! She had never been so humiliated in all her life, and to think she thought him to be like a warrior! Well, he was a warrior alright, but the worst possible kind.

Tearing into her driveway, she opened her car door, grabbed her things, and slammed it shut . She bolted to the front door, unlocked it, and closed it behind her. She slid down onto the cool wooden floor.

The morning's events, her past traumas, her life... they all closed in on her and she sobbed like a child whose most valued possession had been taken from her. She felt like she was finally losing it. Somewhere deep in the recesses of her brain she knew she had overreacted to his jibes.

Still, she was on the edge, and dangerously close to falling off...

she heard the warnings in her head... she had to be very careful from now on.

CHAPTER 14

HE STOOD THERE, SHAKING IN HIS SKIN. What the hell did he do? Never in his sixty years had he ever acted like he just did. His words had cut right through her and opened the barely healed scars she had, whatever the hell they were.

Without thinking, which was something he seemed to be doing a lot of these days, he ran to his office and retrieved her address. Grabbing the paper, he darted back out to his car, got in, started the engine, and headed in the direction of her house. What the hell was he going to say to her? He knew he had to say something, anything, to repair the damage he had done. He had acted like a juvenile, for Christ's sake!

The only plausible explanation he could come up with was that it had been years since he had felt an attraction or had been involved with a woman, and the result was that he didn't know what to do, what to say, or how to act! He had seen her face and the pain that was etched in every line and crease. Fire had exploded from her black eyes, heavy tears had flowed freely down her flushed face, and it tore his gut apart, because he was the one who had caused her anguish.

Finding her house, he pulled in the driveway and parked behind her car. He

saw the "For Sale" sign on the front lawn, and wondered where she was moving. He got out of the car but hesitated.

Not trusting himself, he stood there, staring at the front door, waiting for the courage he needed.

CHAPTER 15

AS HER TEARS SLOWLY SUBSIDED, SHE HEARD A car pull into the driveway. Curious to see who it was, Charlie rose from the cool floor and gazed absently out the window by the side of the door. Cold fury raced down her spine as her heart and pulse accelerated.

What the hell did he think he was doing? She couldn't believe her eyes! He was walking up her front steps and about to ring her doorbell!

She fought to bring her panic under control, because it would do her no good to become hysterical. Panic surged through her as she quickly tried to decide what she should do. She could ignore him. He'd have to go away eventually... but there was a vicious urge deep inside her that wanted to bash in his almighty face!

Startled, she jumped at the sound of the bell, even though she was prepared for it. She stood there for a few beats, then opened the door, confronted with the reality of him standing there on the other side. She tried to slam it in his face, but his movements were too quick. He stuck his foot in between the opening and placed his right hand on the door, applying pressure.

As soon as he saw her, he noticed how pale she was, terrifyingly so, but there was also still a spark in her dark eyes. A wave of tiredness suddenly washed over him. Charlie glared at him making his mouth go dry.

There was an ominous silence building between them as each waited to see who would have the audacity to speak first. She opened the door a crack and turned her face away from him, but not before he saw the flush of raw pain etched across her face.

He silently closed the door and walked up to her back. He didn't know what to say. He stood behind her, silent, then gently lifted a mass of her curly hair in his hand. He leaned down and placed a tender kiss on the back of her neck.

She was totally taken aback and stood very still. Every hair on her body stood at attention. She held her breath, not moving, fearing that if she did her body would crumble to the floor in a heap. Ever so gently, he turned her around to face him.

He placed his hand under her chin and slowly eased it up so he could gaze into her dark, stormy eyes. She stared at him, mesmerized, not trusting herself to speak. His eyes were telling her all that he wanted and needed her to know.

She saw that agony in them now, filled with shame and humiliation at what he had said and done to her.

Not wanting to frighten her, he slowly pulled her to his chest and placed a light kiss on her forehead and cheek. He heard her draw a long breath, then expel it. This woman had touched something deep inside him that he remembered feeling long ago.

He ran his thumb over her mouth and then lowered his lips to hers, softly grazing the silky flesh. Her hands came up and encircled his neck and he sucked in his breath as he fought to hold himself still.

She opened her mouth to share her warmth with him. They started with slow hesitant kisses, their tongues tasting each other, then building to powerful thrusts. A wild frenzied excitement roared through each of them, and he knew he had to fight to regain his composure, or he'd take her right there on the wooden floor.

Abruptly, he pulled away from her, and saw the confusion register in her eyes. He stared at her and took in her rapid breathing and flushed cheeks. "I'm sorry, Charlie, I shouldn't have done that. I won't blame you if you choose not to come back to work."

She was too stunned to speak, but even if she hadn't been, she wouldn't have gotten a word in, because Robert started pacing back and forth and talking rapidly. "I don't know why I did what I did; I mean, I do know why, or at least I think I know why. You see, it's been years since I've felt an attraction or have been involved with anyone. The first time I saw you I felt like I had died and gone to heaven. I think you are the most beautiful creature that I have ever seen, and since the day I met you, I've done nothing but make a complete fool of myself." Charlie quickly interjected, "At least you're consistent!" Robert continued as if Charlie hadn't spoken, "I came here to tell you that if you still want me to train you, I will. I give you my word that I will never touch or kiss you again. I'm sure I'm much too old for you, anyway. So, I hope you will reconsider and come back tomorrow." With that said, he stormed out of her house, slamming the door behind him.

She stood there frozen in the middle of her family room, not knowing what the hell had just happened.

CHAPTER 16

HE DROVE BACK TO HIS HOUSE MORE confused than ever. His thoughts drifted back to times of long ago. In his mind's eye he saw his beautiful wife, Abigail. They met when he had just finished getting his degree in law enforcement, and fell in love immediately. She stayed by his side and always pushed him to follow his dreams. When his agency took off, she was right there beside him, coming in to help, and doing whatever was needed to support him.

Then it came: the big break he was waiting for. Fredrick Constantino, head of the FBI, had waltzed into his office one day and asked him to assist them with an active murder investigation. Robert couldn't believe his luck! He accepted immediately and became fast friends with Fredrick. Eventually the case was solved, and unbeknown to Robert, the man they convicted wanted retribution, and retribution was what he got.

The culprit had major connections on the outside, and had a contract placed on Robert's beloved wife. She was gone from him now... forever. He still blamed himself. He should have had a gut feeling, or something, anything, to warn him. It had happened so quickly and he had told himself if only he had gone with Abigail to the market like she had asked him to. It was the if only that haunted him...

Robert's thoughts returned to that night. It had been late and he was so tired and loaded down with paperwork. Abigail was always so organized, and liked to do the shopping in the evening, because the store wasn't busy. It relaxed her, she had said. He asked her if he could sit this one out. He could still see her face etched in his mind. She stood at his office door and gave him that million dollar smile she had, replying, "I understand, love. You do what you need to do, and I'll beep when I get home."

Smiling up at her, he responded, "You're the greatest, you know that?"

Laughing heartily, she said, "As a matter of fact, I do."

Abigail had begun to leave, but then stopped. She slowly turned around, and said, "Hey, I love you more than anything. Always know that, okay?"

He simply said, "Ditto, my love." Their eyes had locked for the briefest second, and that was the end. She never returned home.

The hit happened in the damned parking lot of a supermarket. As soon as she finished putting the groceries in the trunk, the hit man had aimed at his target and made contact. Abigail died instantly.

He hadn't been the same since. How could he be, when a part of him died with her? Not to mention the immense guilt he felt. The years hadn't eased the pain. Night after night he was bombarded with the same thought... I should have gone with her... I should have gone.

After his wife's death, Robert secluded himself, and threw all his energies into his agency. He couldn't believe that it had been over twenty years since that horrific day. The pain was still raw after all these years, and until meeting Charlie, he never thought he would ever be interested in any woman again, let alone fall in love!

Speaking out loud to himself, he asked, "Did I just say love? I am losing it! I'm much too old for that."

He pulled into his driveway and sat there for a very long time. He had to get a grip on himself! He opened his car window and listened to the waves crash up against the rock wall.

He would do whatever he had to do to fix the situation between himself and Charlie, but only on a professional level.

There was no way he would cross the line and start something he knew deep inside he could never finish.

CHAPTER 17

THE SUN GLISTENED THROUGH THE BOW windows of her bedroom, caressing her awake with a soothing warmth. She rolled over and glanced at the clock. It was six a.m. and she hadn't decided if she was going back to the agency or not. Rolling out of bed, she pondered the logic of her going back... not just going back, she told herself, but going back to him.

By the time she walked to the bathroom to brush her teeth and wash her face, her decision was already made.

As she applied her Elaina Marie Intense Gold Elixir, she made a mental note to herself to let him know just what she thought of his little speech yesterday. It had been after the fact when all of her zingers and retorts had come to mind. At the time she had been too busy standing there like some ancient statue to comment on anything Robert had thrown at her... especially "the kiss."

That was another matter altogether, and she was glad she hadn't driven herself bonkers rehashing it. Oh, it was warm and erotic, all right, it jolted her right down to the bottom of her toes, making them curl. But how dare he tell her that he wouldn't ever do it again! Didn't she have any say in the matter?

She needed to expel the nervous energy that was bottled up inside her; she didn't want a repeat performance of yesterday, that was for sure. She threw on some sweats and went to the home gym that was located in one of her spare bedrooms, and worked out long and hard. She didn't stop until all the muscles and joints in her body were limber and loose.

After a quick shower, she dressed and grabbed the lunch she had made the day before but hadn't touched, and ran out the door. She knew he thought she wouldn't come back, and that fact made the idea all the more appealing to her.

She couldn't wait to see the look of shock on his face when she waltzed through his door!

CHAPTER 18

HE PURPOSELY ARRIVED AT HIS OFFICE AT seven-thirty. He wasn't taking any chances of running into her today in the parking lot. No sir, he did not want a repeat performance of yesterday.

If her glands wanted to work overtime again he was not going to witness the act that followed. He was staying in the safety of his office, grounded behind his desk. Who was he kidding, anyway? She wasn't coming back, and he couldn't blame her, could he? If he were in her shoes, he wouldn't come within five thousand miles of him! Still, Robert found himself turning in his chair every so often to peer out the window that just happened to face the parking lot.

He glanced down at the gold watch on his wrist to check the time. Mumbling out loud to himself, he said, "Well, it's nine o'clock on the dot, Robert." As he turned his chair back to face his desk, he caught her emerging car out of the corner of his eye.

He quickly swiveled the chair to get a closer look. He jumped up and cursed to himself as he banged his leg on the corner of the desk. He hurried to the side of the window so she wouldn't catch him spying on her.

"God, I feel like an idiot," he confessed, but it didn't stop him from cautiously leaning over just a bit. "No good," he decided. If she glanced this way, she'd see him for sure. So he did the most logical thing he could think of... he dropped to his knees and slowly lifted his head just enough so his nose was resting on the bottom of the ledge, with his eyes peeking out.

"Now where the hell did she go?" He saw her car in the lot but she was nowhere to be found. Then it was his turn to feel the heat, hot and thick. A chill raced up his spinal cord and surged straight out through the top of his head. She was in his office, standing behind him. He could smell her perfume.

His mind raced wildly as to how he should handle this delicate situation. Panic rose to his throat as he fought to remember if he had spoken any of his thoughts out loud. Then it happened.

She spoke and he froze, even though he knew she was there.

❦

SHE PARKED HER CAR TOWARDS THE BACK OF the lot, grabbed her purse and lunch, and got out of the car. Thank God for small favors, she was fine today. She was calm and ready to face the situation with Robert head on.

With her free hand, she pushed her sunglasses up on her nose and was proceeding to the side door when a shadow moving in one of the windows caught her attention. Charlie didn't turn her head in that direction because she had a feeling she already knew what the shadow, or rather, who, the shadow was.

She slowed down her pace just a fraction, and shifted her gaze to the left. She couldn't believe what she saw, or rather, what she thought she saw.

A tall man jumped up from his chair and grabbed his knee, then rushed to the side of the window and looked out. She knew it was Robert, but what in God's name was he doing now, she thought?

Her mouth curved into a smile as she saw the figure drop to the floor and slowly raise his head, only his half closed eyes visible over the ledge of the window. Once she knew she was safely out of his range of vision she sprinted into the building and down the curved corridor into his office, before he could realize she was gone.

She froze in front of his desk. He was on his knees, mumbling something about "where the hell was she?"

Charlie assumed "she" was the person he was searching for. Well, well, she thought, how the tables have turned. Clearing her throat, Charlie declared, "SHE is standing right behind you." Her sultry laugh echoed out into the silent room.

Robert remained anchored where he was because he couldn't move. His legs were dead weights. His thoughts raced wildly. I'm a sixty year old man kneeling on the floor of my office with the most beautiful woman I've ever seen in my life standing behind me, and I feel like a moron! What the hell has gotten into me? I think I'd better talk to a shrink; I feel like I'm losing control of all my senses!

She walked around to the back of his desk finding him mumbling to himself. "Ah, Robert, I know I asked you this before, but are you sure you don't nip just a bit in the morning?"

He cocked his head to the right and looked up into her eyes. They gleamed wickedly at him as he fought to stave off the embarrassment becoming evident on his face. "I, uh....I lost something and was looking for it." Struggling to get up, he grabbed onto the corner of the desk and hoisted himself up, a grunt escaping from his throat.

When he finally faced her, she couldn't resist the urge to humiliate him some more. "Gee, that's funny, I could have sworn I heard you say, 'now where the hell is she?'"

"No, I said 'where the hell is Lee,' not 'she'."

"Really, and who's Lee?"

He couldn't think of an answer. He didn't think she'd ask who Lee was. "Um... what did you say?"

"Lee, who's Lee, and why are you wondering where he is?" He rubbed his temple with his fingers, trying to ease the migraine he was suddenly developing. "I, ah..."

"Let me help you out here. You first said that you lost something and were looking for it, so I assume you lost someone named Lee and were looking for him on the floor by your window, is that correct?"

He sighed, throwing up his hands in defeat. He had to laugh at himself. He couldn't dig the ditch any deeper, so he figured once again he might as well try and explain. "You know, Charlie, since the day I met you, all I've done is explain and defend myself to you."

"Well, Robert, maybe that's because you keep saying and doing things that need explaining and defending."

He was powerless, the scent of her perfume was wafting up through his nostrils and it was driving him mad. He took two steps towards her to close the distance between them, and slightly bent his head down to hers until their lips were almost touching.

Their eyes locked as she was about to say something, anything, to fill the unbearable silence that lingered in the air, when he lightly kissed her. He lifted his left hand and caressed her jaw line, sending shivers racing through her body. With his left hand cradled around the back of her neck, he made continuous small circles with his fingers while his lips savored her taste and warmth. Slowly he pulled away from her, his eyes still locked on hers, declaring, "That's what I was doing on the floor by the window."

Gazing into his eyes, she absently nodded, as though what he had just said explained everything. Then it occurred to her, his vow to never touch or kiss her again. Her voice quivered slightly when she asked, "I thought you said you weren't going to touch or kiss me anymore?"

Shrugging his shoulders, he flashed a killer smile, and with a challenging tone simply stated, "I lied."

A knock sounded on the office door, sending them both jumping out of their skin. A tall, very muscular man with dark brown hair and slate grey eyes cleared his throat and stared at Charlie. "Sorry, boss, but everyone's waiting for you in the workout room."

"Come here, Pino, and let me introduce you to Charlie. She's joining our team today."

Pino, eyes never wavering from Charlie's, strode into the room in three steps, extending his hand for her to take. "Well, hello there, beautiful!"

If he shook her hand any harder he'd dislocate her shoulder. Wincing, she flashed a pearly smile and said, "Hi, Pino, nice to meet you."

"The pleasure's all mine, Charlie!"

She glanced at Robert and noticed a quick flush of color on his cheeks.

"Easy, Pino! Charlie's part of the team, not a target, so put your eyes back in their sockets, and tell the fellas I'll be right there."

Pino, who was still holding Charlie's hand, reluctantly let go, and nodded. "You got it, boss."

He turned and walked out the door, and Charlie let out a huge breath.

"Sorry, Charlie, I expect you'll be getting a lot of that. I hope you'll be able to handle it."

Arching one of her eyebrows, she lowered her voice to a whisper, "I think I've already been handling it just fine, Robert." He opened his mouth to say something, then thinking better of it, quickly closed it.

"Are you ready to start, Charlie?"

"Robert, I've never been more ready. Lead the way!"

THEY WALKED OUT OF HIS OFFICE, Charlie trailing only slightly behind him. She had to admit that she liked the view. Gravity hadn't settled on his nice shapely back end yet, and with each step Robert took, she could see his muscles flexing under the sweatpants he wore.

As if sensing her ogling, he abruptly stopped in the narrow corridor and turned to face her. She was still looking down and smashed right into his chest. He reached out with both his arms to catch her from falling back. As his eyes searched hers questioningly, he realized what she was doing and a mischievous smile appeared. "Does everything pass inspection, Charlie?"

Face flushed, she haphazardly swept a hand through her hair, pissed that he had busted her. "Yes, I was just admiring the décor of the corridor, Robert."

Laughing heartily, he said, "Now that's an interesting way to describe my backend, wouldn't you say?"

She couldn't respond. Her tongue somehow got stuck to the roof of her mouth, so she just served up a sly smile. Taking her hand, he led the way to the end of the corridor, turning right at the last door.

When she entered the room, she stopped short. She did a quick scan and noticed that she was the only female present. Gulping hard, Charlie took quick little breaths.

Robert saw Charlie's chest heave up and down and sensing her discomfort cleared his throat. "Gentlemen, I'd like you to meet the newest addition to our force. Her name is Charlie... uh, Charlie...." Damn it, when he read her form he had a hard time trying to figure out how to say her blasted last name! He looked at her, hoping she would finish, but all she did was smile at him! "Charlie Zan... Zanfag... Zanfagna. Yes, that's it, Zanfagna! I want you to make her feel welcome and..." Laughs and sly remarks flowed throughout the room, making her wince and step back.

Robert rested his hand on her arm and said with more force, "Listen, and listen up good! You are not, and I repeat not, to make Charlie feel uncomfortable or out of place here, is that understood?"

When there was no reply, his temper flared, and he shouted, "I SAID IS THAT UNDERSTOOD, GENTLEMEN?"

Voices rang out from all sides of the room, "Yeah, sure, boss!"
"No problem."

"Got it."

"Charlie, join the men on the far side of the room, please."

"Sure." She felt every eye in the room on her as she walked from one end to the other.

"All right! Pino and Toni on the floor, everyone sit and pay attention!"

Two and a half hours later Charlie collapsed on the floor, panting, drenched, and exhausted. Every muscle and joint had been torn from her body. Sure, she had a great deal to learn about hand-to-hand combat, but Charlie thought she held her own. She surmised she'd done okay, despite kicking at least five of the men in their groin, blunders she told herself were all accidental!

Stealing a fast glance at Robert, she noticed that when he slid into his "work mode" he was a different person. She saw a cool, confident man who was in control and knew what he was doing. She was impressed, to say the least.

She wasn't surprised when he didn't go easy on her, not that she expected him to. She knew he needed to test her, to discover how far she could be pushed, and how quick she was on her feet. She glanced around the room, assessing the men, and was relieved to see that they all were sweating and breathing hard, like her.

Robert's voice boomed throughout the room, commanding everyone's attention. "All right, not bad, but not good-my grandmother could have done a better job!"

Loud moans of protest peppered the room, which didn't faze him in the least. "All right, into the conference room, now!" The team got up from the mats they were sitting on and trudged out of the gym single file.

Charlie was the last to leave because she had no idea where the conference room was, and she didn't trust any of these hot-blooded men to walk behind her. She walked halfway down the winding corridor and then took a left into a huge room. She entered the conference room and sat at the far end of the sizable table in the middle of the room, quickly scanning the interior.

Billboards hung across one of the walls with the agent's name, partner, and caseloads. Charlie was shocked to see her name written on the board next to Robert's. He hadn't mentioned anything about putting her on a case with him, but then, he hadn't been the most eloquent person as of late, so this was understandable to her.

Her vision shifted to the wall facing her. It was lined with monitors that scanned and recorded the outside and inside of the complex from different angles. The door was to her left at the far side of the room, and she was glad she sat facing it.

For some reason, she couldn't sit with her back to a door. Wherever she was, she liked to be able to see who came in, and who went out. She remembered how her father always told her to be aware of her surroundings, and was glad she had heeded the advice.

The wall to her left was covered in large maps and graphs. Red tacks had been placed on certain locations, none of which meant anything to her untrained eye. Charlie rotated her chair so that it faced the wall behind her, and examined the large TV screen that was built into the structure. Now she was really impressed! She estimated that it had to measure at least seventy inches across. She made a mental note to ask Robert if she could ever bring in some popcorn and a movie!

The leather chairs surrounding the table were big and comfortable too, much better than any found in a movie theater. Charlie opened a file that had her name on it and proceeded to flip through it. She noticed that all the agents had similar files.

Robert watched her every move. He absorbed her facial expressions and witnessed them change from intrigue to surprise. She had amazed him during the hand to hand combat class. He didn't think she had it in her, but she had held her own, and pride swelled deep inside him. When she defended herself, he saw fire flash in her deep set eyes, like she was fighting off something that haunted her. He knew she was running, but from what exactly, he didn't know. She had many layers of steel armor built around her and he hoped that little by little he would be able to chip away at them.

Now came the next test for her: he would find out how observant she was, which was just as vital as her knowing how to defend herself.

INSIDE THE FOLDER WAS A LEGAL PAD. Charlie took it

out and placed it to the side. She glanced up, and noticed Robert sitting at the opposite end of the conference table, looking at her. Their eyes locked, and she had to force herself to look away. He started to speak when the door flew open.

A man ran into the room and around the conference table, yelling obscenities, and then ran back out, slamming the door behind him. Everyone shifted in their seats while an onslaught of questions flew around the room.

Robert stood and clapped his hands loudly to get everyone's attention. "All right, everyone, pick up your pens and write down a complete list of what you just saw and heard, no matter how trivial." Some of the men raised their hands with questions, but were waved off by Robert. "No questions! You have ten minutes, starting right now!"

Charlie grabbed her pen and wrote furiously. When she flipped the page over she felt eyes on her, and quickly glanced up and scanned the room. Everyone was staring at her.

When Charlie's gaze met Robert's, she saw his eyes twinkling with just a hint of a smile tugging playfully at the corners of his mouth. "Done, Charlie?"

"Yes, sir."

"Good, why don't you read what you have for us, then."

"Okay." She didn't know why, but she stood, then cleared her throat. She tried to control the panic that rose inside her, and prayed her hands didn't shake.

"The man entered through the only door in the room. He wore sneakers: one red, and one white. A red sock was worn with the white sneaker, and a white sock worn with the red. The faded jeans he wore had a hole in the left knee. His right pant leg was rolled up to his knee with a tattoo of a snake visible on the inside of the calf. The second and fourth buttons were missing from his plaid shirt, and the pocket that was sewn onto the left breast was torn. The right sleeve was rolled up to his elbow, while the left buttoned at the wrist. A black cord that had a sterling star dangling from it hung from his right wrist. A red cord that had a red metal snake attached to it hung around his neck. The left side of his face had a superficial scar that jutted from his jawline to his collarbone. His eyes were different colors: one blue, the other green. He had a tattoo of a star over his left eyebrow, and a Mohawk haircut. Well, that's all."

Robert cleared his throat and asked if anyone had anything else to add. When there was no reply, he stood and said, "Everyone put your names on your list and pass them to the head of the table. Take your files with you and disperse. Roll call is at eight a.m. sharp. Don't be late!"

Charlie didn't know what to do, so she sat where she was and concentrated all her efforts on clenching and unclenching her hands. When she felt his warm breath caress the side of her neck, she jumped.

"Oh, my God, you scared me! I didn't know you were sitting next to me! How did you do that without me noticing?"

"I guess you were preoccupied with something. Anything you want to talk about?"

Charlie hesitated before saying, "No, no, I'm fine, but thanks, anyway."

"You look beat."

"I am. My body's not used to being thrown around and manhandled."

A small chuckle escaped from his throat. "Don't be so hard on yourself, Charlie. You have no prior experience in combat training, and I can honestly say that you did remarkably well, and held your own. You should be proud of yourself."

"Thanks, that means a lot to me."

"Um, Charlie, there's something I'd like to ask you."

"Sure, what is it?"

"Well, we're both done for the day, and I was wondering if maybe you'd like to go and get a bite to eat with me. What do you say?"

She didn't know. Panic instantly surged through her body. She wasn't ready, and also knew it was not a good idea to get personally involved with her new boss. Stuttering slightly, she murmured, "Robert, I don't think so, but thanks, anyway. I think I'll go home and soak in a nice hot tub and relax."

Visions filled his mind of her being exposed in all her glory, with him drinking in every naked inch of her. He would have to be patient, he told himself, no matter how much it was going to kill him. He would just have to wait until she was ready. Of course he knew he was going against every fiber of his being as he had promised himself that this to be a purely professional relationship. But something kept pushing him!

She didn't know if she should repeat what she just said. He had a faraway look in his eyes, and he hadn't acknowledged her answer. She wished she knew what he was thinking, or that he would at least say something to her. She was starting to fidget in her seat and feel uneasy.

At last he came back from wherever he had been, and softly answered, "That's fine. I understand. I'll see you tomorrow morning at eight. I'll be briefing you on your caseload, so make sure you have a clear head. Have a good night, Charlie."

He rose, denying her a chance to reply and wish him the same. His movements were too quick for her to keep up with him. He was out the door before she could even turn her head around.

"Now that went over well, Charlie. Good job!"

CHAPTER 19

CHARLIE HEARD THE PHONE RINGING AS SHE unlocked the front door, and rushed to the kitchen and snatched up the receiver.

"Hello?"

"Hi, how'd your day go? Fill me in on every last detail, and make sure you don't leave anything out!"

The sound of Nadine's voice reminded her of the previous promise she made to herself to kill her. Since the two hadn't spoken, Nadine had no idea what had happened over the past couple of days.

Speaking in a frenzy, Charlie rushed on, "You, my friend, are dead, do you understand me? Dead! You have no idea what I've gone through these past couple of days! I was embarrassed beyond repair, not to mention humiliated!"

"Wow! What the hell did you do to the poor guy?"

"Me! What do you mean, what did I do to him? And why are you always taking his side? You're supposed to be my friend, remember?"

"For cripes sake, Charlie, slow down! Let me rephrase the question for you. What happened to you that caused you to be humiliated?"

Deflated, Charlie answered, "Oh, never mind. You're lucky you're not standing here in front of me right now, because if you were, I'd have to follow through with the promise I made to myself and kill you!"

"So I take it you two are getting on okay, then?"

Charlie detected the sarcastic undertone in her friend's voice and felt bad for being harsh. "Look, I'm sorry. I didn't mean to bite your head off, okay?"

Relieved, Nadine softened, "Okay, now would you like to start at the beginning?"

They spoke for nearly two hours, catching up on the events from

71

the past few days. Nadine surprised Charlie once again with sound advice. "Look, you went back! That took guts and stamina on your part. I agree with you that Robert was out of line, but I think it's because he's nuts about you! You drive the man senseless, can't you see that?"

Charlie took a sip of the velvety wine. Absently, she pushed her hair back from her face and sighed. "I feel like an idiot when I'm around him, Nad. He makes me nervous, and I don't like that!"

Nadine, trying to sound reassuring said, "Do you honestly think he didn't know how difficult it was for you to go back? He knows you're serious about this job, plus you said you held your own at the combat and observation class. You should be proud of yourself!"

"I guess you have a point."

"Charlie, you're also forgetting a major issue here."

"Which is...?"

"He also had to face you again after acting like a complete moron. Think about how he feels. The guy's sixty years old and stumbles over his words and acts like he's still a virgin!"

"Well, I wouldn't go that far."

Sensing that Charlie was leaving out something important, Nadine pushed onward. "Why not? What haven't you told me?"

Charlie settled on the window seat and stretched her lean legs out in front of her. Her muscles were achy and she desperately wanted to end the conversation. She gulped down the rest of her wine and felt the cool liquid rush into her body, making her flush. As nonchalantly as possible, Charlie replied, "Nothing really."

"That tells me there's definitely something. Come on, what aren't you telling me?"

Charlie sighed and plunged ahead, knowing that if she didn't level with her friend, Nadine would keep badgering her until she finally broke her down. "Well, after the observation class Robert asked me to get a bite to eat with him, and I said no."

Screaming into the phone, Nadine screeched, "YOU WHAT?"

Nadine's voice pierced right through Charlie, making her shiver. "I said...I said no. I wasn't hungry. There's no crime in saying no to food when you're not hungry, Nad!"

"You are so full of shit right now, you know that? You're afraid, admit it!"

Charlie was weary of the drill, and changed to her cordless phone so she could head upstairs and prepare a bath. "Look, I'll deal with the situation the way that I see fit! It's not a good idea for me to get involved with him. Why can't you understand that?"

Nadine, clearly frustrated, now asked, "Tell me what the reasons are? Go ahead, I'm listening."

"First of all, he's too old! He's sixty years old for Christ's sake, but the most important reason is that I work for him. HELLO! Are you forgetting that? It would cause trouble, heartache, and problems for the both of us if we went that route. Give me some credit, will you? The guy is obviously horny and only thinking with his other head!"

Finding herself getting uptight, Nadine barked into the receiver, "ALL RIGHT, ALL RIGHT! I will point out, though, that you never answered my original question."

Totally exasperated, Charlie gripped the cordless phone like it was a weapon of mass destruction. Her temper was flaring full force now, and she knew she wouldn't be able to control it much longer. "Nadine, I don't care! I'm hanging up now, because every joint, muscle, and bone in my body has been ripped to shreds, and I'm exhausted. I'll speak to you soon, okay?"

Taking a deep breath and sighing, Nadine relented, "Fine, my friend, but do let me know when you decide to admit to me that you feel the same way about Robert as he does you.

After you face that little tidbit you'll be able to admit that you're scared, and that's why you won't go out with him! I hope you feel better after you've had your bath and a good night's sleep, because being BITCHY isn't very becoming to you! Bye!"

She hung up on her! She couldn't believe that Nadine actually hung up on her. She stood in the middle of her bathroom staring at the phone in her hand. "Well, I deserved that." Guilt swelled through her as she ran the water for her bath. Charlie poured in some lavender scented oil, and cursed herself for being so rude to her best friend. She vowed to call her in the morning and apologize.

While the tub was filling, she ran back downstairs to the kitchen, poured herself another glass of wine, and made a small tray of snacks. She was quite in tune with her body, and knew that after her bath she would be too tired to parade down and up the stairs again.

She placed the tray on the night table by the side of her bed, and took the glass of wine with her to the tub. Her body slithered down the cool porcelain. She reached for her Elaina Marie Salt Scrub and massaged it into her weary limbs and sighed.

Charlie knew Nadine was right, but her ego wouldn't allow her to admit it just yet. The age difference meant nothing to her. It was all she could come up with at the time. But the fact that he was her boss being an issue was the truth. She'd seen many relationships go sour because of too much "togetherness," as she called it. In her mind it was inconceivable that two people could have a working relationship and a private, intimate one, simultaneously, without it falling to shreds.

After an hour in the tub her skin glowed. She got out, dried herself off, and put on her silky negligee. Her body felt better, but not her mind. It raced full speed ahead with what ifs.

She fell into the coziness of her bed and switched on the TV. Absently, she ate her snacks and felt herself slowly slip into oblivion. She placed the tray back on the night stand and clicked off the TV, hoping that a good night's sleep would ease all the tensions and doubts that plagued her.

As soon as her head hit the pillow she was sound asleep, but her wish for a peaceful night's sleep would be anything but.

❧❦

WITH EACH TOSS AND TURN SHE MADE, HER body grew hot, very, very hot. Her subconscious mind alerted her to danger. The intense darkness frightened her as alarm surged through her body.

She felt him there, his evil and hatred permeating the room. She felt his hot breath on her face, and slowly opened her eyes. She saw the shank of the silver signet ring he always wore on his huge, wrinkled hand looming next to her cheek, and could feel his flowing black cloak that represented his underworld brush up against her damp skin. She flailed it away as silent screams choked in her throat, and she sprang forward off the bed.

She needed light; knew it was vital to her survival that she have it. His image bore down on her, trying to stop her. She slashed out with all her might, and forced the image to the side. She reached for the switch. Frantically, she clicked the lever up and down, but it didn't work. His deep, dark laughter rang throughout the otherwise silent room. Terror ran through her as she screamed out, "No, no, not again! No more, please!" Charlie needed light, any light, but he wouldn't allow it.

HE NEEDED HER THERE IN THE DARK, because that was her greatest fear, and her fear is what he fed on, what empowered him. He had been coming to her for some time now, and soon, yes, very, very soon, he will have acquired all the power and strength he needed, and when he did, he was going to take her in one final terrorizing blow.

CHAPTER 20

BOLTS OF LIGHTNING AND THUNDER CRASHED THROUGH the dark, dreary sky, as raindrops the size of bullets pounded fiercely against the windows. She lay awake the entire night, too terrified to fall asleep, fearful the demon would return. She stayed on her back, eyes wide open, not moving. She pulled one of her hands out from under the protective comforter and brushed a mass of curls away from her face, and felt how clammy her skin was.

In less than two hours she had to be at work, and somehow she would have to pull herself together. She was in a state of shock and couldn't discern if what she thought to be real, was... or was just another terrifying nightmare. She had been tormented by so many of them she couldn't tell the difference anymore. This one felt so real, it couldn't have been a dream, or could it?

She had felt his presence in her room, his hot breath on her cool flesh, burning her. Then there was the light switch--it didn't work. Hesitantly, she pushed the heavy comforter away and threw her legs over the side of the bed. She needed to know...had to know.

Taking baby steps, she walked to the edge of the room where the light switch was... waiting, just waiting for her to test it. She put her index finger on the switch, inhaling deeply. Slowly, she pushed the lever up, and didn't stop until it clicked into place. Instantly, the room was flooded with a blinding light.

She froze, rooted to where she stood. Her face turned pale...the pallor of the dead. Her breath sputtering out in small controlled heaves as she tried to get air into her diminished lungs. Then the inevitable happened, she opened her mouth and let out one mangled scream after another.

The last thing she wanted was for Robert to see her in this condition. He'd regret hiring her, and she didn't want that. She had to prove not only to him, but to herself, that she could not only do this work, but do it well. She also knew she had to get out of the house as soon as possible. She had to move, and prayed that the terror wouldn't follow her.

Today the real estate agent was showing the house to two interested parties, and Charlie hoped one of them would love it enough to buy it. She herself had three appointments that week to look at some lovely homes on the shore line in Narragansett, and silently prayed that one of the options would be appealing enough for her to finally make the move.

Once in the shower, she let the water run ice cold over her body, hoping the shock would revive her. When she was finished, she got out and examined herself in the steamy mirror.

There were dark circles under her eyes, and creases had suddenly appeared on her forehead that hadn't been there before. She looked like death, and didn't feel much better, either. Haphazardly, she pulled on her sweat suit and sneakers. She thought about applying some concealer and foundation to camouflage the dark circles and creases on her face, but knew it wouldn't do any good.

Slowly, she descended the stairs and made her way to the kitchen to put on a pot of some much needed coffee. She couldn't even muster the energy to make a lunch for herself. She winced when she glanced at the clock on the far side of the wall and saw it was already time to go. She poured the strong brew into a travel mug and grabbed her purse off the counter.

Once in her car, Charlie thought about how she was going to make it through the day, but quickly reminded herself that she had done it before, and could do it again.

CHAPTER 21

SHE PULLED INTO THE LOT AND PARKED AT the far end, where it was fairly empty. She pulled down the visor and looked in the mirror to take a last glance at herself. She gasped at what she saw. She pinched her cheeks, hoping to bring some color to her pale complexion.

Charlie got out of the car, locked the door, and headed for the side entrance. She hoped Robert wasn't engaged in one of his "eye spy" routines this morning, because she was definitely in no mood for it. She entered the building and made her way down the curved hallway to his office. When she reached his door, she found it closed, and hesitantly knocked. His voice bellowed out from the other side, "Come in!"

She pushed the door open, took two steps into the room, ready to attempt a cheerful good morning to him when he looked up at her, gasped, and dropped his coffee cup onto his desk, the hot brew spilling all over him and the documents that were splayed on it. "Charlie! My God, are you all right?"

"I'm fine, Robert, why?"

She couldn't tell him anything; it wasn't the time or place for that type of conversation. She walked to a vacant chair in front of his desk and wearily sat down. Once seated, she unconsciously let out a huge sigh, and felt her body melt into the comfort of the soft leather. His eyes never left her, and she thought she saw concern there, but couldn't be sure.

Why would he be concerned, anyway--he didn't know her well enough to have that kind of emotional response?

HE COULDN'T TEAR HIS GAZE AWAY FROM HER. BY God, she looked like death. She was pale, her body was shaking, and there were deep, dark circles under her eyes.

He was deeply concerned for her, but how did he tell her without crossing the line of proper etiquette? Where the hell was the line, anyway? He was the boss, and that gave him the right to question his employees, which she was, and find out what was wrong.

Trying to keep his tone light, he searched for the right way to phrase the opening question. Since the first day he met her, his articulation and verbal skills had flown out the window, so he knew he had to think carefully, or once again he'd blow it and make a complete fool of himself.

"Charlie, listen, I haven't had my coffee yet, because, as you can see, I had a little accident here, and I didn't have any breakfast, either, so I was thinking maybe we could go down the street to this little diner I know and have some." Nothing.

She stared straight ahead with a blank expression on her face. He tried again.

"You know, coffee and food."

He saw that tears were brimming in her eyes. "Charlie?"

"Um? Oh, I'm sorry, I thought I answered you, Robert. Sure, that sounds great, I could definitely use some coffee and breakfast. Thanks. It's on me though, okay?"

"No, not okay. I invited you, so I pay."

When she raised her hand in a feeble gesture to argue with him, his tone was firm, "This is not open for discussion." She managed a small nod and realized she was so tired she didn't even have the stamina to argue with him. "Let me tell Pino to take over. Wait here, I'll be right back."

Wearily, she nodded in agreement.

When he returned to his office, Robert found Charlie exactly where he had left her. "The diner is small and quiet, so we'll have privacy. If you don't mind, I'd like to bring along some paperwork you need to fill out for tax purposes, and the case file, if you think you can handle it."

"I'm fine. Bring it."

They headed out the door, Robert following close behind her. He was worried now, not just a little, but a lot. She lacked the fire and spunk that usually emanated from her inner soul.

At one point she turned back and glanced into his eyes, and once again was startled by the worry she saw in his eyes. She was so used to being alone and not allowing others to see her when she was vulnerable, that she didn't know how to handle the situation.

When they reached his car, he took her arm, pulling her close to him. He said nothing, just gently rocked her back and forth as though lulling a child to sleep. When he finally felt her body relax, he pulled away. Robert opened the door for Charlie and waited for her to get in.

As he closed the door, pain ripped through his heart for this woman whom he had known for just a short time.

☙◦❧

THEY SAT ACROSS FROM EACH OTHER IN THE quaint diner. Neither said anything; they were both lost in their own thoughts. Robert didn't know what to say or ask, and Charlie didn't know how she was going to stay awake and concentrate.

The two ordered their food and ate in silence. When they were finished, he knew he had to start somewhere, so he gave her the forms she needed to fill out. She was concentrating too hard and going at a snail's pace through each form. He studied her features as she filled out the last of the paperwork, and noticed how incredibly fragile she looked.

When she was finished and looked up into his eyes, he felt his heart being torn from his chest. He didn't want to stare, but he needed to know what the bloody hell had happened to her the night before. Whatever it was, it had shaken her to her core.

"Charlie, I know you don't want me to pry, but please believe me when I say that I am deeply concerned about you. I want you to know that you can trust me with things, and if you need to talk to someone, I'm here for you."

Her eyes glazed over as she forced air into her lungs. Charlie shifted her gaze past his shoulders to the kitchen door at the far end of the diner. She didn't trust herself to speak, so instead she nodded.

He removed a file from his briefcase and handed it to her. She took it from him, opened it, and started to read the contents. He sat back against the hard booth and watched her over the rim of his mug. He knew she would be shocked and confused, and just hoped he wasn't making a big mistake... one that would cost him dearly if she couldn't pull through.

For the first time, her eyes sparkled and showed signs of intrigue as she finally comprehended what she was reading. When she was done, she looked up at him and smiled, then sighed. "Robert, I have so many questions right now. I don't know where to begin."

Relaxing slightly, he encouraged, "Start at the beginning, then."

"Okay. First, there's mention of the DEA. Am I correct in assuming that the DEA is the Drug Enforcement Agency?"

"Yes, you are."

When he didn't elaborate further, she cleared her throat and continued. "There's a man named Antonio Bellesto. He owns two restaurants on Federal Hill and has vast holdings in the warehouse district near Fox Point. I assume he's the lead suspect."

This time he only nodded. Robert didn't mean to make her feel uncomfortable, but he wanted to know how much she grasped and how quickly she could put the pieces of the puzzle together. Charlie fidgeted slightly, shifting her body in the booth. She wanted more than just a nonverbal response, but it was apparent he wasn't going to help her out here, so she went on.

"The DEA suspects Antonio Bellesto is involved in drug trafficking, and wants you to help them find out if their suspicions are correct, and who he's connected with."

Biting down on his bottom lip, Robert coaxed, "Keep going."

"Mr. Bellesto has the reputation of being a lady's man, so the DEA wants a female agent to go undercover and make contact with him." When he didn't answer or look at her, she knew there was more to it.

Charlie's eyes widened and Robert knew the light bulb had clicked on. Charlie let out a long gasp, "Oh, my God. Robert, am I the woman that's going to go under cover? Are you sure I'll be ready for something of this magnitude? Wait! Answer the first question for me. Am I correct in assuming that I'm to be the female agent going in?"

His eyes bore deeply into hers. Robert didn't flinch or blink. He knew he couldn't show her that he was uneasy with the decision he'd made. "Yes, you are correct on that, Charlie."

"But why? The DEA has their own agents--they don't need a PI."

"In this case they do. Fredrick Constantino is the man who's running this operation. He and I go way back and have done many favors for each other over the years. Most of the female agents, which are few and far between, are out on other assignments. Fredrick trusts my judgment and knows I'll send him only the best. In this case, that will be you."

She sat totally still. She didn't move. *What the hell am I doing?*

He sensed what was happening and quickly tried to ease the tension that was growing at the corners of her already weary eyes. "Charlie?"

When she didn't respond, he grasped her hand and squeezed it tightly in his. His stare forced her to acknowledge him and all he had just told her. She lifted her eyes to his, and slowly he continued, trying to calm her fears.

"I believe in you and your abilities. I have no other female agents. I know that with the proper training, you will be able to handle this case. I don't mean to throw you in the deep end here, but something tells me you'd prefer it this way, because it will be more of a challenge for you. Just remember to follow my lead, and you'll be okay."

Charlie nodded in assent. "I always thrive on challenges, but I never encountered one like this before. Well, I wanted excitement in my life, but, my God, this is a bomb, for Christ's sake, Robert!"

When she tried to lean back, he tightened the grip on her hand. "Look at me, Charlie. You can do this. Like I said a few minutes ago, follow my lead, and you'll be fine." He saw doubt mixed with fear flash across her face, and knew that in order for her to make it, she had to let go and trust him. "Charlie, I don't want to pry into your personal life, but at this point, I have to warn you. If you do decide to go through with this, you have to let go of all your fears, and trust me completely. It's vital to this assignment that you believe in me and trust me, with no questions asked. If you can't guarantee me that, then I can't bring you in on this."

Silence loomed between the two. After a beat, he spoke again. "I will repeat the question so there are no misunderstandings between us. Can you guarantee me that you will trust me and not question me on anything pertaining to your training and this case?"

She slowly licked her parched lips and let out a long, deep sigh. *How the hell can I tell a total stranger I will let down all my defenses and put my life in his hands, not questioning him, his tactics, or* motives? This is absurd for him to even ask of me!

He sat patiently waiting for her answer. She was tapping her fingers on top of the table as her legs followed along to the rhythm underneath. He was ready to bang down on her hand. The drumming of her fingers was driving him crazy, but he fought to remain silent and still.

When she finally spoke, it was a mere whisper, and he had to lean forward and strain to hear what she was saying. "I can only promise you that I will try. I will try to trust you, and try to do the best job that I am capable of doing."

His head bobbed up and down in agreement with her words. It wasn't exactly what he wanted to hear, but it was a start. He was determined to break down every wall and barrier that she had built, and prove to her that putting trust in someone could be a good thing, that it didn't always end in disaster and pain. He knew he was in "this" for the long haul with her, and he was willing to wait until she was ready to do the same. He just hoped he'd live through it!

"I think that's a very good start, Charlie. Now, is there anything else you'd like to tell me?"

❦

Her eyes darted back and forth like she was watching a tennis match as she weighed his words, discerning that he wanted to know what happened to her last night. Should I tell him everything? But as she opened her mouth to form the words, she quickly changed her mind and closed it, only nodding instead. She wanted to believe in him and in his words, but just couldn't do it. Not yet, anyway. The horror she lived with would remain deep inside her for a very long time. She wouldn't even know where to begin when it came to what she had been through. It was too overwhelming for her to form the words and relive the past. The other morning when she remembered the last day of her divorce trial and relived the trauma.... it took its toll on her, not just mentally, but physically as well.

"No, no, there's nothing else, Robert. I didn't get a good night's sleep, that's all. I'm sure I'll sleep better tonight."

"You're sure there's nothing wrong?"

When Charlie answered him, he knew she was lying. Her head was bowed and all her concentration was on the tablecloth on the table. "Yes, I'm sure."

He was going to have to teach her to lie better and not fidget so much. God, he had his hands full, but was sure he could handle it.

He could, couldn't he?

CHAPTER 22

IT WAS DARK AND DREARY INSIDE THE warehouse. The only light came from a single bulb. Four men sat around a square card table speaking in hushed tones.

Antonio Bellesto rose from his chair and slammed his fist down hard, causing the table to rock back and forth. His slate grey eyes were mere slits as he fought to keep his demeanor in check. The three men, recognizing the warning signs, kept silent, not wanting to be the one singled out to face his wrath.

Striving for composure, Antonio sat back down and inhaled deeply. Before he spoke, he looked around the table at each of his men, studying their body language and eyes for any telltale signs. One of these men may have betrayed him, and he knew it was vital to his operation to find out which one.

When he felt himself in complete control again, he finally asked the one question that was searing through his brain. "Who betrayed me, and why?"

The silence in the warehouse was deafening. Not one of the men moved or spoke. Antonio's handsome face had disapproval etched across it as he glared from one man to the next, waiting. He could feel his temper flaring up again and strained for composure.

When he finally spoke, his tone was like thick, molten lava. "You each have exactly twenty-four hours to come to me and reveal what you know. I expect that one of you will be able to enlighten me on the incident that almost caused irreparable damage to my operation. If I am not completely satisfied with the information I receive, then know right now that all - and I mean all of you, will pay the price! Is this understood?"

Each of the men shook their heads in acknowledgement and waited for the meeting to be concluded. No one dared move a muscle until the boss gave his permission for them to be dismissed.

85

Slowly Bellesto rose from his chair, and once standing, placed all of his attention on the lapel of his crisp pin striped suit. Though his eyes were lowered, he was studying each of them. He knew one of them was a rat, but which one?

Without the others' knowledge, he had brought a new man on. When he hired him, Bellesto wasn't quite sure in what capacity he would use him. But now, yes, now, he knew what his new right hand man would be doing. His new hire was hungry and ruthless, and Bellesto liked that. He'd have him figure out which one of his tail men was Judas, and when he did, the Judas would face a terrifying and painful death. Antonio Bellesto was known for showing no mercy, and he pitied the poor sucker who would soon be facing his wrath!

"Get out of here, and no more screw ups! Just remember, you each have twenty-four hours to come forward!" All of the men rose quickly, shook Bellesto's hand, and scurried towards the exit of the warehouse. Bellesto watched all of them leave, looking for anything that might tip him off.

Whichever one of these men was his opponent was good, very good indeed.

CHAPTER 23

HE PLACED THE RECEIVER DOWN IN ITS cradle with the utmost care. Everything was moving along as scheduled ...well, not exactly as scheduled. His divorce hampered the timeline a bit, but that wouldn't halt the progress.

During his brief marriage, he succeeded in making contact with the one person that was vital to the success of his heterogeneous operation--his ex-wife's Uncle, Archbishop Giuseppe Zanfagna. Zanfagna flew to Rhode Island from the precious Vatican so he could witness his lovely niece's wedding.

The well-respected Archbishop took time off from handling the Vatican's finances. He worked side by side with the man formerly known as "God's Banker," Roberto Calvi, and Calvi was the key to the success of the plan.

He turned and strode to the opposite side of the dimly lit room and stopped when he reached a painting of a mosque that was located in his homeland of Damascus. He took time to admire its beauty and vastness, for it was quite large, the proportions being eighty inches across by eighty inches down. The artwork was enclosed within an ostentatious gold frame that Darrell thought suited it perfectly. The antique gilt paint glimmered off the canvas into the dimness of the room, sending out trance-like vibes. The frame was so heavy, Darrell had hinges put on one side so it could be easily opened to reveal the hidden safe behind it.

He considered himself to be a devout Muslim and remained totally loyal to the Jihad group. He studied and supported Mohammed's son-in-law, Sidina Ali's, views that all those who did not believe and support Mohammed's words should be killed. Sidina Ali showed no favoritism even with his own people. It was rumored that even after Ali had destroyed all his enemies, he continued to kill off his own people. He also knew that eventually the entire United

States would be under Sharia Law and he couldn't wait...

Darrell's organization took Ali's words literally: All those who do not believe and support Mohammed's words are to be killed. To Darrell, it was clear who the first group to die should be.

He delicately grasped the lower right hand corner of the ornate frame and pulled towards him. The large painting swung open effortlessly on its well-greased hinges, revealing a safe. Darrell pressed in the complex code of Aramaic numbers. He gripped the knob, turned, and waited to hear a click.

Swinging open the safe's door, he peered inside, in search of the files he now needed. A satisfied smile spread across his darkened features as he found exactly what he was looking for. He removed two of the folders marked "Vatican" and crossed back to his desk. He placed the folders down with care onto the gleaming wood.

For a moment he just stared at the red lettering on the first folder, "Vatican/Roberto Calvi," which was written in Aramaic. All the information was written in the cryptic language. He pulled out his favorite wingback chair and sat, his body molding perfectly into the soft grains of the leather.

Reaching forward, he grasped the thick cigar that lay on top of the dark wood and placed it between his teeth. Striking a match, he lit the tobacco, and inhaled deeply. He made continuous smoke rings as he opened the file and began to read.

Roberto Calvi was the chairman of Bianco Ambrossa Bank in Italy. His bank was linked with the Mafia, which was where his new boss, Antonio Bellesto, the Vatican, and the terrorist Jihad group came in, just to name a few.

Darrell's organization was shocked when they heard of Calvi's death. The Jihad had many of their men well-placed within the walls of the Vatican's confines, and soon found out that the Vatican had asked the Mafia to assist them in permanently removing Calvi, because he was not only backing the Jihad terrorist group, but also had been transferring the Jihad's laundered money throughout the Vatican for them.

Calvi knew too much about the Vatican's and Mafia's finances, and their interwoven dealings with one another, and he needed to be eliminated, pronto. To make matters even worse, Calvi owed an astronomical amount of money to the Cosa Nostra.

"Big mistake, Bellesto... big mistake, Vatican," Darrell said to himself, as he shook his head disapprovingly.

It was then that Darrell's organization decided to accelerate their plan. It was all over the world news. Calvi was found dead, hanging under the Blackfriars Bridge in London. A wide scope probed Calvi's business as well as personal affairs, and it became public knowledge that Calvi was not only a Freemason, but a member of the elite Grand Orient of Italy Lodge P2.

The media was having a field day. The Vatican's standing as the wealthiest institution in the world was now being questioned. What kind of organization was it, really? It became public knowledge that the Vatican's Archbishop Giuseppe Zanfagna - with the Vatican's support - gave two hundred and fifty million dollars to Calvi's creditors! It's "holiness" was tarnished by the ties it shared not only with Calvi, but also with the Mafia.

Another main figure tied to Calvi's bank and Bianco Ambrossa, was Luigi Gellico. Gellico was the Grand Master of the P2 Masonic Lodge. He was revered within the Masonic organization, for he alone initiated thousands into their society. It was a fact that many of these Freemasons and members of the elite P2 were splayed throughout the inner walls of the Vatican. Gellico got off easier than Calvi; he was sentenced to house arrest, but more importantly...he was allowed to live.

Placing the file back on the desk, Darrell stretched and rose from his seat. He had been reading for over an hour now, and his back was stiff. The cigar had long been smoked down, but the filmy hues of the vapors still hung heavily in the air.

Silently, he paced around the office, his mind reeling. This was more...much more than he ever could have hoped for. His voice was laced with sheer excitement when he spoke into the dimness of the room. "What a tangled web of lies and deceit, and all from the holiest, not to mention richest, state in the world. But... for how much longer!"

Stopping by the window, he peered outside and saw that dusk had arrived. His stomach ached for food, but such an indulgence simply would have to wait. He must finish reading the second file before he would allow himself to give in to his bodily needs. He pulled out the chair and collapse heavily into the worn leather. He inhaled the rich scent the leather gave off, and heard his stomach grumble.

Ignoring the pangs of hunger, he leaned over and took the file that simply said "Vatican" on it. He rubbed his hands together in anticipation at what juicy information he would read about this vast institution. He flipped open the folder and stopped dead. His eyes grew wide at the bold red letters that splayed across the top of the page. "Vatican's Secret Mafia." The encoding of this file was much more direct and gave less explanation than the first. It was more in outline form.

Finally relenting, Darrell had to turn on the light now, for outside was nothing but pure blackness. He preferred his office to be as dark as possible; it gave him the feeling of power and control.

He pulled the brass cording that hung from the Tiffany lamp perched on the edge of his desk. The room was instantly illuminated with blinding light, making him blink and cover his eyes.

"Damn!" he screamed out into the stillness of the room. Red dots played back and forth like a visual ping pong match. Waiting for his eyes to adjust and the dots to go away, Darrell massaged his aching temples. Absorbing all of this information was tiring...very tiring. He reread the first line, then continued on.

Catholic Churches Religious Orders: Opus Dei, Jesuits, Legionarios of Christ, Freemasons, P2.

These orders are more harmful and dangerous than any Mafia family.

All are Roman Legions.

Vatican is the richest Independent State in the world. Vatican has the largest collection of priceless art treasures. Vatican's Bank-The Institute for Religious Works suffered severe losses due to Calvi's dealings.

1978- Pope John Paul I murdered by the Vatican Mafia 33 days after his election.

Vatican gave the order to have him killed because John Paul was signing documents that would completely cut off the Vatican's dealings with Calvi and his bank.

September 1978 - Pope John Paul I tells his Secretary of State to initiate a detailed and thorough investigation into the Vatican's Bank operations.

September 28, 1978 - The pope demands over one hundred resignations from many of the cardinals and bishops working within the Vatican. The Pope found out these men were members of the Freemason's Group P2.

September 29, 1978 - Pope John Paul I was found dead in his bed by his Secretary of State. His Secretary of State removed all key evidence of what John Paul I was working on. All documents signed by John Paul I were removed from his bedside table.

Secretary of State gives false statements to the media in regards to the Pope's death.

Secretary of State orders the Pope's body to be embalmed immediately so no autopsy could ever be done.

October 1978 – Pope John Paul II replaced Pope John Paul I

None of John Paul I last wishes were known or carried out.

Satisfaction flowed as he placed the documents back inside the second folder and closed it. There was much to do now...yes, much. He picked up the two folders and pushed back his chair. He strode to the side of the room where the safe was still open. He eased the folders back into place, shut the vault, locked it, and guided the painting back into position.

He had a meeting to go to now; his dinner would have to be postponed for a while longer. As he turned off the light, he reflected on many things. They, meaning his organization, had to proceed with extreme caution. His organization was based in his homeland of Syria, but stretched far and wide to all corners of the world, including the almighty Vatican.

It was no coincidence that he ended up in Rhode Island. He not only needed Charlie for her connection to the Archbishop, but he also needed to make contact with the infamous Antonio Bellesto. He, too, hadn't ended up in this lovely little state for no reason. No... he came to the Ocean State straight from the inner workings of the Vatican itself. He not only succeeded in making contact with the most auspicious crime boss, but he went one step further and was made his right hand man!

This plan had taken years to perfect and now the wheels were finally in motion. They were going to destroy the most powerful state in the world... the Vatican!

And when that was done, there would finally be a one- world religious government...the government of the Islam.

CHAPTER 24

WHEN THEY REACHED HIS CAR, HE HESITATED by her door. He knew she'd probably turn him down again, but he was willing to take the risk. "Ah, Charlie, I was thinking that maybe you could come to my house and relax."

He felt her body stiffen next to him, and quickly continued so she could hear him out completely. "You see, I live by the ocean, and it's such a beautiful day that I thought we could take a walk and you could rest, and then later we could review the photos and information on all the suspects that you need to memorize. By then I'm sure you'll be hungry again, and we could have some dinner together and..."

Charlie's face turned a bright pink and she laughed out loud. *He is so endearing!* "It sounds like a great plan Robert! It's a beautiful day, and a walk by the shore would indeed do me some good. I had some appointments to look at houses. I'll call and cancel them."

I'm going to do something I haven't done in years... Taking one step forward, she tilted her head up to meet his and placed a tiny peck on his lips. She slowly pulled back so she could gauge his reaction. He stood looking at her with his mouth wide open. She didn't know if that was a good thing or not. "Robert?"

"Uh, yes...., yes, sure, that sounds wonderful, I'd love to. Thanks."

Her sultry laughter exploded into the air as shock and embarrassment registered on his face. "I'm sorry, I guess you threw me off a little there. I wasn't expecting that, and anyway..."

"Robert?"

"Yes, Charlie?"

"Be quiet. Open my door and let's go, okay?

A huge smile spread across both their faces, and for the first time in years they each felt carefree and at peace within themselves.

CHAPTER 25

WHEN THEY PULLED INTO HIS DRIVEWAY SHE let out a shriek of delight. She could hear the rustling of the waves through the open window as she inhaled the crisp clean air. "I don't know about you, Robert, but I feel better already!"

He glanced over at her and was delighted to see her eyes wide and sparkling, with a huge smile spread across her face. He got out of the car and ran around to her side and opened the door for her.

"Thanks."

"You're welcome..."

Tilting his head to the side, he studied her face silently. As if mesmerized, he said, "You know, Charlie, the ocean air agrees with you-your face has a soft glow to it now."

She bowed her head demurely as color flooded her cheeks. Startling her, he grasped her hand and together they walked up the cobblestone path that led to his front door.

She took in as much of the breath-taking view as possible. All the flowers were in bloom; the lawn gleamed and was manicured to perfection. He opened the door and stepped aside for her to go in first, and when she did, she let out a long sigh. She took in the vaulted ceilings and the warm, creamy colors. There were no walls or barriers, just fluid motion across the open floor plan. Her eyes were wide saucers as she entered the kitchen and noticed that it also had stucco walls and light, cheery colors. Copper pots hung from the ceiling, and huge plants adorned the angles of the walls to give each of the rooms a more uniformed feel.

"Robert, this is beautiful! You've done a wonderful job."

"Thanks. I'm glad you like it. Come on, and I'll finish showing you around."

As he led her from room to room, she finally got a sense of who this man really was. Each room was large and spacious. There were neither masculine nor feminine tones, but, rather, soothing and tranquil colors that heightened all one's senses. In the lower level of the house was a huge workout room filled with weights and universal equipment.

"I'm impressed, Robert, this is some layout you have here. It's a comfortable home; I'm sure you must be quite happy here."

He didn't respond. *What can I possibly say to that statement? I want to tell her that it isn't a home, it's just a house. She has no idea my nights are spent in solitude and the stillness drives me crazy most of the time.*

She stood directly in front of him by the bench press, and took in the faraway look in his eyes. Sadness filled the blue pools and her heart tugged at the seams when she saw them cloud over.

Instinctively, she gently placed a hand on his arm, her eyes never leaving his. He pulled away from her gesture and abruptly said, "Come on, let's go for that walk."

It felt like he had just slapped her hard across the face, and she took a step back. Hesitantly, she answered, "Okay." He said nothing more to her.

He turned on his heel and strode to the door, leaving her no choice but to follow after him.

❧∘❦

THE GLIMMERING SUN WAS A BRILLIANT orange color as its rays poured over the soothing waves, giving it a glass-like appearance. They walked side by side in silence, each lost in their own thoughts.

The sudden sound of his voice made her flinch. Sweeping a hand through her hair, she regained her composure and waited for him to speak again.

"Sorry, I didn't mean to scare you."

"It's okay, Robert; I guess I was lost in my own thoughts. What did you say?"

They both stopped and stood on the shoreline, facing each other. There were so many things each of them wanted to say but didn't know how. The water was warm as it gushed up to their toes, making them both inhale and sigh. "I was asking you why you had a For Sale sign on your front lawn."

The sun hit her eyes, making her squint. She raised a hand to block it so she could see him better, and explained, "I'm selling it."

A sudden roar of laughter escaped from the depths of his throat, and all the tension from the day instantly dissipated.

Smiling and laughing, she replied, "Well, you asked why I had a For Sale sign on my front lawn, and I told you. I figured you didn't quite grasp t what 'for sale' actually meant."

"Ha, ha, smart ass. Okay, let me rephrase the question. Why are you selling your house, and where are you moving?"

"Ah, now, that's two questions, not one."

He took in the mischief in her eyes, and noted how they gleamed like mink. He couldn't help what he said next, it just came out. "Are you aware of how striking you are? My God, Charlie, you are the most sensual, beautiful woman I've ever seen."

She was never good at accepting compliments, and felt her face grow hot. She lowered her head and pretended to study the water flowing over her feet. She merely whispered a thanks, and he realized just how humble she was. She had to be aware of her beauty. Any woman with her looks and breeding had to have heard at least a million times how attractive they were, right?

Sensing her discomfort, Robert dropped the subject, and asked if she wanted to go back. Still looking down at the waves, Charlie nodded her head in agreement. He started walking first, but still managed to steal a few side glances at her.

He realized she never answered his question about her house. But he knew not to push her--he'd wait until the door of opportunity opened again, and when it did, he'd walk right through.

The few minutes of comfort they shared vanished, and he considered how they constantly traded off putting their walls up and blocking the chemistry that surged between them.

When they reached his house, they took another moment and silently gazed out at the vast sea, each lost in private thoughts. His phone started to ring, making them jump and jolt back to reality.

She watched him turn and run into the house, and hoped that someday they wouldn't each feel the need to put up steel walls to protect themselves--that someday, they would be free to just be.

CHAPTER 26

Robert WAS ON THE PHONE FOR AT LEAST twenty minutes. Charlie moved one of the lounge chairs to the edge of the patio, faced it towards the ocean, laid down on it, and closed her eyes. She felt uncomfortable going inside while he was on the phone, and thought it best to give him his privacy.

He walked over to where she lay, and knelt down next to her. His face was creased, the tension in him palpable. Concern rushed through her as she sat up and turned to face him.

"Is something wrong, Robert?"

"That was Fredrick. He has some information that he needs to give me immediately. We're going to meet halfway so he can give me the documents."

"Oh, I'll hurry and get my things."

He put his hand on her shoulder to stop her. "No, no, I don't want you to go, Charlie. I'll be right back, and I need you to wait here so I can show you the documents. They pertain to the Bellesto case you'll be working on."

She sat there, not knowing what to say.

"I would like to ask a favor, if you don't mind."

"Of course, what is it?" she said.

"I thought we'd barbeque on the grill, if that's okay with you?"

"Sounds great, so what's the favor?"

"I took out some hamburgers and hot dogs and put them on the counter. Would you mind making a salad, some fixings, and get the grill going for us while I'm gone?"

He was only a few inches from her and she could feel his warm breath on her face. *This is crazy! I don't know him that well and he wants to leave me in his house? How the hell am I supposed to find anything?*

From the wide doe eyed look, he knew what she was thinking, and rumpled her hair and laughed. "Charlie, I trust you in my home and have no problem leaving you here. I want you to feel comfortable, okay? I don't know if you realize this or not, but you are going to be spending more and more time here, starting now."

Confusion swept across her face as she fidgeted on the lounge chair. Before she could utter a word, he clarified what he just said so she would understand.

"Charlie, you saw part of my facility downstairs. I also have a target room that you still haven't seen yet. You'll have to learn how to handle different types of firearms, and practice target shooting. You'll be doing that training here and on the compound."

Before he could continue, she cut him off. "Compound? What compound?"

"I'll get to that later. It's not important right now. What is important is that you stay here, so ...."

His eyes locked with hers, and they both waited. He waited for her to answer his original question, and she....she just waited because she couldn't remember what the bloody question was! *He's too close to me, he's making my brain all foggy.*

A smile played at the corners of his mouth as he posed the question again, and then it hit her. "Oh, right--barbeque, salad, fixings. No problem, I'd be happy to, Robert."

"Good."

He stood, helped her to her feet, then walked behind her, admiring the curves of her hips and the way they gently swayed back and forth. Once in the kitchen, he gave her a quick run through of where things were, and reassured her that she could rummage through whatever she wanted until she found what she needed.

"The grill is on the patio under the kitchen windows with the coals and lighter fluid on the ground next to it. Anything else?" he asked.

"I don't think so. How long do you think you'll be gone?"

"Hopefully, not more than an hour."

"Great, that'll give me more than enough time to get things ready here."

"Thanks, Charlie."

"Anytime."

They stood in the middle of his kitchen, staring at each other. He wanted to embrace her and kiss those silky lips of hers, but thought twice about it. She wanted him to leave because he was making her feel uncomfortable again.

"Okay, I'll be back as soon as I can." He abruptly turned and walked to the door, not glancing back. When the door closed behind him, she exhaled long and hard.

She hadn't realized she had been holding her breath.

☙◦❧

AFTER ROBERT LEFT, CHARLIE WENT OUT TO THE PATIO and saw the grill under the kitchen windows. She made a mental note to ask him why half of the patio was wood and the other half brick.

Not paying much attention to what she was doing, she lifted the bag of coals from the ground and dumped the entire contents into the grill. If she had paid attention to what she was doing, she would have noticed the grill was on its last legs and had seen better days.

But her mind was on Robert and she wondered where this thing with them was going. Then her thoughts shifted back to the patio-- she really wanted to know why half was wood and the other half concrete, damn it!

She picked up the bottle of lighter fluid. Her talents were limited when it came to fire and coals. She had a hard enough time with her gas grill, and all she had to do was turn a lousy knob.

"It figures, no directions. How much do I use?" She felt the weight of the bottle and assumed it was full, so not wanting to risk not using enough, she poured half the contents over the coals.

Charlie was good at many things, but anything that involved matches and fire was a dangerous mix for her. She also had the tendency to be accident prone, but thought it unwise to inform Robert of this, due to the nature of her new occupation.

She placed the now half-empty container in close proximity on the picnic table, in case she needed more of it later on, and went inside to prepare the salad and vegetables. She found his stereo system, put on Gary Puckett and the Union Gap band, and sang her heart out.

When she went back outside, she was delighted to find that he had speakers placed all around the area. The music soothed away the tension and she felt good. She found a book of matches on the table, picked it up, and proceeded to strike one to light the grill, but had a fleeting thought that maybe she should move it away from the windows. Talking aloud, she reasoned, "I'm sure it's fine where it is, or Robert wouldn't have it here, now, would he?"

Charlie struck a match and dropped it onto the coals. As soon as the match made contact with the lighter fluid, a mini eruption occurred. Her reflexes kicked into high gear and she jumped backwards, almost tripping over her own feet. The flames were high, hot, and flaring up against the kitchen windows. In a coma-like trance, she stood open-mouthed, watching in horror as the fire jumped up and licked the windows, instantly charring them.

She was afraid the intense temperature from the flames would blow the windows out, and got the bright idea to pull the grill forward away from them, just in case. Bracing herself, she grasped the handles that were on the side.

But what she hadn't realized was that the legs of the grill were broken, and the top portion was only resting on the base. So when she went to pull the grill forward, the top part started to flip over in slow motion, or so it seemed to her, and its trajectory was aimed straight for her legs. Charlie let out a shriek, flipped the grill's top to the side, and jumped out of the way. The wooden part of the patio caught on fire, and smoke began to encircle the area.

She acted on instinct, and started to blow on the flames and flap her arms up and down like a bird ready to take off for flight, when it finally dawned on her that this wasn't helping the situation. She ran to the kitchen and found the biggest pot she could and filled it with water. Charging back out to the patio, she dumped the water onto the flames. She repeated this tactic three more times until the flames finally were out. She made a mental note to tell Robert to put a spout outside somewhere for emergencies like this.

Charlie stood there, appraising the damage, and cursed aloud to herself. "Who the bloody hell has a wooden patio, anyway?" She glanced at her watch and saw that forty minutes had gone by and Robert's return was imminent.

Fighting off panic and the sudden urge to throw up, she willed herself to think of a solution. She quickly picked up the grill and brought it to the far end of the patio. She retrieved all the coals off the ground, threw them back into the grill, and started striking matches like crazy.

Frustration took over when she couldn't figure out why the damn coals weren't lighting. It wasn't until she went through two books of matches that it occurred to her that you couldn't relight wet coals.

Running back into the kitchen, she put the oven on, threw the hamburgers and hot dogs onto a cookie sheet, and literally threw it in the oven. She ran around the kitchen like a madwoman searching for his dishes and silverware. She set the table, and placed the salad and vegetables onto platters, then ran back out to the patio so she could survey the damage.

She stood with her legs apart, hands on her hips, and slowly shifted her head from side to side so she could absorb everything. She mumbled to herself as a feeling of doom spread through her. "Wow! How the hell am I going to explain this one? He's going to wring my neck! The poor guy leaves me alone for one hour and I set his patio on fire!"

She took in the black soot, burnt wood, and foul smell, and felt like crying. "He entrusted me with his home and belongings and I nearly destroyed it all!" She thought she heard a car pull into the driveway and ran into the house. She rushed to the front window and peeked out through the curtain.

It was him.

"Shit!"

She began to hyperventilate; her body rocked back and forth as panic took over. She tried talking to herself, but that didn't work. "Damn." She heard the car door open and close. "He's walking up to the door and any second he's going to come through it!"

Robert opened the door and a look of surprise flashed over his face at finding Charlie standing there. Her skin was a chalky white color, and she was shaking. His smile froze midstream as he stopped dead in his tracks. He stood perfectly still as he watched her pace around his family room.

"Hi, how's it going?"

She stopped pacing and faced him. She tried to drag out the inevitable and evaded his question.

"How's what going?"

Something alerted him of danger.

"Uh, oh."

Robert shifted his weight from one foot to the other. His hand was still on the doorknob as he slowly pushed the door closed, his eyes never wavering from hers.

"Why do you look like the cat that ate a mouse?"

She dropped her gaze to the floor and began counting all the different colored specks she could see in the carpeting. Now she was scaring him. He couldn't begin to imagine what could have possibly happened in the short amount of time he was gone.

Raising his voice just a fraction, he asked, "Charlie, what happened?"

With her head still lowered, she slowly walked to where he stood. She stepped on the balls of her feet and whispered into his ear, "I can't tell you."

He placed a hand under her chin, tilted her head back and hesitantly asked, "Why not?"

Still whispering, she replied, "Because if I tell you my life expectancy is going to be drastically reduced."

He let out a small laugh and leaned back so he could look directly into her eyes. "Come on, Charlie, it can't be that bad. Can it?" Robert turned his head from side to side, sniffing.

"What the hell is that smell?"

She cleared her throat, and her voice took on the tone of an announcer. "I have good news and bad news--which do you prefer to hear first?"

The smell seemed to be getting stronger. "I guess I'll hear the good news first, that way it'll soften the blow for the bad."

She let out a feeble laugh, and her voice croaked when she said, "I don't think so, but ....uh, the table is set and the hamburgers and hot dogs are ready, so we can eat."

Slowly, he said, "Okay, that's good, thanks... now the bad news is?"

"Well, you see, I had a minor mishap while you were gone."

"How minor are we talking here?"

She was totally flustered now, and grabbed his arm while talking fast and dragging him out to the patio area. "I might as well just show you so you can kill me first and ask questions later!"

When they reached the patio he said nothing. He stood there at first, not comprehending what he was actually seeing, and then as the dawn filtered through his brain, his eyes grew huge and looked like they were going to pop out of his head. Shock was etched in every line and crease on his face, and Charlie held her breath, waiting for the explosion to happen. His motions were slow and concise as he shifted his head from side to side, assessing the damage. His reply was calm and collected as he turned to face her. A smile tugged at the corners of his mouth as he said, "Looks like the patio was on fire."

"Mm, hmm." She was saying as little as possible. She knew volcanoes erupted when one least expected, and didn't want to add any more combustible material to this one. What he said next caught her totally off guard.

Robert started to laugh, grabbed her hand, and said, "Well, it's a good thing my insurance is up to date!" Tears filled his eyes as his laughter grew louder and harder.

She didn't know why, but out of sheer nerves she started to laugh too, and found she couldn't stop. He started to pull her back into the house while still roaring. "Let's eat, I'm starving!"

He waited until they were seated at the table and said, "Charlie, I think we'll have a nice bottle of crisp white wine tonight and watch the sun set. Then you can explain to me exactly what happened here. I'm intrigued as to how you managed to almost torch my house down."

Every time he glanced at her over the course of their meal he would burst out laughing.

She had to admit that she finally found the situation quite humorous, now that she knew her life wasn't going to be cut short on her.

❧

SHE OFFERED TO CLEAN UP AFTER DINNER since he was being such a good sport about the fire.

"Charlie, I can help you."

"No, you're not. You go sit and relax, and I'll take care of everything here."

"I guess I can start going through the files Fredrick gave me, and get them organized."

"Great, you do that."

"Are you trying to get rid of me?"

"No, not at all. I just don't want you hovering next to me and getting in my way."

"Now I'm in your way and hovering?"

102

He gave a small pout and lowered his head like a child who had just been ostracized for doing a no-no.

She put the pan down in the sink and let out a laugh.

"Good God, will you give me a break. I'm not playing, little one, so be on your way now, and let me be."

"Okay, but I need to know something first."

"What now?"

They were facing each other, she with her hands on her hips, face flushed from the heat of the water, he with a small grin pulling at the corners of his mouth, relishing the radiance of her skin and the closeness of their bodies. He wanted to be careful how he phrased the question that he'd been needing to ask her since he returned home.

"Things seem to happen to you--am I correct in assuming this?"

"What sort of things, Robert?"

He knew she wouldn't make this easy for him, so he bravely plunged ahead. "I guess I'm asking you if there's anything I need to know about you?"

Her voice raised just a fraction and put him on alert that he was treading in dangerous waters now. "Like what?"

"You're not being very helpful, Charlie."

"And you're not being very clear as to what you want to know!"

"Okay, here it goes. Ah... are you by any chance accident prone?" He jumped back just in case she decided to try out one of the hand maneuvers she had learned in class.

Her voice was a screech when she finally found her vocal cords and pointed her index finger into his chest. "NO! I AM NOT ACCIDENT PRONE! The fire was your fault, anyway!"

He choked on his saliva and gasped. "What do you mean *my* fault? I wasn't even here!"

They squared off, facing each other now, and were ready to do battle. What they didn't realize was how much they were enjoying the little combat session they were engaged in with each other.

"I'm fully aware that you weren't here. It's what you didn't do before you left. Understand?"

Here I go again. I'm holding a fishing reel and winding it in, just like Charlie's doing to me again. "No, I don't understand what it was that I should have done but didn't do before I left. So why don't you enlighten me and tell me just what it was I should have done? My

God, I'm repeating myself now!"

She took a step back from him so she could count on her fingers as she began her tirade. "You didn't tell me the grill was old, broken, and decrepit! If you had, I never would have used it, which means that I wouldn't have lit it, tried to pull it away from the windows, and I wouldn't have needed to put out a frigging fire! And by the way! One, you need to put a damn spout out there for emergencies like the one I had today! Two, you need to get a new grill, and three, who the bloody hell has a WOODEN PATIO?!"

He didn't say a word, not a single syllable. He stood with his legs apart and mouth wide open. *My God, I actually understand what she is saying and the sick thing is I'm actually inclined to agree with her, and I don't know why.*

Robert responded as seriously as possible, "I totally agree with you, Charlie. It's my fault. I definitely should have told you about the grill, and I promise you the next time I leave you alone in my house, I'll give you a more detailed walk through of the working order of all my possessions. How's that?"

"Why do I feel like you're humoring me?"

"I don't know, why do you feel that way?"

She realized how foolish she must not only look, but sound, and started to laugh at herself. "All right, all right, you're off the hook. Now leave me alone so I can finish cleaning up in here."

"I'd be happy to, Madame, and when you're finished please join me in my office."

"Oh, so formal, now." She gave a low bow and turned back towards the sink, put the water on full blast, and all but dismissed him. He stood there a second longer, admiring her backside, and grateful that she was opening up and being more like her true self.

He liked that, indeed he did.

WHEN SHE WAS FINISHED IN THE KITCHEN, she made her way to his office. She quietly crept down the hallway so as not to disturb him. When she reached the doorway to his office, the sight of him stole her breath away, and she sucked in long and hard.

He looked incredibly handsome sitting behind the huge mahogany desk. He was unaware of her presence, and she enjoyed observing him without his knowledge. The curtains behind him were drawn back and the moonlight filtered into the room, casting shadows of light across his face. He was feverishly writing on a yellow legal pad, and his glasses were down on the bridge of his straight nose. His brows were creased in consternation, and she wondered what he was thinking. She softly cleared her throat, which made him jump in his seat.

He looked up at her and smiled that million dollar smile he had, and her heart melted. "Charlie, I have to ask you something."

She entered the room and said, "Sure, what is it?" She plopped down onto one of the oversized leather chairs and put her feet up on the desk.

His smile spread further as he said, "Make yourself comfortable."

"Thanks, but I believe I just did."

He liked this side of her. Quick wit always excited him, and she definitely had it. He didn't realize that she was staring at him, waiting.

"Uh, Robert?"

"Hmm?"

"Hello."

His face flushed, and he thanked God he was seated behind his desk.

Laughing out loud now, she said, "Hi, nice trip?"

"Very funny, Charlie! Sorry... I was thinking of something else."

"That was obvious."

Oh, God, he hoped his facial expressions didn't give away his thoughts.

"I believe you wanted to ask me something."

"Yes, I do. Can you by any chance, by the grace of God, lip sync?"

She must have heard him wrong. She could have sworn he just asked her if she could lip sync. She dropped her legs from the top of his desk and swung them to the floor, sat up erect, and asked, "Did you just ask me what I think you did?"

He leaned forward and placed both his arms on top of his desk and smiled. "That depends on what it is you think I just asked you?"

"If I could lip sync?"

"You heard right, then."

"Why do you want to know if I can lip sync?"

"Answer the question, and then I'll tell you."

"Okay, yes, as a matter of fact, I can."

He fell back in his seat, mouth hanging open. "You can? Are you kidding?"

"Robert, you're starting to irritate me now. I answered the question, now tell me why you need to know that?"

"Wait a minute, you're telling me that you've actually done it?"

"Done what?" If he wanted to play games she'd follow right along. She was actually enjoying the banter between them. It had been a long time since she'd let her guard down and had fun. She knew she could be quick witted when she wanted to and she was enjoying herself immensely.

"You know 'done what.' Come on, and fill me in on the details. It's important."

Letting out a dramatic sigh, Charlie stretched her arms above her head and looked him dead in the eye. "Oh, all right. I've done some singing and entered a few lip sync contests for fun. Nothing much to tell."

"How many contests have you been in?"

She placed her hand on her chin and mentally took count.

What the bloody hell is taking her so long to answer a simple question? Women!

When she finally answered him and said thirty, Robert almost fell off the side of his chair...

In response, Charlie let out a loud laugh.

He rolled his chair back, stood, and walked around to the front of his desk and sat on the edge. He peered down at her and had to make sure he understood what he'd just heard.

"You said 'thirty.' You've been in thirty contests?"

Her smile was like a cat on the prowl when she confirmed, "Yes, I believe I did."

"Do you mind if I ask how many of them you won?"

Her eyes gleamed wickedly at him as she flashed him an erotic smile, which made him grow hot inside. He shifted his weight and waited for her to answer. Her voice was sultry and deep when she said, "All of them."

My God! I know absolutely nothing about this woman. I am going to find out everything I can about this intriguing woman if it's the last thing I do. My God! Thirty!

"You're not kidding, are you?"

"No. Now it's your turn to fill me on why you needed to know this."

I can visualize her on stage in some sexy outfit, holding a mike, mesmerizing everyone in the audience. Man...

"Robert?"

"Yes, oh, sorry."

Stifling a laugh, she said, "Let me guess--you were thinking of something else?"

"Ah, sort of."

"Would you like to fill me in on the specifics now, or would you like to continue to think about whatever it is that has you smiling from ear to ear?"

"No, I don't think so."

"You mean you're not going to tell me why you asked me if I could lip sync?"

She was playing with him now, and he knew it. He turned around, reached behind him and grabbed the file on his desk. He glanced down at it so he didn't have to make eye contact with her. He needed to get his composure back, and quick.

He cleared his throat before beginning.

༄∞ঔ

"OUR MAIN SUSPECT, ANTONIO BELLESTO, owns two restaurants that have nightclubs attached to them. He's having a series of lip sync contests, and Fredrick and I thought it would be an excellent way for you to make contact with him. If you win the semifinals, you will get five hundred dollars cash and a dozen roses. The grand prize is one thousand dollars, a dozen roses, and a free dinner at his restaurant."

"No problem. That'll be easy money for me, and I do love flowers! I just hope I'll be able to make contact with him."

Locking eyes with her he replied, "I don't think you'll have any problem with that, Charlie. Mr. Bellesto loves beautiful, intelligent women, and you are both."

Charlie blushed, mumbling a quick "Thanks."

"I'll be in the club at the time of the contest with two of

Fredrick's men. You are not to acknowledge either us in any way." He handed her the file, and she glanced through the photos of Antonio Bellesto.

"He's a very handsome man.... But there's something dark and foreboding about him."

As Charlie read through the notes on Bellesto, Robert quietly left the room. Over an hour went by, and when he returned, he found her still mulling over the file he had given her.

Charlie looked up and said, "I've memorized all the facts and pictures. I know it's vital to the operation to know as much as possible about the men I'll be dealing with."

Bellesto had moved here from Italy, was a lady's man, and at the moment, unattached. In addition to his two restaurants and clubs, he owned three warehouses that shipped local seafood in and out of the state. He was a tall man, standing six feet tall, with shiny black hair that had silver streaming through the temples, and the darkest eyes she had ever seen. His moustache was trimmed to perfection, and the suits he wore in the photos were tailor-made to define his muscular frame.

"Money. He has it, and lots of it."

"That's right, he does."

She placed all the papers back in the binder and put it on the desk. "Do you want to quiz me on the information?"

"Good idea."

He pulled a chair next to her so they could face each other. Their knees touched and Robert felt bolts of electricity surge. He knew this wasn't the right time to get sidetracked, and let out a long sigh and settled in. He quizzed her for the next two hours, and was pleased that she retained so much information in such a short period of time.

"Excellent, Charlie. You're a quick study, and that's a good thing to be in this job."

"Thanks, Robert."

He looked into her eyes and saw fatigue. She tried to stifle a yawn as he patted her knee. "I think you've had enough for tonight. Fredrick will be giving us another file on Bellesto. This one only skims the surface."

She interrupted him before he could continue. "Wait, what do you mean by only skims?"

He placed his hand on the top of her head and playfully ruffled her hair. "If you didn't interrupt me I would have answered that next. Patience, grasshopper."

She smiled wide, tears springing to the forefront of her eyes when he said that... 'patience, grasshopper.' *He has no idea what he just said to me... I'm a little girl back on my daddy's lap. He's caressing my hair and patiently explaining to me, as best he could to a child, why people sometimes made wrong decisions in their lives, even when they knew they were the wrong ones. He told me time would bring wisdom, and then I would understand why people sometimes did the things they did. I badgered him again and again with more questions. Finally he replied to me, "Patience, my little grasshopper, patience."*

Robert instantly saw the transformation in her. She slouched back in the chair with tears filling her eyes, threatening to spill over. Her face had a faraway look. It appeared she had mentally left the room and was somewhere else now. He hated to interrupt her, but saw how tired she was. Speaking softly so as not to scare her, he asked, "Charlie? Are you okay?"

"Oh, sorry. I was just thinking about something."

"Do you want to talk about it?"

"No...no. I'm fine, really. Now finish telling me about Bellesto."

Not wanting to push her, he switched gears and explained that Bellesto came to Rhode Island from Italy. He had ties with not only the Mafia there, but had worked right inside the Vatican itself. In what capacity, they didn't yet know, but Fredrick was trying to uncover as much information as possible.

Robert brought the meeting to an end. He rose from his chair, took hold of Charlie's hand, and said, "Let's get your things and I'll take you back to your car.

CHAPTER 27

THEY WERE SILENT AS HE DROVE HER BACK. When they reached her vehicle, he cut the engine and glanced over at her. Her head was back against the headrest, her eyes closed. He watched her breathing, and knew from the small even breaths that she had fallen asleep. He didn't want to wake her; she looked so peaceful. Carefully, so as not to scare her, he leaned over and gently placed a hand on her shoulder.

"Hey, sleeping beauty. Wake up."

Her thick lashes slowly fluttered open, and, unbeknown to her, a small seductive smile spread across her face. He felt his throat constrict, and fought to get air into his lungs without making a fool of himself. She was so damned beautiful, and she didn't even realize it. It was that modesty that made her all the more appealing to him.

"Um....sorry, I must have fallen asleep."

She stretched her arms above her head as he fought off the urge to grab her. "Are you going to be okay to drive home?"

"Um... sure, I'm awake now."

"I think I'll follow you home just to make sure you get there, all right?"

Stifling a yawn, she replied, "Robert, I'm a big girl. I can drive home fine, but thanks for the offer, anyway." Without thinking, she leaned over and placed a small kiss on his cheek.

Instantly, he grew hot, and couldn't believe the effect this woman had on him.

"Drive safe and sleep well. I need you at your best tomorrow."

She arched one eyebrow and let out a small laugh. "Who are you fooling? You need me at my best every day!"

He found himself smiling as he watched her get into her car and drive   away.

CHAPTER 28

SHE UNLOCKED THE FRONT DOOR, TOOK TWO steps in, and instantly felt the blast of cold air. She knew she had closed and locked all the windows before she left, and wondered where the chill was coming from. Nothing seemed out of place on the first floor, but as she made her way up to her bedroom, she felt cold air circulating throughout the entire floor. She went from room to room and found everything just as she had left it that morning.

An eerie feeling ran through her body as she crossed to the fireplace opposite her bed and kindled the logs. Once the embers were crackling, the coolness subsided, and a glow of warmth filled the room.

She no longer felt safe in the house. She contemplated calling Robert and asking him if she could spend the night there, but decided against it. That would open a can of worms, and she was just too bloody exhausted to have to answer the many questions she knew he would have.

She got undressed and slid under the comforter, letting out a long sigh.

She hadn't realized how tired she was until her head hit the pillow and she fell into a deep sleep, dreaming of the demons and how they were coming for her.

THE TEMPTATION WAS TOO HUGE FOR HIM TO pass up. He came back again; he had to. The only sound in the house came from the swishing of his long black robe. She had underestimated him, which was a fatal mistake. He was going to teach her a lesson she'd never forget, before he killed her. She had no idea he was watching her, or that he knew about her new job and the pending sale of the house.

He was killing two birds with one stone. He needed to make contact with the infamous Antonio Bellesto. Achieving that task had been more than successful. He was hired on by the man himself to be his right hand man! And to his sheer delight, she had gone and gotten a new occupation--private eye! He couldn't believe her very first case was investigating his new boss. He couldn't have asked for a more ideal scenario.

His people had done an excellent job with the paperwork. He knew Bellesto would have his background checked out. Well, his people gave him nothing less than sterling credentials. Bellesto himself had said it was an honor to have him in their family now.

He wasn't going to tell his new boss about her and the operation she was involved in. No, he would wait for the right moment to do that. He was going to use the both of them to his advantage, and when the time was right, he would let his boss know just who she was and what she was up to.

He went from room to room, checking the recorders and bugs he had planted long ago. Every conversation in the house was being taped. A sardonic smile spread across his face as he reminisced about the day he had tried his key in the door and found that it still worked. For months now, he came and went as he pleased, and she was none the wiser. He quickly changed the tapes and checked the bugs.

When he was finished, he just had to look; he couldn't resist the urge. Slowly, he climbed the stairs to her bedroom. He reached the open doorway and watched her turn over onto her side. Such beauty, a vision of peaceful slumber. It was a shame he was going to have to kill her.

He had no choice, he had to do it. It didn't matter that she was just a decoy in the plan. No woman disrespected him or left him.

She needed to be taught a lesson, the end result being that she simply pay with her life. After all, everyone knew that the almighty Allah created women for only two reasons. The first was to bear children and the second was to serve their husbands and be subservient to them until the day they died!

He was tempted to leave her a little trinket to let her know that someone was near and watching, but thought better of it. He inhaled deeply and told himself he had to remain patient.

Silently, he turned and made his way back down the stairs, out of the house, into the darkness of the night.

In his mind, he was infallible, and no one, and nothing, could stop him.

CHAPTER 29

FOUR MONTHS LATER

FOR FOUR STRAIGHT MONTHS SHE STUDIED every day, and then some. When she first started out on the job, she had no idea how much she would need to know, and Robert was relentless with her. He demanded that she study everything on firearms: she learned to take them apart and put them back together; when it came to drugs: she researched their chemical make-up, identified who was known for dealing them, and traced where they derived from. She also became literate in the history of the Mafia, their leaders, where they came from, what they dealt in--the list went on and on.

Fatigue was a common feeling for her these days. She didn't want to let Robert down, but more importantly, she didn't want to let herself down. He was placing a lot of stock in her and her abilities. She questioned her physical strength, along with her ability to comprehend what she was learning, on a daily basis, but fought off the panic because she knew Robert wouldn't keep her on and push her to the limit if he didn't believe she was capable of handling it all. So Charlie plunged ahead into the unknown every day, not knowing what was on her agenda.

His voice was harsh when he spoke to her. He was on edge because time was closing in on them. "Charlie, follow my lead and you'll be fine! Block me, for God's sake!" Showing her no mercy, he lunged at her again.

She dove with all her might and pushed her fist into his gut when he came for her. Using his weight to her advantage, she grabbed his arm and flipped him onto the mat.

She wiped away the sweat that streamed down her face with the back of her hand, cocked her head to one side and smiled. "You mean like that?"

He looked up at her with a stunned expression on his face. "All I wanted you to do was block me, not flip me!"

They had been working out for two hours and were exhausted. Every muscle and joint in her body was burning. He pushed himself up to his feet and asked, "How are you feeling?"

She glared at him for asking such a stupid question. Exasperated, she said, "Like I went through a paper shredder a couple of hundred times! How the hell do you think I feel?" Her patience was wearing thin and she, too, was on edge.

Soon she would be making contact with Bellesto. Three potential buyers on her house fell through, and the latest offer she made on a house was rejected by the sellers.

She felt like there was some sort of curse on her. Her bid came in at the full asking price, and the sellers still rejected her offer. The buyers for her home said they'd had a change of heart. Something was going on... she could feel it in every bone in her body. She just didn't know what it was yet.

Robert had assigned her other cases to keep her busy. To her and his utmost satisfaction, she cracked them all. She had finally earned the respect from the men in the firm and now felt comfortable in their presence.

Out of the corner of her eye, she saw Robert staring at her. She still felt uncomfortable when he did that.

He cleared his throat before speaking. "Charlie, did you find an outfit to wear for the contest?"

She turned and faced him as a smile spread across her face. She flashed him her pearly whites, knowing that when he saw the outfit on her he would have a heart attack. "As a matter of fact, I did."

"Do I get to see it?"

She waited a fraction of a second before replying, "If you want to."

"I would."

"Why don't I go take a shower and then I'll try it on for you and you can tell me what you think."

A huge smile spread across his face as he said a little too eagerly, "Fine by me."

Charlie turned and left the room, knowing how he would react. For the past four months, she had made sure to wear loose clothes. He had no idea how she loved the feel of leather, not to mention how great the tight material looked on her body. Her muscle tone was more defined now, and she had gained some bulk to her curvy frame. The extra weight actually suited her just fine. As she made her way into the shower, she realized that she and Robert had grown accustomed to each other's ways and moods, but she still held many things back from him.

What neither of them consciously realized was that she was spending more and more time at his house. She had moved some of her personal belongings into his spare bedroom, because they worked into the wee hours of the night and he wouldn't allow her to drive home.

As the hot water cascaded down her back side, easing her tight muscles and joints, Charlie reluctantly admitted that Robert's protectiveness was more than okay with her, since she didn't relish going home to that house, anyway. She was afraid of it and what it represented. Here at Robert's, she knew she was safe. The nightmares hadn't happened once, and for that she was relieved. They established a comfortable routine together, and for the most part, still guarded their feelings towards each other.

She begrudgingly got out of the refreshing shower, dried off, and put the black leather jumpsuit on. She knew it looked stunning on her. The intense training from the past four months had defined her muscle tone, and she looked toned and lean, though society would still probably deem that she was on the hefty side.

The jumpsuit was backless, with the front open just enough to display some cleavage. She added the final touch, her black boots, then strode out of the room to find Robert.

She went down the stairs and found him sitting on the couch with his long legs stretched out in front of him. His eyes were closed and he appeared to be sleeping.

She hated to wake him up just to show him the outfit. Silently, she turned to make her way back up the stairs when she heard a gush of air escape from his throat. Charlie stopped. She turned to face him, and what she saw shocked her. His sensuous mouth was curved into a seductive smile as his smoldering gaze raked over every inch of her body. She was unable to tear her gaze from his eyes, which told her he approved of her outfit.

He rose from the couch, his eyes never leaving hers. *My God she's mesmerizing, and powerfully arousing and she's not aware of it.* An ominous silence filled the room. She was holding her breath waiting to hear what he thought. *Now what do I do, my tongue is stuck to the roof of my mouth.*

She could feel his eyes undressing her, and instantly felt her insides shift.

He knew it was all over for him. All his self-restraint and control flew out the window. He no longer even wanted to try to control himself. He just hoped she would finally let go and allow herself to feel. He strode towards her. When he stopped, his body was no more than two inches from her. His eyes darkened to a navy blue, full of passion as he lowered his head to kiss her. For both of them, it was a long awaited moment of aching and longing.

He finally conceded that he wanted her more than he could ever begin to imagine. His kiss intensified as his fingers caressed and massaged the silky skin on her back. Knowing he had to have her, he pulled back, searching her eyes, looking for some kind of confirmation that she, too, was feeling the same thing he was. She stared into his soul, never flinching, the corner of her mouth tilted slightly, giving her a most alluring look.

He lifted her into his arms, his eyes never wavering from hers, and carried her to his bedroom. They stood facing each other by the side of his bed. He lifted his hands and placed them behind her neck, then unclasped the back of her jumpsuit and slowly peeled it down to her feet. He gently guided her onto the side of the bed and lifted each foot to remove the black leather cowboy boots, then grasped her hands to pull her up again to stand before him.

Kneeling down, he removed the last of the jumpsuit. When he stood, he looked into her eyes and saw that they gleamed wickedly at him. There she stood before him in all her naked glory. He had never seen such an intoxicating sight.

Gently, he eased her onto the bed, and in the blink of an eye, he had removed all of his clothes and thrown them haphazardly onto the floor. Charlie's hair gleamed around her face as she laid her head back against the pillow. She looked up and studied his hard, muscular frame noticing that his skin glistened like satin.

He eased down onto her body, kissing and caressing her. He wanted to taste every inch of her, and fought to restrain himself. He wanted to go slowly, very slowly, and savor every sensation that surged through him. His body threatened to explode from her warmth and softness. His eyes clasped shut as he reeled in the emotions that took over for him. He lifted his head and gently placed his warm lips on hers and gave her the lightest brush of a kiss.

In that very moment Robert knew that without Charlie, his life was meaningless. Hesitantly at first, he slowly began massaging her breast, and heard a soft moan escape from her. She shivered as his tongue played with her sizzling skin.

He lowered his hand, frantic to have her and please her, until he found the soft flesh between her legs and eased his fingers inside of her. He became more aroused as he watched her twist and moan under him. Lowering his head, he placed erotic kisses on her stomach as his fingers continued to tantalize her.

Losing any and all sense of control, his animal instincts took over and he planted his mouth where he knew he most desired to, and made her cry out his name as his tongue began a slow, seductive dance on her warm flesh. He wanted to bring her over the edge, and didn't stop his relentless licking and sucking until she arched her back and moaned.

He quickly straddled her, holding on to her hips with both his hands and lifted her high off the bed so he could plunge deep into her. He pushed hard, his motions frenzied, and threw his head back as she tightened herself around him. They didn't stop until they brought each other higher and higher, to the point of no return. She opened her eyes and saw his flushed face and dark, fierce eyes, and when he looked into hers, he exploded, screaming out her name.

CHAPTER 30

HE SAT TRANSFIXED, LOOKING AT NOTHING, but seeing so much. Placing his hands on the gleaming wood of the mahogany desk he sat behind, he indulged himself in the pleasure of thinking back to the days of not so long ago when his life was full, and he had everything he dreamed of and more.

He wasn't happy with his new position in Rhode Island. It was a small state, too small for his comfort. He didn't like that at all. He was better when he was home in Italy and his men ran the businesses for him. He need only return to RI three or four times a year, and that suited him just fine.

Now he felt confined, and was suffocating. There was so little time...little time for him to think back and meditate on life's twists and turns. This was one of those rare occasions where he indulged himself with memories of a much happier time in his life.

Lighting a cigarette, Bellesto dragged heavily and returned to that fateful day, the day that changed his life.

Few knew of his other life, and they never would. Bellesto exhaled slowly as smoke rings floated effortlessly through the air. Stubbing out the freshly lit cigarette in the crystal ashtray perched on the side of his desk, the visions materialized slowly, and quite clearly...the visions and memories of a totally different world...a world he was once a part of.

THE VATICAN

THE VAST HALLWAY WAS STILL BUT FOR THE light

clatter of Antonio Bellesto's Italian loafers. Sunlight streamed in through the ornate stained glass windows that filled the dome of the Vatican. Stopping in mid stride, he allowed himself for the briefest moment to admire what many considered an ostentatious display of gold leaf, priceless artwork, and an overabundance of exquisite Italian marble.

He had no idea why he had been summoned to such a godly place at such an ungodly hour. The sun was just rising over the soft peaks of trees that lined the outer courtyard as he recollected the phone call that had come two hours ago, rousing him out of a sound sleep.

The conversation was short, direct, and to the point. "This morning, seven a.m., be in the office, and don't be late." A loud click boomed in his ear, as the person on the other end slammed the receiver down.

Bellesto was early by about fifteen minutes, so he didn't rush. Moving to the next window, he glanced out and what he saw took his breath away.

Each and every time he walked down this particular corridor and looked out the windows to the outer courtyard, his feeling was the same; one of reverence for the dedication of the men and women who kept the Vatican, in his opinion, one of the most beautiful places in the world. His eyes slowly absorbed the vast landscape of perfectly manicured trees, the never ending fields of grass the color of mint, and the thousands of flowers budding an array of colors. The scene was truly breathtaking.

He was one of the chosen few who had complete access to the inner realms and workings of the Vatican. His job was to make sure "The Family" was always in complete order. What thousands of unsuspecting Catholics would never know is that their precious Vatican was not ruled by their Pope, but by The Family. The Family guided the Pope with a heavy hand, and if he didn't comply, they would take care of him the same way they had dealt with the former Pope John Paul I.

Forcing himself to turn away from the intricate beauty, he quickly glanced at his wristwatch which gleamed in the sunlight. He loved the solid gold Rolex almost as much as he loved his dear mother, God rest her soul.

He was so absorbed in his thoughts that the fifteen minutes had escaped him. He quickly made his way down the rest of the corridor, and started a slow jog as he turned the bend. The striking sound of his shoes hitting the hard marble floor echoed off the walls. Without a minute to spare, he reached his destination and bent at the waist to catch his breath. Pulling himself totally erect, he inhaled deeply, then knocked twice on the heavy wooden door that gave off a foreboding energy to those on the outside.

A LOUD VOICE BELLOWED FROM THE INSIDE, "Come in!" Hesitantly, he reached for the large ornate brass knob, and slowly turned. Inhaling deeply, he pushed the large mass open and stepped inside. There, sitting behind a large cherry desk, was his boss, Pidori Luciano.

Looking tired and bedraggled, Pidori beckoned Antonio with a sharp wave of his hand to sit on one of the leather chairs placed in front of his desk. Antonio didn't know if it was his imagination or not, but Pidori's hair seemed to have thinned considerably, not only on the top, but also on the sides of his head.

Something was definitely up, and it wasn't good. He could feel it deep in his bones. Pidori seemed preoccupied with a lone sheet of paper clasped in his hand. As Pidori kept reading, Antonio took in the ashen color of his skin. When he finished reading, Pidori placed the sheet of paper down on the gleaming wood and slowly slid it across the desk to the edge where Antonio sat.

Their eyes locked, neither man saying anything. Antonio reached out and picked up the paper. The first thing he noticed was the encrusted seal on the top of the ivory stationery. As Antonio read the document, his eyes grew wide. Further down, his lips parted into a snarl. When he was finished, he placed the sheet back on the desk, and imitated the exact movement his boss had, not a moment ago.

Antonio waited for the man who was not only his superior, but his friend, to speak. He knew all too well that if he uttered one syllable it would throw off his friend's equilibrium. This he had learned after years of working side by side with him.

The two men would often joke that their friendship was the closest thing to a marriage. They knew one another's good and bad points, yet still had a bond that was unbreakable. They also realized that the level of trust they shared could not be penetrated by anyone. Each man had put the other through numerous tests over the years, and it was in both their interests that they had passed with flying colors.

Before trying to explain, Pidori shrugged his shoulders heavily and let out a long sigh. "I hate to be the one to give you the bad news, but at the same time, I insisted that I be the one, if that makes any sense to you, my friend."

Antonio, too stunned to speak, merely nodded, his eyes locked on his friend's enthralling beams of chocolate brown.

"Things are spinning out of control in Rhode Island, my friend. Your presence is needed there to straighten things out, as time is of the essence. We suspect there's a leak inside The Family. We need you to find out how many there are, and extinguish them."

Antonio could not find the right words to say. No matter what he argued, he, in the end, could not refuse direct orders from the head of The Family. Standing, he paced around the vast room trying to think of a way, any way, he could avoid leaving his home.

Things were heating up inside the Vatican as well, and his intuition told him there was much more to this "leak" in Rhode Island than he was being told right now. The Family would not send him away unless what was happening in RI could somehow directly influence the dealings in the Vatican.

Stopping in mid stride, the fog began to clear for Antonio. They would never tell him to leave, he was far too valuable here. He once again locked eyes with his friend. He remained riveted to the spot in which he stood, and spoke for the first time since entering the office.

"What's the rest of it?" That was all it took; one sentence. His friend smiled so wide, it looked like the creases on the sides of his face would slide off any minute. Letting out a hearty laugh, Pidori slammed his fist down on the desk, and leaned back in the mahogany leather chair, all the while laughing. It disappeared as fast as it came. Within seconds, the laughter was gone, the crease lines firmly set back in their place, his eyes hard.

"Sit down, my friend." Antonio was not unnerved by his friend's abrupt change in demeanor. He was quite used to Luciano's colorful ways, so he did as he was told, and what he heard next shocked him.

Almost an hour had gone by, and Pidori was still talking. As the time wore, on his voice escalated, his hands grew more animated, and the color of his face had turned beet red.

Then he stopped. He could speak no more. After a half hour, both men had moved to the oversized chocolate brown leather couch that was placed in front of the fireplace. A fire roared as both men sat, their bodies angled so they could face each other.

Letting out a long sigh, he tried in vain to make light of the situation. "Ah, my friend, I fear the stress is getting to me these days. I'm not as young as I used to be, you know." He ended his sentence with a weak smile.

Antonio reached out and grasped the older man's hand and squeezed tightly. "It is alright, Pidori. Whatever their plan is, they will not succeed, I promise you. I will make sure of this."

Sighing audibly, Pidori nodded his head in agreement, and replied, "We have been foolish, my dear friend. In the very beginning, my gut instinct told me that we should not allow the Jihad Muslims to mingle within the confines of the Vatican. But, alas, man's desire for money and power superseded our judgment. I just hope we can stop them before they do any irreparable damage to the Vatican.

"We cannot, and I repeat, my friend, we cannot allow this to filter out of the confines of the Vatican. The damage will shake the church to its foundation, not to mention the thousands of followers we would lose! The Catholic Church will be ruined if one word leaks out."

Highly perplexed, Antonio rose from the comforts of the soothing couch and started walking in concise circles throughout the room, thinking out loud. Pidori allowed his friend to air out his thoughts. He knew Bellesto had quite an eccentric air about him, and over the years Pidori had grown used to his quirks and odd sense of humor. The ironic thing was it was Antonio's eccentricity that made him a genius.

"The Jihad has infiltrated all the families. They are with us here in the Vatican. They have millions of dollars floating in and out of all the outlets and have a substantial amount of power, much more than they should have. How has this happened?"

Pidori didn't respond, because he knew his friend was not actually speaking to him. So he watched with interest as Antonio's movements became more sharp and erratic. With a sudden jerk, he stopped and seemed transfixed by the intricate design woven into the ancient Persian rug beneath his exquisite Italian loafers.

Looking up, he glanced into his friend's eyes and inhaled sharply. When he finally spoke, his voice was a whisper. "Pidori, I have a strange feeling that the Jihad's end game is to destroy the Catholic Church."

Suddenly both men were sick beyond comprehension. Pidori's first reply was adamant denial. "No, no, my friend, it couldn't be!"

But as soon as the last word was uttered, he knew that what he had just said was the farthest thing from the truth.

CHAPTER 31

THE INTENSE BEAM OF LIGHT SEARED HIS EYES, making them tear. He was strapped onto a steel chair, slipping in and out of consciousness. His captor hadn't bothered to blindfold him after apprehending him, and he vaguely remembered where he was-- Fox Point, the warehouse district in Providence.

He couldn't take any more. It was over for him, but he'd never fink. He was many things, but not a snitch. He'd rather die than give any information to this sick bastard! Hot, thick blood oozed down from his forehead, seeping into his already burned eyes, making them sting.

He had made a fatal mistake and would now pay for it with his life. He had found out valuable information about the case his boss was working on, and had failed to fill him in. He'd only wanted to confirm that what his sources had told him was accurate. Now he knew it was.

He hoped both his boss, Robert, and Charlie, his co-worker, would somehow, someday, find it in their hearts to forgive him; that is, if they lived through this. He had procrastinated on giving vital information to Robert only because what he had discovered was so bizarre, he wanted to make sure he had gotten it right.

Charlie was in danger. She had no idea what was lurking around the corner for her, and he prayed that somehow she would survive what this bastard had in store. He was the Judas they were searching for, and he knew his boss meant what he had threatened.... he would be shown no mercy and die a most painful and horrific death.

Once again he felt the cold steel make contact with his gut as he heaved forward in the chair, almost toppling over. A strong hand stopped his fall and steadied the chair. His left eye started to swell shut, with the other following close behind, and he strained to see the man standing beside him. Cold fury and rage pulsed through his body as he recognized the figure.

It couldn't be, could it?

The man let out a soft, dark laugh, "Why, yes, my dear friend, it is. I'm surprised you recognized me, but just think, my face is going to be the last thing you see before you die. You're a lucky man. After I finish with you, I'll be able to put the rest of my plan into action. Don't worry about not seeing any of your people again, because when I finish with them, they'll be joining you in the afterlife!"

There was no way he could warn them, especially Charlie. None of his people had any idea of the magnitude of trouble that was headed their way, unless they were warned and tipped off.

As if reading his thoughts, the man said, "There's no way you can warn them, my friend, especially her, but I'll make you a promise. Before I kill her, I'll let her know how concerned you were about her and the rest of your cronies! It's the least I can do, after all. Now, is there anything you'd like to tell me before I kill you, because I'm on a tight time schedule, and I need to have this little task completed before the night is over?"

The man looked into those steel eyes with what compromised vision he had left, and saw that he was crazed. The man's eyes were huge and glassy; like he was there, but not really. He prayed for his friends' safety, and knew that if anyone could trip up this psycho they could. They had to, or they too would face what he was facing...an untimely death. His last words before he was silenced by the final blow that took his life were, "She'll get you before you get her, my friend, and then we'll see who has the last laugh! ROT IN HELL!"

He saw red. No one would, or could, ever outsmart him! The silver signet ring gleamed in the dim light as he raised the steel weapon and then brought it down, crashing into his target over and over until the arms and legs were severed, thumping heavily onto the cement floor. Throwing the steel blade down, he took a handkerchief out of his pocket and attempted to wipe away the river of blood that saturated his clothes. He turned and walked out of the warehouse. He had to call his boss and inform him that the problem was taken care of and the other men could come and dispose of the body.

As he closed the door to the warehouse, he stopped momentarily and smiled.

Behind him, he heard the faint echoes of his humming fade into the stillness of the night.

CHAPTER 32

THE RINGING OF THE PHONE JOLTED THEM both awake. Robert grabbed the receiver and hoarsely croaked, "Hello?" He bolted upright and jumped out of bed. "WHAT! WHAT DO YOU MEAN, HE'S MISSING?"

Terror ran through Charlie's body. She had never seen him like this. Whatever news he was hearing was bad, real bad, and she wasn't waiting for him to fill her in. He was running around the room, grabbing any clothes he could find. She scrambled out of bed and did the same. Within seconds, they were haphazardly dressed and sprinting down the stairs and out of his house.

She knew better than to ask anything; she'd be finding out soon enough. They jumped into his car, both slamming their doors. He thrust the key into the ignition and waited for it to turn over, and when the engine roared to life, he peeled out of the driveway, clocking a hundred the entire way to his office.

Neither spoke a word as he sped to the complex, but she knew from the end of the conversation she'd heard that Victor Pedro, one of Robert's top agents, was missing. He was posing as one of Bellesto's inside men. Victor hadn't reported in. Charlie knew something was desperately wrong. Pedro was Robert's right hand man, and always reported in.

They reached his office complex in half the time it usually took to get there. He sped into the lot and jumped out of the car, leaving it running. She turned the car off, grabbed the key out of the ignition, and hustled to catch up with him. Robert was already in the building and down the hallway opening his office door when she finally rounded the corner. She ran into his office and found six of his men already assembled, pacing and waiting.

❧❧❧

"All right, gentlemen, what do we know so far?" Robert rushed around to the back of his desk, not waiting for a reply, picked up the receiver, and dialed Fredrick's number. While the phone rang, he looked impatiently at Lou Moretti, his other right hand man. When Lou answered, his voice was tight.

"He never reported in, boss, so Tom and I went to the warehouse district to see what we could find out. We saw two of Bellesto's men carry out two duffel bags. I followed them to the river, east of Fox Point, and saw them weigh the bags down with cement blocks, and then watched them hurl the bags in. There was no sign of Victor anywhere."

Robert held up his hand, halting Lou's recap, while he explained the situation to Fredrick. He looked up and asked the exact location where Bellesto's men dumped the bags. After Lou gave him the particulars, Robert relayed it to Fredrick and hung up.

"Fredrick and his men are on their way there now." He ran around his desk, barking orders to, then grabbed Charlie's hand. "Come on, you and I are going to meet Fredrick at the site."

Minutes later as they pulled into the lot, they saw Fredrick and his men. Charlie's heart pounded as fear coursed through every nerve in her body. They got out of the car, rushed to where the men were, and watched them dive into the dark, murky water.

Fredrick put a comforting arm around Robert's shoulders lamenting, "I'm so sorry, Robert. I don't know what to say. If it is Victor down there, my men will find him."

Robert's shoulders slumped as he bowed his head. He couldn't breathe. He couldn't think. All he knew was that he was responsible for his men's safety and lives. In all his years on the force and in private practice, he had never lost a man.

If it was Victor down there, Robert silently vowed to personally kill whoever was responsible.

Charlie walked to his side and said nothing. She merely put her hand in his and tightly squeezed. He glanced at her, his eyes red and full of pain. She nodded her understanding of what he was feeling; her expression told him that she felt the same.

There was nothing they could do now but wait and pray. The

winds picked up force, and the air grew cooler. They stood huddled on the dock, waiting patiently. There was always the chance that Fredrick's men wouldn't find the body. The water was frigid, the visibility poor. Then there was the issue of the air tanks. The men could only stay under for so long. Once their air supply was nil, they would have to surface and replace them. This would take precious time they simply didn't have. It also didn't help that Bellesto's warehouses were directly in back of them.

Three hours slowly ticked by. Everyone was afraid to say what they all were thinking. Things were not looking good. Suddenly one of Fredrick's men surfaced and yelled, "Boss! We found something! I think it's what you're looking for." Anticipation was high. Everyone held their breath as the divers hauled two grey duffel bags out of the water. Fredrick and Robert rushed to the edge of the dock to help drag the bags over.

Charlie, face white, lips quivering from the cold, asked the men, "Why do you think there are two bags?"

Both Fredrick and Robert stopped what they were doing and glanced up at her. They looked at each other, not wanting to reveal their thoughts for fear that they might be right.

Robert stood and took her hand in his. "I'm not quite sure yet, but we're about to find out." Fredrick opened one of the bags and sighed long and hard. He looked at Robert and said, "I don't think you want or need to see this."

Robert bent down and took hold of the opening from Fredrick, "No, I need to know what happened to him." He looked in the bag and instantly turned white.

Robert covered his face with his hands and let out a long, anguished cry. She didn't have to kneel down to see what was in the bag. An arm was visible, with part of a foot jutting out of the opening.

When he did look at her, she saw something she had never seen before: acid, anger, and the silent vow to repay the bastard that did this to his man.

And she knew Robert would.

CHAPTER 33

THEY LIVED OUT REST OF THE WEEK IN A DAZE. Robert personally went to notify Victor's family. He took care of all the arrangements and insisted on paying for everything. Guilt was etched in each line and crease on his face, and Charlie felt helpless.

There was nothing she could do, and a part of her reasoned she shouldn't try. Everyone handled stress and trauma differently, and their choices deserved respect. If this was how Robert chose to cope with the situation, then who was she to interfere and say it was wrong? Her needs and ways differed greatly from his, but it was her loyalty to him that meant far more to her.

The agency was closed for the week, and caseloads piled up. His men were extremely supportive and kept things going for him. There was a storm brewing deep inside Robert, and it was only a matter of time before it erupted. Little did she know, part of his wrath was about to be unleashed on her.

❧❦

The night was dark and stormy, and it matched the way he felt. Thick pellets of rain slashed hard against the windows, making him cringe. He had made a drastic decision and knew it wasn't going to go over well with her, but that was just too bad as far as he was concerned.

She didn't have any say in the matter, *he* was the boss, and she would do what he said or face the consequences. He didn't know exactly what the consequences were yet, and just hoped the situation wouldn't come to that.

Robert didn't like giving ultimatums to people, but in this case he had no choice.

CHAPTER 34

HE WAS SEATED BEHIND HIS DESK, SIPPING the crisp white wine he had brought in for the two of them. He heard her make her way down the stairs, and his heart constricted. He couldn't breathe, and a headache spurred to life, his head pounding ferociously.

❧❧❧

She hesitated in the doorway of his office and casually leaned a shoulder against the frame so she could observe him before entering. But sensing her presence, he lifted his gaze to meet hers, and instantly, she was on alert. The strain around his eyes was pronounced and his usually golden skin had a yellowish tinge to it.

"Hi, how are you doing?" Not waiting for him to answer, she walked into the room, her eyes never leaving his.

He rose from his seat and moved to draw a chair out for her. As she sat down, he swept a mass of her fiery chestnut hair to one side, leaned down and placed light kisses in the crook of her neck. Her skin ignited into flames, sending shivers through her entire body.

When he finally answered, "Better, now that I've made some changes," she detected the terse quality in his voice. She studied his eyes and noticed the dark currents that swirled beneath the calm surface. He walked to his chair and sat down. He crossed his arms over his chest, saying nothing.

She didn't know why, but she was starting to feel uneasy. Shifting slightly in her chair, she tore her gaze from his, drew a long breath, then expelled it slowly as she looked out the window behind him.

He grasped the stem of her wine glass and handed it to her. She leaned forward and took it from him, trying to smile. She had a feeling they were about to have their first major fight, or "disagreement," as Robert would call it. At our age, he reasoned, "We don't fight, we disagree."

Whatever the hell that meant, she thought. To Charlie a fight was a fight, and she could feel one coming on fast and furious. She took a sip of the crisp wine, and surveyed him over the rim of her glass.

He regarded her with an inexplicable smile, and then as quickly as it appeared, it vanished, leaving his handsome face taut with a look of reproof. He shifted his attention past hers and cleared his throat.

"Charlie, there's something I need to discuss with you."

As she looked at him, his relaxed demeanor was quickly unraveling. Quietly, she answered, "Okay, I'm listening."

He saw the flush and pain that flashed across her face, and felt terrible for what he was about to say to her, but knew he couldn't turn back now--it was too late. Once he made up his mind, that was it, and this situation would be no exception. He wanted to be as direct as possible and not beat around the bush on this, so he just came out with it.

"I've decided to take you off this case."

She edged forward in her chair, and leaned her elbows on the hard desk as she asked, "I'm sorry, Robert, but can you say that again for me, because I don't think I heard you correctly."

"I said I'm taking you off the case."

Her body instantly stiffened and her tone sharpened when she asked, "And may I inquire as to when and why you made this decision?"

Robert merely shrugged and cocked his head to one side as he coolly replied, "I don't owe you any explanations, Charlie. That's one of the perks of being the boss. I do what I want, when I want, and I want you off this case."

❧⚭❧

She fell back against the soft leather, placing her hand on her cheek as if to ease the pain from the slap he just gave her. He raised a blond eyebrow at her, waiting for a response, but for the moment she maintained her silence, not knowing what to say. She couldn't believe the way he had just spoken to her, or even the tone he had used. She had fallen in love with this wonderful man, yet now didn't know who this one was sitting across from her. Rage was something she didn't like feeling. It shrouded her in a cloak of dark and violent urges. But now it was running free within her, and she couldn't stop it.

Charlie leapt from her chair and slammed both fists hard on the desk, but kept her expression cool and remote. Her tone was filled with fury when she roared, "WHO THE BLOODY HELL DO YOU THINK YOU'RE TALKING TO? You can't pull me off this case! I've been working my ass off and I'm supposed to make contact with Bellesto! You're jeopardizing this entire case because of your guilt about what happened to Victor!"

Robert snapped. The storm that had been brewing deep inside him since Victor's horrific murder came to a head and took aim directly at her. "I'LL TELL YOU WHO I'M TALKING TO--ONE OF MY EMPLOYEES! AND MAY I REMIND YOU THAT I PAY YOU TO DO WHAT I SAY WHEN I SAY IT! YOU DON'T QUESTION MY DECISIONS. DO YOU UNDERSTAND?"

She was frozen, rooted to where she stood. When she spoke, her breath came out in small spurts. She knew he was hurting and felt guilty, but she wouldn't be an enabler and allow him to destroy all of their hard work.

"Is that all I am to you now, just an employee, and someone you fuck when it suits you?"

Her words cut right through him, and now it was his turn to feel the slap or her words. The air was thick, and the tension between them could be cut with a knife. Neither broke their silence as they faced off like two bulls that had entered a ring for a deadly match.

He fought with all his might to regain his composure. Slowly, he sat back down in his chair, taking three deep breaths.

She stood by the front of his desk with her hands tightly balled, her knuckles white. Her posture rigid, Charlie glared at him, and quickly made her way around to the back of his desk where he sat.

He couldn't, and wouldn't, back down now. He pushed his chair back and rose to face her. He towered over her, hoping to intimidate her. He saw fury and anguish swirl around her features, making his heart skip a beat. What she did next he would never forget for as long as he lived.

She took both her hands, balled them into fists, and then quick as lightning, smashed him square in his chest, sending him reeling backwards. Screaming in pain, he reached for the edge of the desk to break his fall.

When she spoke, her tone was deadly, and he knew he had pushed too far this time. "You take me off this case and I will walk out of your life forever. I will leave here, and go to Fredrick, and ask him to take me on. He will, because I was trained by the best, you asshole! He's seen what I can do, and Lord knows, you've spoken highly enough of me for him to recognize just what I am capable of doing. The decision's yours. But I strongly suggest, before you open that mouth of yours again, you think long and hard as to why you're doing what you're doing. Then I would think VERY HARD about the consequences that will follow when you make your final decision."

He saw her pained expression, which she tried to conceal by turning her face away.

She said nothing more, nor did he answer.

He couldn't, it was too far gone now.

Her body was like Jell-O as she turned from him and walked quietly out of the office, closing the door behind her. She never glanced back. If she had, she would have seen the tears streaming down his face.

CHAPTER 35

SHE SLOWLY MADE HER WAY UP THE STAIRS that led to the bedroom. Her legs felt like lead and she couldn't breathe. She walked into the bathroom, then slumped onto the toilet seat. As she lowered her head into her hands, she became nauseous, and tears flowed freely. Without warning, loud wails escaped from her throat. She crumpled onto the cool tiled floor, grabbing her legs close to her body, and rocked back and forth for a very long time.

When there were no more tears left to cry, she got up from the floor, her body aching from sitting in the same position for so long. The house was silent and she wondered if Robert was still there.

She contemplated driving home, but knew she was too emotionally and physically spent and was in dire need of some sleep. As she stripped off her clothes, it was clear what she had to do now. In the morning, she was going to pay Fredrick a visit and ask him to take her on. There was no way she was backing out now. She didn't care what Robert would think, or how angry he would be. He had made his decision and now she had made hers. She was the major link in this case. No one else could make contact with Bellesto--only Charlie. And, by damn, that was exactly what she was going to do!

She tossed and turned all night and watched the sun rise over the horizon through half open eyes. She stretched her aching muscles and dragged herself out from the safety of her bed. She walked to the bedroom door, and as quietly as possible, opened it and stuck her head out. She listened for any sounds or movement in the house, but heard nothing.

Hesitantly, she made her way down the stairs to Robert's office and found it empty, as was the rest of the house. She went to the front door and peered out the windows that faced the driveway. His car was gone. She turned, ran up the stairs and into the bathroom. She took a quick shower and threw on the first thing that she grabbed off the floor.

She never bothered to look in the mirror, which was a blessing, because if she had, she would have been shocked at what she saw staring back at her. Her skin was pale, devoid of all color, and there were deep, dark circles under her puffy, red eyes. She grabbed her bottle of Elaina Marie Intense Hyaluronic Gold Elixir off the counter and applied it all over her dry face and throat. There was no need for her to see what she was doing for she had this ritual down pat. "Do your magic Elaina Marie, I need it now more than ever." When she finished she twisted the cap back on the . She had a sinking feeling where Robert was, and knew she had to hurry before he convinced Fredrick not to recruit her.

CHAPTER 36

THEY WERE SEATED ACROSS FROM EACH other in his plush living room. Sighing, Fredrick leaned forward and said, "Robert, you need to seriously think about what you're doing. I can't agree with you that Charlie should be taken off this case. She knows what she's doing; you know that as well as I do!"

Robert hadn't slept all night and was running on fumes. He sat hunched over on a pull out bed, cradling a glass of scotch in his hand. Last night he hadn't known where to go. He left after he heard Charlie's sobs, and it killed him. He had gotten in his car, driven around aimlessly, and had finally somehow ended up at his best friend's house.

He knew she planned on going to Fredrick's, and a part of him needed to be there to try and stop what he knew was inevitable. "Robert, I think the liquor and your personal feelings are clouding your judgment. I know you feel responsible for Victor's death, but you have to understand, you couldn't possibly have known or controlled what happened! Can you look me in the eyes and tell me it never crossed your mind that Charlie would at some point be in danger? ROBERT! DAMN IT, LOOK AT ME, MAN!"

Robert slowly lifted his head to meet his friend's gaze. Deep down in his gut, he knew Fredrick was right, but his guilty conscience continued to eat away at him. When he finally spoke, his voice was harsh and hoarse. "She's off the case and that's it. I'm not changing my mind."

Fredrick was getting exasperated and could feel his temper rising. "Robert, I have known you for many, many years. I have to give it to you straight, because you and I have done nothing less with each other in the past. This is the most unwise decision I have ever seen you make. This case, your reputation, and your personal life are all in jeopardy. Are you prepared to lose everything you've worked so hard for over the years? Are you ready to lose the woman who's responsible for that shit-ass grin that's plastered all over that ugly face of yours?"

He hesitated only a fraction before answering, "Yes, I am."

"Very well, then, my friend. You leave me no other choice but to take her on."

Anger raced through every vein in his body as he jumped up from the couch, spilling the scotch down the front of his pants. He stood face to face with his best friend, panting, trying desperately to find control; it was difficult because he felt like Fredrick had just smashed him in the face. "You'll do what?"

"I'll hire her to work for me. Is this what you really want?"

As he slumped back onto the couch, the glass of scotch slipped from his fingers, smashing onto the hardwood floor. He was completely numb, his head throbbed, and he couldn't think. Neither man took notice of the shattered glass or the thick liquid seeping into the expensive wood.

They stared at each other until Robert bowed his head and began to weep uncontrollably. Fredrick strode to the couch, sat, and placed a powerful arm around his friend's shoulders. Fredrick was worried now. Never in his life did he conceive that his warrior friend would crash and become a broken man. When Robert spoke, his voice was the merest whisper, with defeat ringing heavily in his tone.

"Fine, Fredrick, I'll keep her on and allow her to finish out the case, but heed my warning: if one bloody hair on that woman's head is so much as ruffled, I'll kill whoever is responsible myself. My way. Understood?"

Fredrick knew Robert meant every word he said. He also knew that deep in the recesses of his friend's mind he was reliving the tragedy that had ripped apart his life years ago with the loss of his first true love. If anything happened to Charlie, Robert would hunt down his prey and show no mercy.

Nodding to his friend, Fredrick whispered, "Understood."

SHE PULLED INTO FREDRICK'S DRIVEWAY AND saw Robert's car parked off to the side. "Thank God! At least I know he's been in good hands." Charlie knew if anyone could talk sense into his thick head it would be Fredrick. He would tell Robert the way it was, whether the stubborn oaf wanted to hear it or not. Taking a deep breath, she opened her door and got out of the car. She closed it as gently as possible, not wanting to alert them to her arrival.

Slowly, she made her way up the cobblestone path, praying she made the right decision. It never occurred to her that Fredrick might agree with Robert and not take her on. She reached the front door and stood there. She lifted her hand and pressed the doorbell. She heard the chimes ring inside the house, followed by sound of footsteps.

Fredrick opened the door, and relief spread across his face. He gave her the smallest of smiles and led her into the foyer. Once the door was closed behind them, he pulled her into a warm embrace. When he finally released her, she stepped back and looked up into his eyes.

Tears flowed freely down the brawny man's face as she fought to choke back the flood of her own welling up inside of her. "Robert's in the family room. I think I'll leave the two of you alone so you can talk. I'm bushed and going up to bed, so feel free to stay as long as you like."

"Thanks, Fredrick, I knew I could count on you." He gave her one last hug, walked to the bottom of the staircase, but abruptly stopped, and turned to face her. "Charlie?"

"Yes, Fredrick?"

"Go easy on him, he's a stubborn man and isn't used to taking back anything, you know what I mean?"

"Yes, I believe I do. Thanks."

She watched him turn and climb the stairs. Once he reached the top, she waited for him to go into his bedroom and close the door. She walked to the archway that led into the family room and leaned her weary body against the hard structure.

Robert was seated on the couch with his head in his hands. Tears instantly filled her eyes as she observed the man, once so strong and sure of himself, but who now resembled the shattered glass on the floor by his feet. She didn't move a muscle. She just stood there trying not to choke on her saliva. After what seemed like forever, he finally lifted his head and turned to look at her.

Their eyes locked, neither of them knowing what to say or how to say it. Each was waiting for the other to make the first move. When Robert could feel the circulation in his legs again, he stood up and extended both arms out to her. Like a child who was lost and now found, she ran with all her might and jumped into his loving embrace. They stayed that way until he felt his arms go numb, and then he slowly put her down.

They held on to each other for dear life, both crying tears of frustration and guilt. He cleared his throat to make sure he could find his vocal cords and said, "Charlie, I..."

"Not now, Robert. Come on, I'll drive us home."

All he could manage was a feeble nod of acceptance. They locked the front door behind them and made their way to her car.

She opened the door for him and helped him get in. She smelled the strong liquor on his breath and prayed he would fall asleep. By the time she made her way around to the driver's side and got in, he was out like a light, and for that she was grateful. He slept the entire way, and by the time they pulled into his driveway she, herself, felt like she was sleepwalking. Every muscle and joint screamed out, and her eyes were at half-staff. Gently she rocked him awake and watched as his eyelashes slowly fluttered open. "Hey, sleepy head, come on, your bed is more comfortable, trust me." She coaxed and soothed him like she would a small child, and obediently he stretched and opened his car door.

Before he got out, he turned back to her. "Charlie?"

"Yes, Robert?"

"I.... do trust you.... with my life."

She didn't know what to say. Her heart felt as if it was going to explode. She nodded her head, displaying a brave smile. She knew how difficult it had been for him to say what he just did, but more importantly, she knew he wouldn't have said if he didn't mean it. Knowing this rocked Charlie to her core.

CHAPTER 37

SHE OPENED HER EYES AND LOOKED AT THE clock on the end table by the bed. When they had first arrived home, she had planned on going to her own bedroom, but he had put his arm around her and told her he needed her with him, not just now, but forever, and she had willingly agreed.

"Three o'clock. I can't believe I slept that long."

"Me, neither."

She hadn't realized he was awake, and the sound of his voice made her jump.

"Sorry, didn't mean to startle you."

When she rolled over and looked into his eyes, she saw everything she needed to know. Grinning widely, she tore herself from his warm embrace and got out of bed.

He feigned a look of panic and wondered, "Where are you going?"

Momentarily stunned, she replied, "To the bathroom, why?"

"Are you going to come back to bed with me?"

"I don't think that's such a good idea. We have a lot to do today. I'm making contact with Bellesto tonight, remember?" Letting out a sigh, he said, "Always the voice of reason, not to mention the biggest party pooper I've ever met!"

She threw one of the pillows at him, hitting him square in the face. "You're lucky that's all I had in front of me, fella."

"Oh, really, and why's that?"

"Keep that up, and I'll have to kick the shit out of you."

"I think I'd rather enjoy that."

"I bet you would."

She laughed as she made her way to the bathroom and took care of business. When she returned and looked at him, she gasped. He was sitting up with all the pillows plumped up behind him, looking very smug while cradling a small package in his hand. When he spoke, his voice was husky.

"Come here, Charlie, I have something I'd like to give you." Her legs were like lead as her mouth hung open. "Come on, I promise I won't bite.....too hard."

She was glad he had his sense of humor back. It was one of the many things she loved most about him. She let out a soft chuckle as she made her way to the bed and gave him a sly smile. "You think you're funny, don't you?"

"As a matter of fact, I do."

Laughing, she said, "Oh, God, here we go." She slid under the covers and looked up at him.

Like tides shifting, his face grew serious, and when he spoke, his tone had a somber quality to it. "This is for you, Charlie. I've been waiting for the right moment to give it to you, and I know that moment is now." Gently, he placed the brightly wrapped package on her lap.

She knew whatever was in the small package would alter her life drastically in some way. She propped herself up and rested her head against the headboard. He took two of the pillows out from behind him and placed them behind her head so she would have better support. She held the package in her hand and admired the cobalt blue paper and the bright lemon colored bow. He remembered these were her favorite colors and the gesture touched her heart.

He was holding his breath as he watched her facial expressions change. He knew she would be touched by the fact that he remembered her favorite colors and it showed on her face right now. He swallowed hard and waited patiently as she carefully undid the bow, and then the paper. The box was no larger than a deck of playing cards. He wished she would hurry up and open the damned thing already. She was staring down at the box, not moving a muscle.

He figured she needed a little coaxing, so he obliged, "Go on and open it, it won't blow up or anything, I promise."

Playfully, she elbowed him in the side and he feigned pain. Slowly, she lifted the cover off the box and gasped when she saw the contents. Thick tears streamed from her ducts and flowed down the sides of her flushed face. She grabbed her throat with her free hand and moaned.

She took the object out of the box and was transfixed by what she now held in her hand. It was a gold detective's badge with her name engraved in large letters on it.

"Turn it over, Charlie."

She did as he asked and saw that there was an inscription on the back.

"Read it out loud."

She managed a whispered "Okay." Taking a deep breath, she whispered what the phrase said: "To my partner in life forever. Love, Robert." She couldn't move, speak or blink. Her flood gates opened at full force as she wept for what seemed like an eternity.

He wrapped his arms around her, gently rocking her back and forth like he was holding a baby, and whispered soothing endearments in her ear.

When she finally spoke, her voice was hoarse with emotion. "This is.... Oh, my God.... Robert, it's magnificent! I don't know what to say."

"Just say you love it, and that you'll be what it says: my partner forever."

A lump formed in Charlie's throat. She couldn't swallow. She didn't know what he meant by "partner for life." Was he asking her to marry him, or was he just referring to them working as partners forever? She looked deeply into his sapphire eyes, searching for any clue that might help her answer this question. Finding none, she played it safe and said, "I think we're on the right track, let's just make sure page it's the one we both want to stay on together, okay?"

Her answer seemed to pacify him, and when he answered, "Okay," she still didn't know what he meant, but thought it best to drop it for the time being. "I'll tell you what, beautiful, why don't I make us something to eat, and then you can do whatever it is you need to do before you make contact with Bellesto tonight."

Wiping the last tears from her face, she sniffled and said,

"Oh ...I'm too nervous and upset to eat anything right now." Sniff, sniff, sniff.

"Come on, just a little something...for me?"

"Well, I guess just a little something. Nothing big, just a little salad, some corn...," sniff... "on the cob, and a couple of lobsters, and maybe just a small dessert. Nothing too big because I'm not that hungry."

Laughter exploded from him as he watched her. One of the things he loved about her was her ability, at times, which he thanked God wasn't often, to consume large quantities of food and think it was a "little tidbit to hold her over."

"You're sure that will be enough now?"

"Yeah, I just want something to hold me over."

"If you consider the list you just gave me to be on the *light* side, I can't wait to see you when you're ravenous!"

Playfully, she slapped him, and then pushed him off his side of the bed. She got up and placed her badge on the end table. Sunlight streamed in through the bay windows and danced on the shiny metal, sending rays of light onto the walls and creating a beautiful mosaic of color.

Right now, she felt like the richest woman in the world, and her heart felt like it would take flight from her chest. She was unaware that he was watching her from where he sat on the floor. When she turned and looked into his eyes, she saw nothing but understanding and love for her. Clearing her throat, she said, "Let's get going. I have a lot to do before my meeting tonight."

Hoisting himself up from the floor, he smiled and said, "You got it, boss."

CHAPTER 38

SHE PULLED INTO BELLESTO'S LOT AT TEN P.M. that evening. She got out of the car Fredrick had provided for her and locked the doors. Her name was Maria De Testo, single, mid-fifties, and self-employed.

Taking a deep breath, she walked to the front door of the restaurant where a mint green and white striped awning hung overhead. A bald, burly man stood at the entrance greeting the patrons. From the size of his gut it looked as though he consumed way too much of Bellesto's Italian food. As she approached him, he flashed a smile, which sent shivers running down her spine. His two front teeth were solid gold, and with his mouth open, the light from the overhead lantern glared off them and gave him an eerie look.

"Good evening, ma'am."

"Good evening."

"Will you be dining alone this evening?"

"Oh, I'm not here for dinner. I'd like to go to the back bar and have a drink."

"What a shame."

"Excuse me?"

"It's a shame such a beautiful woman as you is alone. If you'd like some company later I can assist you with your problem."

Fighting off the urge to smash him square in the jaw, Charlie curtly replied, "Funny, I don't recall stating I had a problem."

Flinging her long chestnut hair over her shoulders, she walked through the door the bouncer held open for her and was then greeted by an anorexic woman. Charlie did a quick scan of the woman's appearance. She estimated the young to be about mid-thirties, a bottle blonde, with narrow green eyes, straight, white teeth, wearing a very expensive silk dress. Charlie noticed the hostess was engaged in her own assessment, and by the icy tone she conveyed,

146

Charlie gathered she wasn't a fan of the competition.

"Good evening, and how many are in your party this evening?"

She always wondered why the hostess asked that, when the number of people were usually standing right there.

"One."

Charlie suppressed the urge to slap the scrawny chick right across the face as her icy tone took on a condescending quality. "Oh, my. Will you be dining with us this evening?"

Her nerves already frayed, Charlie bluntly asked, "Is there a problem?"

"No, no, not at all. Which would you prefer, the front or the back of the restaurant?"

Charlie purposely took one step forward to breach the little bitch's comfort zone. When she spoke, her tone took on a hard edge that said, *Do not fuck with me.* "To answer your first question, no, I won't be dining with you this fine evening, and to answer your second, I'd like to go to the back bar where the club is."

"Yes, of course you would."

Charlie felt her temper rise, and realized she already wanted to give the once over to the first two people she'd encountered at this place, and she wasn't even in the establishment yet! She bit down so she wouldn't give the retort that was right on the tip of her tongue. Not wanting to give the impolite hostess another chance to zing her, Charlie pushed past her and made her way to the back of the restaurant, absorbing the interior layout en route.

The walls were red brick, with tiny lights lining the length of the room. Large, gold mirrors hung at even intervals along both sides of the restaurant. The tables and chairs were a deep cherry wood embellished with intricate carvings, which she assumed were crafted individually by hand. The tablecloths were crème on crème, perfectly matching the upholstery on the chairs, and in the center of each table were beautiful frosted glass hurricane lamps, each with a lit candle in the inside. She mumbled to herself, "Mr. Bellesto definitely has expensive taste."

She walked into the club area and sat on one of the high back chairs at the bar. A bartender resembling Tom Cruise approached her and flashed a cheery smile.

"Good evening, madam."

Reading his name tag she said, "Good evening, Sylvester."

"Ah, you're observant... I like that in a woman."

She gave a demure smile, and said, "Thank you."

"And may I inquire as to who you are?"

"Maria."

"Well, Maria, I hope you don't mind me saying that you are a very beautiful and classy woman."

"Thank you again."

"What can I get for you this evening, Maria?"

"Do you have any Pinot Noir?"

"We certainly do, shipped in directly from Italy."

"Wonderful, I'll try one of your finest, please."

"Coming right up."

As Sylvester walked to the other end of the bar to pour her drink, she swiveled her chair around so she could take in the details of her surroundings. She spotted two men seated at a table at the far end of the room, and knew they looked familiar to her, but couldn't quite place them. She noticed two briefcases on the floor by their feet and the legal pads that were on the table. They were both writing vigorously, but their eyes also were scanning the bar.

Interesting. Her thoughts were interrupted as Sylvester placed her wine down onto a beautiful lace napkin.

He stood there waiting for her to taste it and tell him what she thought. Languidly she lifted the glass by its delicate stem and brought it to her nose to sniff the contents. Slowly she swiveled the glass around to see the legs of the wine. She took a small sip and savored the combination of the oak and fruit. "This is wonderful, Sylvester, the wood and fruit is in perfect harmony and it slides down my throat like silk, with no bite or aftertaste."

"I'm glad you like it. Please let me know if you need anything else."

"I will. Thank you."

$$\infty$$

AFTER AN HOUR, THERE WAS STILL NO SIGN OF Bellesto. As Charlie finished her second glass of wine, a slight buzz rang in her head. The bar was filling up with patrons who had finished their meal and wanted to enjoy some music and an after dinner aperitif. She turned in her chair so she could face the entrance of the club, and suddenly spotted Bellesto talking with another man. Letting out a small burst of air, Charlie mumbled to herself, "Finally."

He was definitely striking. Standing about six feet tall, he resembled a tower of strength. His hair was jet black with silver blending in on both sides of his temples. His eyes were black marbles, and though they sparkled now with amusement, she knew that if angered, the look could turn instantly deadly. She didn't know why, but she didn't like the energy this man emanated. There was something cold and calculating about him, and it made her uneasy.

His mustache was perfectly trimmed and his suit was tailored to fit his muscular build. He must have sensed her staring at him, because he turned and locked eyes with her. She could feel her armpits moisten, and fidgeted in her seat. She didn't know what to do, so she lifted her glass to him in a toast and flashed him one of her award winning smiles. He kept his eyes on her even as he finished his conversation with the patron, then he ambled towards her.

When he stood no more than a few inches from her, he lifted one of her hands off her lap, brought it to his mouth, and placed a light kiss on it. When he spoke, his voice was like silk. "You are definitely one of the most beautiful women I have ever seen."

Charlie thought to herself, *Boy, he doesn't waste any time.* She cleared her throat, which seemed to have closed up on her, and replied, "Thank you."

"Please, call me Antonio... and you are?"

"Maria."

"May I refresh your cocktail for you, Maria?"

"Yes, thank you, Antonio."

His stature spoke volumes. At the opposite side of the bar, Sylvester was watching the exchange, and had already started to pour a fresh glass for her by the time Antonio waved him over. Sylvester brought the wine glass to her and placed it on a fresh lace napkin. "Your usual, Mr. Bellesto?"

"Yes, thank you, Sylvester."

"He knows what you like, Antonio. I'm impressed."

"I demand only the best, Maria. My help is a reflection of me; so, yes, they are trained thoroughly. Is this your first time here?"

"Yes, as a matter of fact it is."

"I thought so."

"Why's that?"

"Because if you had been here before, I would have definitely noticed you. You are not a woman who could slip by undetected. But I'm sure this is something you've heard many times throughout your life."

"Thank you. Now, it's my turn. Are you the manager?"

"I guess you could say that." He chuckled and lifted her hand again to place another kiss on it. His dark eyes bore into hers and a cold shiver ran down her spine, they were so intense and brooding. He was still holding her hand when he declared, "Actually I own this fine establishment."

Feigning surprise and embarrassment, Charlie lifted her hand to her mouth and allowed a small sigh to escape. "Really?"

"Really." Not knowing what else to say, she lowered her eyes, and concentrated on the rim of her wine glass.

"Are you blushing, my beauty?"

She raised her eyes, meeting his penetrating gaze, and cleared her throat. "Maybe, I've never been one to take compliments."

"Well, get used to them, because for as long as we know each other, and I hope that it will be for a very long time, you will be showered with compliments."

She had tired of the small talk, and got to the point of her visit. "Mr. Bellesto, I...."

At the sound of his last name his jaw went rigid. She knew something was wrong by the look on his face. His eyes bore into hers, questioning something, but what?

"I'm curious about something, Maria."

Little balls of perspiration formed on her temples as she racked her brain over what blunder she could have made. "And what is that?"

"I'm curious as to how you knew my last name when I haven't told you yet?"

Anxiety raced through her as she quickly tried to think of an answer, and then lightning hit! "Why, Mr. Bellesto, Sylvester called you by it, so I assumed it was your last name."

Relief spread across his face as a small smile formed around the corners of his mouth. "Please call me Antonio, Maria. We are past the formalities, are we not?"

"Yes, of course we are. I'm sorry, *Antonio*, I heard you are going to be having a lip sync contest here."

Startled by her question, he pulled back from her and tilted his head to the side with a questioning gaze. When he made no reply, she went ahead with the rest of her explanation.

"You see, I'm interested in entering. Can you tell me where I can sign up?"

"My, my, but you are full of surprises, now aren't you? So you want to join the contest... tell me, have you ever done any performing?"

"Not really. But it sounds like fun, and the prize is very enticing. Besides, how hard can it be?"

"It's a lot harder than most people think, Maria. Remember, everyone knows that the performers are not really singing. You must make them all forget that. Do you think you can do that?"

"I don't know, but I'm willing to try."

"Good enough, then. I'll put you on the list myself."

"Oh, that's very kind of you. Thank you, Antonio."

At that moment, one of the waiters came and asked Antonio if he could come to the kitchen to address a slight problem. "Excuse me, Maria, but duty calls." "Of course. Thank you for the drink."

He began to leave, then stopped and turned back to face her. "I think we should get to know each other better. What do you think?"

"Oh, I agree, Antonio, I agree."

With that said, Bellesto bowed and placed a final kiss on her hand, letting his lips linger longer than necessary. "Till we meet again, my beauty." He turned, and with two strides he was gone.

Charlie was exhausted and needed to sleep. She knew Robert would be waiting up for her when she got home. He would be dying to hear all the details. She just hoped she could stay awake long enough to give them to him.

CHAPTER 39

AS HE PULLED INTO BELLESTO'S LOT, HIS MIND reeled over the conversation he had just had with his leader in the Jihad group. They were not happy with him or his progress. He knew he had to tread ever so carefully now. This was not the time to piss off his superiors. He knew better. He also knew that if they concluded he was of no use to them or the cause any longer, they would not hesitate to eliminate him immediately. He had seen it before and knew what the consequences were. They were not pretty.

He steered into an open space and killed the engine. He leaned his head back against the cool leather headrest, reprimanding himself for his foolishness. He silently vowed that he would not deviate from the plan anymore. His intentions were admirable, but fleeting.

He had yet to look up and notice the beauty exiting the restaurant. He was just about to open his car door, when he looked across the way and saw her saunter out the restaurant door. His heart pounded wildly as he watched her get into a car that he knew wasn't hers. By God, she was beautiful!

He gripped the steering wheel hard, causing his knuckles to turn white. His breath heaved in and out in small spurts. Unclenching his hands, he massaged his fingers and casually turned the silver signet ring. All his intentions to abort the intricate plan involving his exotic ex-wife were quickly forgotten. He was mesmerized as he watched her close her car door and start the engine.

The warnings and reprimands from his superior were long forgotten. The light from the lamp post caught on the silver shank, and the skull that was engraved on it looked as though it suddenly came to life.

He waited for her to drive off. He took a deep breath and opened his door. He had a meeting with the boss. He couldn't believe his good luck when he saw her walk out of the door of the restaurant.

There was no doubt what she was up to, but now wasn't the time to let his boss in on what he knew, nor would he. He would wait until the time was right when his boss would also fall... yes, he would stick with the plan to eliminate his boss. He would just weave his ex-wife into the plot, and have them both disappear together.

Slamming the door shut, he hummed a little Arabic tune over and over as he made his way to the entrance. The Jihad would just have to wait a little longer--this was more important to him and his own cause.

CHAPTER 40

WHEN SHE ARRIVED HOME, SHE WAS surprised to find Robert asleep. She tried stirring him, but he didn't move. She watched him sleep for a while and noticed the fatigue around his closed eyes. His breathing was heavier than usual and his body was tensely rolled up into a ball. She made an executive decision to wait until the following morning to give him the scoop.

Outside the air was heavy as the sun raged. She slept late and was surprised to find when she woke up that Robert was gone. The silky sheets clung to her body as she rolled to get out of bed. As she walked to the bathroom, she thought she heard something coming from downstairs. It sounded muffled, but she could have sworn it was Robert's voice.

An instant later, she heard him running up the stairs. She turned as he blasted into the room like a streak of lightning.

"How fast can you be ready?" His chest was heaving up and down, his eyes drawn as he strode to the bureau and yanked out some of her clothes. Without turning around, he haphazardly threw them at her. Her reflexes were still sleeping as she stood in the doorway watching him. Her pants and shirt sailed through the air, hit her square in the face, and then floated down onto the plush carpeting.

Her voice cracked just a hair when she said, "Well, good morning to you, too!" She had seen him like this before and knew something was up. She just didn't know if she was ready for it yet; she needed her time in the morning to get acclimated and have her coffee.

As if reading her mind, he said, "I'm sorry, honey, but you don't have time to shower or have your morning ritual of coffee and prayer. Last night Bellesto received a large shipment of crates, and my men working on the inside transferred some of them over to our warehouse. We have to get there right away and see what's in them."

154

Her head was getting dizzy as it moved from side to side, watching him pace back and forth in the room. There was no need for her to ask anything, nor would she have the chance, because he stormed out of the room and ran back down the stairs. As she splashed cold water on her face, she could hear the distant sounds of drawers banging, and then the front door opening and slamming shut.

She dressed hurriedly while simultaneously trying to brush her teeth. She fell twice, once almost swallowing her toothbrush. When she was finished, she flew down the flight of stairs and out the door. She dashed to the car that was idling in the driveway, opened the door, and threw her body onto the passenger seat just in time. The car had started to roll down the driveway even before she had a chance to close the door.

When she said, "Thanks," it was with a touch of acid.

"Thanks for what?"

"For almost killing me, that's what! Couldn't you at least have waited until I was in the car with the door closed before you peeled out of the driveway?"

"Sorry, Honey, I'm preoccupied right now."

Sighing heavily, she turned to face him, and smiled. "All right, I forgive you. Now fill me in on all the details."

"I really don't have much to add to what I've told you already. The crates have tuna marked on them, but as far as the men know, there is no tuna in them."

"How do they know? Did they open up any of the crates?"

"No."

Letting out a sigh, Charlie raised her voice just a fraction.

"That's it, no?"

"Yes."

"You know, Robert, I really hate it when you do this."

"Do what?"

"Not answer my question! How do they know there isn't tuna in the crates, damn it?"

"I don't know. I didn't think to ask, now that you mention it." Laughter exploded from them as the car breezed down the highway.

Still laughing, Charlie said, "I can tell this is going to be one of those days."

Nodding his head in agreement, Robert said, "I think you just might be right, Charlie."

Before they reached their destination, Charlie took the opportunity to fill Robert in on her meeting with Bellesto. As soon as she mentioned Bellesto's name, Robert slammed down the accelerator, and the car took off like a rocket.

⌒∂∽⌒

WHEN THEY ENTERED THE WAREHOUSE, Fredrick and Robert's men were already there, pacing and waiting. The two friends hugged and slapped each other on the back. Fredrick hugged Charlie tightly and placed a light kiss on the side of her face. "You look great, Charlie, how's the old geezer treating you?"

"No complaints so far, though I was deprived of my morning coffee."

"Well, you have me to thank for that. We didn't want to open the crates without the two of you here."

"It's okay, Fredrick, I'll survive." They walked over to the platform where five large crates marked with tuna were. For what seemed like an eternity, no one said anything. They stood and processed what was in front of them. Robert was the first to speak.

"Okay, everyone, let's take a look and see what we have here." Robert stepped back as two of his men went to work opening the first crate. Once the top was off, Charlie stepped forward, took a switchblade out of her purse and removed the seal that was blocking the interior contents. Pulling back the seal, she inhaled deeply and groaned.

"Oh, someone is really trying to piss me off this morning!" None of the men moved a hair, as they were all used to Charlie's sudden outbursts. All eyes were trained on Robert. It was one of the codes they shared, and this one was saying "don't just stand there, say something comforting to try to ward off another outburst."

Robert stepped forward and looked down into the crate. He couldn't help but smile as he said, "Sorry, Charlie."

Eyes wide, Charlie let out a loud laugh as she said, "Really, Robert, couldn't you think of something more original? You sound exactly like that old tuna commercial.

Fredrick cleared his throat and said, "Can we continue now,

156

folks?"

Sighing, Charlie said, "Sorry, Fredrick, but this damn container is covered with the best smelling coffee, and as you know..."

She was cut off by the men saying in unison, "You didn't have your morning coffee!"

Ignoring the jab, Charlie gave the contents of the container her undivided attention. With quick, sharp movements, she managed to clear half the coffee off to the side. Peering inside, she froze at what she saw. "Jesus, look what we have here. This doesn't look like tuna to me."

Robert and Fredrick were standing next to her, speechless. Charlie reached into the crate and pulled out the item. She examined the weapon, the cool steel glittering in the silvery light of the warehouse. She turned it over, looking for a serial number, aware that everyone was watching her. The long hours of intense studying and her love for history was about to pay off.

Robert thought out loud, "Is this what I think it is?" Charlie answered right away, "It's an air gun."

Bobby, one of Robert's men, looked puzzled, and asked, "What the bloody hell is an air gun?"

Gripping the gun tighter, Charlie took two steps back so she could face everyone. "Well, I know this much about them. They date back to the 1500's. They were preferred over Black Powder Rifles because they didn't produce any smoke. They could be loaded faster than the rifles, because the user didn't have to worry about getting the powder wet or worry about getting burned, and it was much quieter. The air gun was also made in large and small calibers, which were used for hunting big and small game."

Before she could continue, Robert raised his hand to silence her. Everyone present seemed to have the same question in mind, but no one but Robert wanted to ask the question for fear of sounding like a male chauvinist pig. "Curiosity is killing me, Charlie, so I have to ask this... Okay?"

Standing totally erect, she was unnerved by his comment. She already knew what was coming. "Shoot."

"How do you know all this?"

Flashing a wide smile, she explained, "I was trained by the best-- my father. He was a great marksman, and taught me everything he knew, not to mention I have a love of history and spent long hours studying, remember? For four months, you had me research all different types of firearms and ammo. I found a book on air guns and thought they were interesting, because I'm also a history buff. The fact that they dated back to the 1500's intrigued me, so I read the whole book. It was fascinating."

The men looked at one another, trying to hide the smirks that threatened to come out full force on their faces.

"May I continue now?" No one spoke. They all bobbed their heads up and down.

"They were pneumatic air guns, which were effective up to one hundred and fifty yards."

Pino, who couldn't believe this woman was outsmarting him, interrupted her. "I'm sorry, Charlie, did you just say pneumatic?"

"Yes Pino, it means pump."

"Well, why didn't you just say pump, then?"

Ignoring him, Charlie arched an eyebrow in disgust and resumed her intel. "After one pumped the air reservoir tank anywhere from 100-1000 times, the air gun could produce twenty shots as a repeater at speeds from anywhere between 650 fps up to 1,100 fps on one charge."

"Hold on a minute," said Fredrick, "who the hell wants a gun you have to pump 100 to a 1000 times?"

Nodding in agreement, Charlie answered, "I honestly don't know, Fredrick. Your guess is as good as mine. Robert, what about you?"

"No idea, Love. Please carry on, though; I'm enjoying the history lesson." He was all smiles, and she knew in her heart he was bursting with pride.

"The air gun is both silent and deadly, as I'm sure you've already figured out." Everyone let out heavy sighs. "Wait, I have more. After the cartridge bullets were perfected, the caliber rifles started to fade away, but today there has been a huge comeback of high-powered, large caliber air guns. What I'm holding in my hands is what we call a Super Max High Powered Spring Piston Air Rifle. It can shoot at 1000 fps. It is so powerful that it can shoot a pellet right through a three- quarter inch panel of plywood."

Robert took a box out of the crate and handed it to Charlie. She passed the gun to Fredrick and opened the box. She took out one of the pellets and examined it. "These are Crossman Pointed Pellets. They're solid, and the best when it comes to penetration. Hunters tested these pellets in the Super Max. They found that the Crossman pointed pellets went through both sides of a hard tin cracker can at seventy feet with no problem. They went through a half-inch thick piece of plywood with ease, and the pellet kept going. I...."

Robert cut her off. "That was extremely useful information, Charlie. Great work." Blushing, she lowered her head and nodded. "All right, guys, let's open up the others and see what we have." After the remaining four crates were opened and they examined the contents, and knew they had hit pay dirt.

THE OTHERS LEFT, LEAVING ONLY CHARLIE, Robert, and Fredrick. Together, they went over the inventory displayed on tables in front of them. Robert's voice was high with excitement as he and Charlie discussed what they thought Bellesto was doing.

"Look at these weapons! We've got a load of 9mm calibers. These babies are great personal protection weapons! They have less kick, the ammo is cheaper, and they are much better for range shooting."

Charlie was showing just as much excitement as Robert when she offered, "Look, Robert, these are Colt Gold Cup Trophy Handguns! They give a great single shot, have smooth action, and are good weight!"

Fredrick was standing off to the side, observing his friend and his love. They were like two kids in a candy store! He also noticed the slight competition going on between the both of them. They were trying to show each other they knew just as much if not more than the other. Well, they definitely were formidable opponents. Thank God they were both on the same side. Suddenly, they both stopped what they were saying and turned to look at Fredrick.

Robert smiled at his lifelong friend and asked, "What are you doing?"

"Oh, not much, just observing the brilliant minds before me."

Charlie let out a giggle and said, "Well, come here, we have something to show you."

In three strides, Fredrick was by Charlie and Robert's side. "What is it? Wait, no ... please don't tell me that's what I think it is? Is it? Wait!" Fredrick carefully took the weapon from Charlie's hands and inspected it with awe. "This, if I am not mistaken, is a Taurus Titanium Tracker Model 617TT .357 Magnum. My God, I started out with one of these!"

Now that Fredrick was caught up in the moment, Charlie egged him on. "Really? What do you know about it?"

"I know that it is a seven shot revolver. It is also the first total titanium target sighted sport and field revolver. It has a medium frame with a four inch revolver that weighs only twenty-four ounces. Every component in the gun that should and could be made of titanium, is."

Charlie was momentarily baffled. "Why's that, Fredrick?"

"Because titanium is stronger and more elastic than steel."

"Oh, I see."

"This baby is great to use on both light and dark colored objects and in high and low conditions."

Now it was Robert's turn to look baffled. "What?"

"It simply has to do with its tracker's red-insert front and white outline rear sights."

"Do I need to understand what you just said?"

Chuckling at his friend, Frederick said, "No, you don't. May I continue?"

Charlie and Robert exchanged smiles with each other now, realizing that this must have been what they looked like only moments ago. In unison, they invited, "Please do."

"Don't worry, I'm almost finished. The last tidbit I have is this--this gun has super accuracy. It has what is called a Yoke Detente System. Now before you raise your hands and ask the question, let me answer it for you. The Yoke Detente System is a spring-loaded latch in the top of the yoke that makes sure the cylinder stays tightly shut within the frame at the moment of firing. I personally love the fact that it has soft elastomer ribs that deform and squeeze together to shape themselves to specifically fit the person's hand! The spring then goes back into place after the hand lets go.

"Well, that's about it. Class dismissed"

CHAPTER 41

THERE WAS A MOMENT OF SILENCE IN THE warehouse. You could have heard a pin drop. The sudden sound of a door creaking set them jumping in their skins. Two sets of heavy footsteps could be heard on the unforgiving cement floor. They were getting louder as they turned a blind corner. Not knowing what, or who, to expect, everyone's reflexes kicked in immediately, and guns were drawn in precise unison.

Two of Fredrick's men, Agent John Dagastino and Agent Tom Lynch, walked around the corner and froze mid-stride when they saw everyone standing with guns drawn. Everyone let out relieved sighs.

Fredrick broke the tension. "Sorry, guys, I was so engrossed in what we were doing, I forgot you were coming."

The two agents looked at each other and were grateful they still had all their limbs intact. Speaking at the same time, they answered, "Sure, boss, no problem."

Dagastino and Lynch had worked as partners for over ten years. They were constantly harassed by the other men because the two could, and often did, read each other's minds and finish each other's sentences. It was said they were long lost twins, though they looked nothing alike. Actually, they made quite a comical pair. Dagastino was tall and lean, with fire red hair and freckles all over his face and body. Lynch was just what his last name sounded like: he had no neck, and was short and round. He looked like he had been lynched and then someone had taken his head and placed it back onto his shoulders. While his counterpart had a thick head of hair, Lynch had only a few strands left on the sides of his temples.

Fredrick gave his agents instructions then turned them loose. He approached Charlie and Robert and said, "Okay, guys, we're done here for the time being. My men are watching Bellesto closely. I'm sure once he realizes these crates are missing, the shit's going to hit the fan, big time."

Charlie and Robert headed for the exit of the warehouse. "Okay, Beautiful, what's next?"

"If you don't mind, I think I'm going to go home and check on the house. The real estate agent was showing it today, and I want to check in with her."

"Sure, do you want some company?"

"Thanks, but I think I'd like to be alone. I have to figure a couple of things out. I'll give you a call later, okay?"

"Are you sure? Is there anything you'd like to talk about? You do know you can talk to me, Charlie. I don't care what it is--I'm here for you always."

Her heart pounded at the sound of his words. How did he do that to her? She could feel her face flush as she lowered her gaze to the cement floor. When she finally answered him, it was the merest whisper. "I know you are, and I thank you for that, but there are some things that I need to deal with that you can't help me with. I need to handle them by on my own."

He cupped his hand under her chin, and slowly raised her face so her eyes met his.

"Sometimes in life, Charlie, it's okay to ask for help. You are one of the strongest women I have ever known, so please understand that sometimes when one asks for help, it's not a sign of weakness."

Her eyes filled with tears. She blinked them away, then walked to the door. When she turned around to face him, she was all smiles. "Thanks, but I just need some time alone. But I promise I'll call you later."

As he escorted her to the parking lot, it dawned on Charlie that they only had his car. As if reading her mind, he offered, "It's okay, take mine. I'll have Fredrick take me back."

"Thanks."

He opened the door for her and watched her slide behind the wheel. He hated to see her like this. Her moods changed so quickly that he found it frustrating when he couldn't keep up with them. It was like she was haunted by something. He wished she would let him in, but at the same time, he didn't want to push. The last thing he wanted to do was drive her away.

Once she was settled in, he closed the door and watched her place the key in the ignition. She smiled one last time before she drove out of the parking lot. He stood there for the longest time. He didn't know why, but for some strange reason, he felt very uneasy, a premonition of some sort, and it wasn't good. He feared Charlie was in trouble and something terrible was going to happen to her. He admonished himself for being such a worrywart, and hoped he was wrong. Quickly, he said a silent prayer. Please watch over her. You already took one love from me...

He had to stop; he didn't like where his thoughts were going. Wiping a lone tear from the side of his face, he made his way back to the warehouse.

CHAPTER 42

HIS RAGE COULD BE FELT THROUGH THE entire building. He called a meeting and demanded an answer, or "heads were going to roll." Four of his top men were present and accounted for when Bellesto burst into the room. Everyone sucked in the thick, suffocating air. The silence was deafening as Bellesto's intense stare went from man to man. His gaze was livid, his eyes on fire and penetrating. Everyone stood at attention, awaiting what would come next.

When Bellesto spoke, everyone had to strain to hear what he was saying. His words were delivered in a measured whisper, but the tone was icy and chilled them all to the bone. "I want to know what the fuck happened to the missing crates. Someone here had better be able to tell me."

No one moved a muscle. The outrage Bellesto felt roared within him. Cold fury raced down his spine as his heart pumped furiously. Suspicion flickered in his mind as he silently reviewed the sequence of events. When he spoke again, there was a threatening quality in his voice, although dark currents swirled beneath his now calm demeanor.

Bellesto raised an arm and pointed at one of his men. "Everyone is dismissed but you." Loud sighs were heard all around the room, and the three dismissed men couldn't escape fast enough. Scurrying like pigeons discovering a feast of crumbs on a sidewalk, the three henchmen bolted from the room all at once, pushing and shoving to get out of there as quickly as possible.

Once they were gone, Bellesto strode to the door, and ever so quietly, closed it. He sensed no fear in the man standing behind him. Since the day he'd hired him, Bellesto had a feeling about him that he couldn't quite put his finger on. Well, now was the moment of truth. If he didn't come clean, he would make sure this man faced the most agonizing death.

Exuding complete composure, Bellesto resolutely faced the man he believed to be his very own Judas. Walking to the table, he pulled out one of the chairs and sat down. Straightening his jacket, he motioned for the man to also sit. Looking Bellesto straight in the eyes, the man slowly pulled out a chair and sat. Sitting totally erect, like he hadn't a care in the world, the man placed both his hands on top of the table and carefully laced his fingers together, waiting.

When Bellesto spoke, his tone took on a congenial air. "So, my friend, we've come to a crossroads. I'm curious as to which path you have chosen. You see, in my mind there is a puzzle, a complicated one. Do you know why?"

Bellesto was staring the man down, but the possible traitor wasn't flinching .... yet. "It's complicated, because some of the most important pieces are still missing and I believe that you have them. Now please tell me if I'm wrong here, or feel free to interject when the mood strikes you."

Bellesto leaned back in his chair and studied the man sitting across from him. There was no way he could have imagined what this man was about to tell him. The information he was about to receive was not only going to shock him, but would put a whole new twist on his operation.

❧❦

BELLESTO'S FACE WAS A CHALKY COLOR. HE was too stunned to speak, so he merely sat with his hands folded on his lap, absorbing all the information he had just heard. This man was no Judas! He was a godsend. If it wasn't for what this man knew and had just revealed to him, Bellesto would be spending the next twenty years of his life behind prison bars!

Bellesto's eyes locked with those of the secret weapon seated across from him. He cleared his throat before speaking. "You will be rewarded handsomely for your allegiance. I think we both know what has to be done next." The man nodded and gave what Bellesto thought was the most depraved smile he had ever seen. He had clearly underestimated this man, but was glad they were on the same side for the time being.

But something nagged him in the dark recesses of his brain. Bellesto knew the man had a few screws loose and could potentially become a hindrance in the future. He would make sure to keep a tight leash on him, and down the road, if he proved to be too much trouble, he would be dealt with accordingly.

One rule Bellesto learned at a very young age, and still lived by today, was that everyone could be replaced, and this man would be no exception.

CHAPTER 43

ALL OF HIS SENSES WERE OPERATING ON OVERLOAD. He swung the heavy steel door open and squinted at the brightness of the day's final rays. He left the warehouse feeling like a mighty warrior. Nothing and no one could, or would, ever come close to the brilliance he had. The moment he had been waiting for was coming. He couldn't contain the excitement that surged through every fiber of what he thought was his immortal being.

He decided to take a little drive that evening after concluding his meeting with Bellesto. He knew exactly where he was going to go. Swinging the door open, he slid effortlessly behind the wheel of his new silver BMW. He revved up the engine as his heart pounded fiercely in his chest. He was actually getting aroused just thinking of all that was finally going to come to fruition in the very near future.

Speaking out loud to himself, he wondered, "Why not give her a little prelude of what's to come? After all, it's the least I can do." He peeled out of the parking lot humming and laughing, "Star light, star bright, now I know the time is right."

CHAPTER 44

CHARLIE GAVE NADINE A CALL. MY GOD, SHE felt like she was the worst friend on the face of the earth. Thank God, Nadine understood. The two pals talked for over an hour, filling each other in on the latest dilemmas and details of their lives.

After she hung up with Nadine, Charlie contacted her real estate agent and finally heard the words she wanted to hear. The house was sold! The agent explained it wouldn't be more than a month for everything to be completed.

Charlie felt as though a huge lead weight had been lifted off her shoulders. To celebrate, she went to the private stock of selected wines in her cellar and picked one out. She normally didn't drink, but at times she did appreciate a fine wine. "Ah! A nice Pinot Noir from Italy!"

As she wiped the dust off the bottle with the rim of her t-shirt, a sudden and unexpected chill raced down her spine. Slowly, she made her way to the foot of the stairs. Something hit her deep inside just as she positioned her foot on the bottom step. Carefully, she set the wine on the stairs and turned around. What was it that was nagging her? Something was out of place, but she couldn't figure out exactly what it was.

She checked the windows and found them all locked. She traced her steps back to where the wine racks were, and paced around, looking for anything awry. When she was finally satisfied that everything was accounted for, she attributed her uneasiness to the fact that she had been spending less and less time in the house since she and Robert had become an item.

She retrieved the bottle of wine and slowly made her way up the stairs. When she reached the top she clicked the light switch off, closed the door, and made her way to the kitchen. What she neglected to do was to bolt the door after she closed it. This little oversight, among others that night, would prove a huge mistake.

If she had known what was going to happen to her that evening, Charlie never would have gone home at all.

CHAPTER 45

THE TWO MEN WERE WATCHING HER THE entire time. They shared many things in common, one being their lust for her. Bellesto spoke first. He knew the thoughts that were racing through this man's head. "You must restrain from doing anything harsh right now, my friend. Patience is the key here."

As he looked into Darrell's eyes, he detected nothing but darkness and death. He was primed for violence, and although that would come in handy in the very near future, he had to make sure his energy was directed to the right place. He was fearful Darrell would act hastily and jeopardize what they had planned. They had collaborated on a scheme they both knew couldn't fail, but extreme caution had to be used every step of the way.

"Don't concern yourself with me. I know what I'm doing." Darrell's eyes were like steel, his voice crisp like ice, when he continued, "If it weren't for me and the information I shared with you, you'd be a dead man in no time. No one knows her better than me, so I will decide how the rest of this plan goes down. Understood?"

Bellesto froze. Darrell already showed signs of coming apart at the seams. He had such vengeance and hatred for this woman that his thinking was impaired. Bellesto's mind concentrated on how to calm down this loose cannon and keep him focused on their objectives.

Bellesto knew at that moment that Darrell was no longer an asset to him, but had become a liability. He would have to make some quick adjustments to their plans. "I'm well aware of your inside track, Darrell, but just keep in mind all that we stand to lose if we are not careful. Understood?"

Darrell nodded feigned agreement. I have to get rid of this albatross now so I can get back to the monitor and finalize my plans for tonight. It's none of his business, anyway. Nobody tells me what to do. Relaxing his facial features, he smiled and nodded in agreement once again. "Sure, no problem. Whatever you say."

Bellesto was wary--he didn't believe a word Darrell said, but he had no choice. He had to leave to tie up some loose ends, and couldn't babysit this wacko. "Fine, I'll meet you later at the warehouse."

Darrell walked Bellesto to the door. Darrell watched him continue on to his car and get in. Once the engine started, and the car backed out of the driveway, he couldn't move fast enough to get back to the monitor to see what she was doing.

CHAPTER 46

THE SUN SET, LEAVING AN ORANGE GLOW HIGH IN THE SKY. It was a beautiful night to sit and relax. She called Robert and gave him the good news about the sale of her house.

They chatted for awhile and he told her he was thrilled for her. They finally admitted to one another what each had been keeping close to the heart. They wanted to be together all the time now. They both felt strong enough now to release their private demons and move on together.

After she hung up, Charlie grabbed one of her favorite novels and a glass of wine and went out to the back patio. She laid on one of her lounge chairs and sipped the cool crisp liquid. Placing the glass on the table next to her, she picked up her book and started to read. After a while, the sky turned an eerie shade of black, totally devoid of any stars. She hated to go in, but exhaustion took over.

She got up from the lounge chair and stretched her tired muscles. She picked up her empty glass and book then headed for the French doors that led to the kitchen. Once inside, she closed the doors behind her, and walked over to the sink to wash her glass. She headed upstairs and decided to take a nice, long, hot bath and get a good night's sleep.

Tomorrow night was her lip sync performance at Bellesto's. She wasn't nervous about the contest itself; she was nervous about what was going to happen after. Pushing all thoughts of Bellesto and the competition from her mind, she went into the large bathroom and filled the oversized claw tub with hot water and fragrant oils. She stripped herself of all her clothes and lowered herself into the steamy liquid. When she was settled, she placed the headphones of the compact CD player that she kept on the ridge of the tub over her ears. The soothing sounds of harps put her in a tranquil state that she loved.

Unbeknown to her, at that very moment, an angel of sorts was entering her house. This angel had a name all his own-- Angel of Death--and he was coming for her.

CHAPTER 47

HE WATCHED HER STRETCH LIKE A SEXY VIXEN. He was mesmerized by her sultry gait and found himself getting hard. God, how he wanted her, but he knew that piece of enjoyment would have to wait. First he would inflict tremendous amounts of pain on her, then take her violently. He'd see how much of a prima donna she'd be then!

He watched her saunter into the house. He'd bet any amount of money she hadn't locked the door. But even if she had, he could get in through the cellar, or better yet, he could waltz right in the front door, because he still had his key! How she ever became a detective was a puzzle to him. After all this time, it never occurred to her to change the damned locks on the doors, let alone lock any of them!

He rocked back and forth on the balls of his feet, pulling the black cloak tighter around his body. He looked up into the dark sky and smiled to himself. He would bide his time and wait. Soon, very, very soon, he was going to enjoy scaring the bloody hell out of her!

Actually, tonight was merely a small glimpse of what she would be getting tomorrow night, and he couldn't wait!

CHARLIE FINISHED HER BATH AN HOUR LATER. SHE looked like a raisin, but it was worth it. Her muscles were loose, and she knew as soon as her head hit the pillow she'd be out for the night. She quickly blew her hair dry and slipped her silk nightgown over her head. Tomorrow she would start the tedious task of packing her belongings. She was looking forward to moving in with Robert and finally letting go of the past.

Smiling, she walked into her bedroom and turned down the bed. She went to the bay window and opened it. A soft breeze caressed her face as her mahogany curls swirled playfully around her face.

She inhaled deeply, and was grateful once again that her house had finally sold. It would be all but impossible to truly start over while still living in the same home she had once shared with Darrell. Just the thought of him made her blood boil. Purposefully, she forced all thoughts of her ex-husband out of her mind. She didn't want to waste any more of her precious energy on him!

She turned away from the window and made her way to the bed. She climbed in and got comfortable, and just as she had predicted earlier, the moment her head hit the pillow, she was out like a light.

❧◦❧

IT WAS TIME; HE HAD WAITED LONG ENOUGH. His gut told him she was fast asleep. Slowly and methodically, he made his way through the bushes. He crept to the side of the house where the hidden door was for the ancient bomb shelter. The last time he was here, he made sure to grease the hinges so they wouldn't creak.

Carefully, he lifted the hatch and descended the stairs. The only sound that could be heard was the faint swishing of his cloak. A twisted smile spread across his face as he reached the last step.

He inhaled deeply, savoring the anticipation of what he knew was to come. He walked to the far end of the cellar and removed the tape that was in the hidden camera. Earlier, he saw her look of apprehension. He knew she sensed something. Too bad she didn't realize her every move was being monitored. There was no need to replace the tape. After tomorrow night, her very existence would be exterminated.

He went to the bottom of the stairs and hesitated for just a fraction of a second. In his mind a video played. He remembered a day soon after they had gotten married. He had sneaked downstairs while she was searching for a bottle of wine, and quickly took her from behind. He hadn't been able to resist the urge when she bent over and her shapely backside was in full view.

She never knew what hit her. She had made him promise that he would never do that again. Women! When they wanted it rough they denied it, but he knew better. Even though she protested, he knew deep down inside she had enjoyed every minute. He promised himself before he finished her off tomorrow night, he would have her one last time, and he knew he would have her begging for more.

҉

HE REACHED THE DOORWAY TO HER bedroom. It was open for him, inviting him in. He pulled the hood of the cloak closer to his face so she wouldn't see him--not that she could anyway. While he was in the cellar, he had shut off all the circuit breakers. Even if she managed to make it to the switch, nothing would happen.

He had a little surprise for her, and with every step he took, his excitement mounted. He carefully eased the rope and handkerchief laced with chloroform out from the inside of his robe. He hesitated at the doorway. How he loved to watch her sleep. She resembled an ancient Greek goddess. Her skin was velvety, like satin, and her fiery chestnut hair gleamed.

She lay on her left side facing the windows. Like a little angel, she had her hands cupped beneath her head. He watched her breathing pattern--slow and even. His eyes wandered to her firm behind, and he stood in awe at the luscious shape. She had improved her muscle tone, that was plain to see; she was trim and fit. What a waste he had to finish her off.

҉

SHE WAS DREAMING AGAIN, BUT THIS TIME IT was a full blown nightmare... or so she thought. He was back in full force, whoever he was. She felt his hot, thick breath on the arc of her throat, and his hand on her thigh. She could hear his evil whispering in her ears. She tried to move, but couldn't. She was paralyzed with fear. Slowly, she felt his hand slide up the middle of her leg. He was telling her how he was going to have her sexually.

Fumbling out into the darkness, she tried to grab at what was holding her down. She couldn't breathe. Muffled screams echoed out into nothingness. She was pinned down onto the bed, then felt something being placed over her nose and mouth. She desperately tried to fight off whatever it was, but the force was too powerful. The last thing she heard before she slid into total oblivion was a dark menacing voice taunting, "Wait, my love, this is just the beginning of the end for you."

Satisfied that she was unconscious, and would not wake up, he stood back to admire her. If only she knew what was in store for her tomorrow night. For a split second, he pondered the possibility of her not going through with the contest or the plans she and Lover Boy had worked out.

"Oh, but you will, won't you, my love? I know you better than anyone. Your pride and ego won't let you quit! This, my dear, is your biggest downfall, and always has been. You never know when it's time to ease back and quit. Well, we'll just see what you choose to do!"

He quickly took the rope and tied her hands and legs together. When she woke up in the morning, she wouldn't know who, or what, did this to her. He felt himself get hard, and fought to restrain himself. But the urge was too powerful, though. Placing his right hand under his cape, he unzipped his trousers. Freeing himself in the darkness, he began a slow and steady rhythm on himself. With his free hand, he began to massage her breasts. Low groans sprang from his throat as his rhythm increased. Slowly, he slid his hand down her flat smooth stomach until it reached her silky flesh. The feel of her skin ignited the fire that was boiling deep inside his loins, and then like a bomb going off, he climaxed and screamed out her name.

ABJECT TERROR FLOODED THROUGH HER entire being. Her head was heavy, her thoughts muddled. It felt like she had a massive hangover. Her eyelashes slowly fluttered open. Her mouth was bone dry. When she attempted to move her arms and legs, she found she couldn't. Her whole body ached from the lack of circulation, and the skin where she was tied was raw and bleeding.

Panic raced through her. Fighting desperately to gain control, she took small, deep breaths, filling her lungs with as much air as possible. She closed her eyes, hoping it would help her concentrate better. Whispering out loud, she said, "I have to stay calm and be rational." She knew if she could roll herself off the bed and onto the floor, she could then get up. Rocking from side to side, she kept moving closer to the edge. Finally, she rolled off the edge and fell to the floor. She landed hard and let out a faint scream.

Pain rippled through every limb as she tried to get up. She pushed her weight against the side of the bed to gain some leverage. Once standing, she found her legs weak and sore. "Don't complain; you're alive, you idiot!" Anger now rippled through her veins at the thought of an intruder in her home. She couldn't even remember what the hell happened!

She leaned against the bed for support as she slowly made her way to the phone that sat on the end table. Though her arms were tied behind her back, she could at least pick it up and dial. Turning her head as far around as she could, she picked up the receiver, placed it on the edge of the bed, and pressed in Robert's number. She kneeled down on the floor and placed her ear against the receiver.

Charlie prayed he would still be home, and panicked when three rings had gone by and he still hadn't answered. Tears stung her eyes as she fought to remain calm. She counted the rings: five, six, seven, Come on, already! Be there! Finally, on the eighth ring, she heard the voice she needed to hear.

He sounded out of breath as he said, "Hello?"

She tried to speak, but started to cry, and choked on her words.

Panic riddled through Robert's voice when he asked, "Hello? Hello, Charlie, is that you?"

She couldn't stop, and try though she did, she only cried harder now.

"Oh, my God, honey, what's wrong? Are you all right? Charlie!"

She inhaled deeply and whispered only one word: "Help."

Robert, now in a frenzy, yelled into the phone, "Charlie, don't move, I'm coming right over! Do you hear me, Charlie?"

Relief spread through her as she wearily answered, "Yes." The next thing she heard was a click on the line, and knew that he was probably already down the stairs and out the door.

She lay down on the edge of the bed and tried desperately to collect her thoughts. She had to think! What was the last thing she remembered from the night before? She had her bath then went to bed. She had what she thought was a nightmare again, but this time she knew it was no dream--it was real! Someone had snuck into her her house and knocked her out with something; the throbbing in her head was relentless!

An eerie feeling swept over her as she thought of the contest to be held that night at Bellesto's. She knew Robert would be dead set against her going, but she was determined, now more than ever, to find out who was behind this little scare tactic. She hated to admit it, but it had worked; she was scared shitless!

Whoever it was was hoping she would back out, but they were wrong, dead wrong.

She was going to make sure that whoever did this paid. As her head began to clear, another thought crossed her mind. Whoever came into her house knew something. Thinking aloud, she tried to make sense of the situation. "How much does this person know, and is it just one person, or more than one? What is it they know and exactly how much do they know? How did they find out what they know?"

She could feel the pressure building again around her temples and she took a deep breath. She closed her eyes and replayed every one of her movements from the night before, but nothing stood out as odd. "Damn!" Just then, she heard the doorbell. It was ringing insistently and she wondered how the hell she was going to make it down the stairs.

CHAPTER 48

ROBERT JABBED THE DOORBELL WITH HIS index finger, then left it there. He could hear incessant ringing from inside of the house. Something bad had happened, but just how bad? "Christ, I never should have left her alone yesterday!"

Guilt swirled deep inside him as he fought the urge to break down her door. Losing any and all of the composure he had, he started yelling her name as loud as he could. "Charlie! Charlie, can you hear me?"

When she still hadn't materialized, he went around to the back of the house. He jumped over the hedges that led to the patio and the back doors. He tried the handle and found that it opened. "Christ, the damn door was open all night, or was it?" Once inside the kitchen, he frantically called out her name again. He ran from room to room on the first floor, checking all the closets as he went along. Finally, he heard her. Her voice was coming from upstairs.

He bounded up the stairs two at a time and reached her bedroom. When he saw her tied up on the bed, he stopped. He stood rooted to where he was, taking in the horrific sight before him. Charlie was the first to speak. "Robert, please come and untie me." Her voice was hoarse and she looked like shit, but thank God, she appeared to be okay.

Running to her side, he grabbed her and cradled her in his arms. "My God, who did this to you?" Releasing his grip, he started to untie the rope that cut deep into her wrists and ankles. He noticed the black welts and dried blood. Rage filled his entire body, and he silently vowed to find and kill the animal who had done this to her.

As quickly as his fingers would work, he finished loosening the rope and led her to the bathroom to help clean her up. When they had finished, he helped her get back in bed, propping some pillows behind her so that she would be more comfortable. He went downstairs to make her something to eat, which he then brought up to her. He sat in silence and was in awe at the appetite she had. He didn't think she'd want anything, but sitting before him was a woman who was totally ravenous.

Slowly, the chalky color of her skin was replaced with a pink glow. When he took the tray from her, she managed to give him a faint smile. Robert smiled back, and couldn't believe how strong she was. He hoped that she wasn't going to fall apart later.

Something told him she was putting up a brave front for his benefit. Clearing his throat, he said, "I'll bring this downstairs. Is there anything I can for you while I'm down there?"

Letting out a huge yawn, she replied, "No thanks, honey. That was a great breakfast. I can't believe I ate as much as I did!"

Letting out a small chuckle, he said, "I'm glad to see you ate it all. It's a good sign that you're on your way to recovery. I'll be right back."

"Okay, and Robert?"

"Yes, Love?"

"I love you."

Sighing heavily he managed to reply, "I love you, too." He turned and walked out of the room. When he returned he found the love of his life fast asleep. He pulled the covers up and quietly left the room.

He had some calls to make.

CHAPTER 49

BELLESTO CALLED AN IMPORTANT MEETING. All of his top men were present and accounted for. They sat in one of the large conference rooms around a large oval mahogany table that was situated under his warehouse. The atmosphere was strained as the men waited for their orders. The "Boss" seemed to be in a foul mood again, and they silently wondered what had happened now.

Minutes passed as Bellesto paced around the table, not uttering a word. His brow was creased and he was deep in thought. Pulling at the lapel of his crisp, pinstriped jacket, he pulled out his chair and sat. No one dared move a muscle. Bellesto was about to speak when the door flew open and Darrell strode in.

Slamming the door behind him, he made his way to the nearest chair and pulled it out. Arrogance was written across his face, and it caused Bellesto's blood to boil. To think that he had the audacity not only to be late for such an important meeting, but then offered no explanation for his tardiness.

Their eyes locked. The other men in the room could feel the tension between the two; it was so thick it could be cut with a knife. Bellesto was the first to break the unbearable silence.

"All right, guys. There have been a few changes to the original plan. Listen up, because we could stand to lose everything if one, and I mean one, little mistake is made. I want my orders carried out to a tee. Is that understood?" Everyone nodded in agreement.

Bellesto stopped when his gaze fell on Darrell's. When he spoke again, his voice was impervious, and directed to him as if challenging him. "I do not, and I will repeat this so all of you will understand: I do not want anyone to deviate from the plan. Is this understood?" Again, no one spoke a word. The only sound that could be heard was the rustling of the men in their seats.

Bellesto knew Darrell was trouble. He had had one of his men tail the miscreant the night before. When he received the report, he was livid. He was going to have to eliminate him along with the others. It was such a shame he was going to have to get rid of Charlie, alias Maria. She had guts, he'd give her that, but truth be told, she was going to have to suffer for what she had almost accomplished.

No one betrayed Bellesto. Oh, a few here and there tried, but they never lived long enough to finish what they started. He made sure to always stay one step ahead of the game, and to do that entailed keeping his enemies right in his own back yard.

Pushing his chair back, he stood and straightened his jacket. When he spoke, his voice rang with authority. "All right, listen up. Here's what we're gonna do...."

CHAPTER 50

WHEN ROBERT FINISHED HIS CONVERSATION with Fredrick, he wearily hung up the phone. He was exhausted. He was so engrossed in his thoughts he didn't hear the light patter of footsteps. He jumped when Charlie appeared in the doorway and cleared her throat. He pushed his chair back and rushed to her side.

Pulling her into his arms, he hugged her tightly. After a few moments, he pulled back and gazed into her eyes, searching. Searching for what, he didn't know exactly. The color in her face had a healthy pink tone, and her eyes were clear and devoid of any trauma or stress.

A small smile curved on her mouth as she asked, "How are you doing?"

He couldn't believe that at a time like this, she was more concerned for his welfare than her own. He silently reprimanded himself, because knowing her the way he did, he should have known she would place his needs above hers. This was just another attribute he admired about her.

His voice was husky with emotion when he said, "I'm doing fine, but it's me who should be asking you that question, don't you think?"

Hesitantly, she said, "I'm fine, but there are some things we need to discuss right away."

"Okay, let's go and make some tea. We'll talk in the kitchen."

Nodding in agreement, she took his hand in hers. Silently, they made their way to the kitchen. He led her to one of the bar stools that was placed by the counter. "You sit and talk, and I'll make the tea."

"Deal." She knew that once she told him what she was planning on doing, he would erupt. She started to get nervous and looked down at her hands, tightly clenched in her lap. She hadn't noticed that Robert had stopped what he was doing and was watching her.

"Charlie?" His tone was beckoning her to go on, so she took a deep breath and plunged ahead. As he placed the steamy mug of tea on the counter in front of her, his heart felt a stirring of tenderness and protectiveness towards her. This didn't surprise him, as he lifted his mug and took a long sip of the soothing mixture. But now he saw a flushed look of panic, which she unsuccessfully tried to conceal by turning her face away.

His concern for her was heavy now as he coaxed, "Come on, Hon, it's all right. I'm here for you, I always will be." When she made no effort to respond, he kept talking, hoping he could break down her wall. "Whatever it is, we'll take care of it together. We're a team, remember?"

This elicited a reaction from her. She looked sharply at him and frowned. Her mind was reeling, because she knew the last thing he expected her to say was she still planned to attend the contest that night, and follow their original plan through to fruition. What she didn't know was that he was already prepared for this.

He prided himself on knowing what made her tick, and knew how strong her character and morals were. He knew she would never allow anyone or anything to stop her from reaching her goals. Once she started something, she made sure she worked hard and finished the task to completion.

Pulling out one of the stools, he dragged it closer to hers and took her hands in his. He caressed her smooth skin lightly and smiled. "I'm ready when you are...what's the matter, are you afraid of me?"

This definitely got her going now. Answering with more force than she intended, she raised her chin up, her nostrils flaring out, and said, "No! I am not in the least bit afraid of you, or anyone, for that matter."

He couldn't help chuckling as he said, "Good, I'm glad to hear that. So what do you have for me?"

As she fidgeted in her seat, she felt some of her confidence wane a little. Stalling for time, she licked her lips and picked up her mug. She took a large swig of the hot tea, burning her mouth, then spitting it onto the counter...and Robert.

"Thanks, just what I needed, a burnt crotch!"

She finally realized how stupid and childish she was acting. She sat perfectly erect and locked eyes with him. "All right, here it is: I'm going to follow through with the contest tonight. I figure whoever came here last night and tried to scare me will be there waiting to see if I show up. After I've won the contest, I'm still going to go with Bellesto and see what I can find out."

Tilting his head, he asked her, "Are you sure?"

"Yes, I'm sure."

"You sure are cocky, you know that, beautiful?"

She looked bewildered, not sure what he meant.

"Excuse me; did you just say I was being cocky?"

When he answered her, he had a mischievous look in his eyes. He knew she wasn't catching on to his little joke. "I believe I did, why?"

"What am I being cocky about?"

Sensing that she was beginning to get agitated, he clued her in on his humor. "If you recall, you just said, 'when I win the contest.' To me, that's being just a little bit cocky, don't you think?"

Playfully, she slapped him and laughed. "Ha, ha! You wait and see who has the last laugh, my friend. I have no intention of losing that contest tonight, and like I said, then I'll meet with Bellesto and find out as much information as I can."

As he looked into her black beams, he could have sworn he saw lightning bolts shoot out from her pupils. He knew not to argue with her, because she was right. He, on the other hand, was going to make sure he stayed as close to her as possible. He was going to find out who the maniac was that scared the shit out of her, and take him out himself.

His eyes were still locked on hers when he finally asked the question that was searing the inside of his brain. "Okay, now I want you to tell me what happened last night. Start from when you pulled in the driveway, and don't leave anything out, no matter how small you think the detail is."

CHAPTER 51

EVERYTHING WAS IN PLACE. HIS HEART pounded wildly with anticipation. He couldn't wait to see the look on her face when she found out that it was him all along who had been tormenting her.

As he straightened the collar on his crisp, white shirt, he smiled at his own shadowy reflection in the mirror. He liked what he saw, and knew she'd be begging for him to take her again, just like he used to. Well, maybe he would, just for old time's sake.

He purposefully strode to the wingback chair in the corner of his dimly lit bedroom, picked up his sports coat, and methodically wiped any traces of lint off it with the brush that was placed next to it. A sardonic smile formed on his lips as he thought about the arrangement he had made with one of Bellesto's own men.

Everyone had a price, and he had paid that piece of scum handsomely for his services. Darrell assured him he was not going to deviate from the original plan--too much. He wanted to make sure he was the one who got her first, not Bellesto. Oh no, that pleasure belonged to him, and him alone.

He carefully put on the jacket, not wanting to cause any unnecessary wrinkles in the fabric. He wanted to look perfect for her...after all, he was the last person she was going to see before she died. He walked to the door, grabbed the knob, and turned it. He suddenly remembered that he had forgotten something.

He sauntered to the oak bureau and opened the lid of a deep mahogany box that sat on top. There, glimmering atop a cushion of burgundy velvet, was his silver signet ring. He carefully removed it and placed it on his left ring finger. Admiring the engraving, he smiled, and now knew that everything was complete.

This ring held many powers for him. It gave him strength and knowledge, and made him infallible. He quietly closed the lid on the box, made his way back to the door, and slipped silently out of the house into the darkness in search of his prey.

CHAPTER 52

THE NIGHT WAS WARM, WITH A DEWY MIST that hung in the air. Charlie gripped the steering wheel with both hands as she drove towards Bellesto's. She knew Robert and Fredrick were already there. They went for dinner at the restaurant, and then afterwards, made their way into the lounge for the contest. Fredrick had two of his men also in place at the disco.

She had called to find out which contestant she was. There were twelve in all, and thankfully, she was last. She was always right in the beginning or at the very end, never in between. So far, Charlie had entered thirty of these contests, and won them all hands down.

She tugged absently at the front of her jumpsuit, then stole a quick glance at the work she had done with makeup to cover the small blue and black welts that had formed on the inside of her wrists. She was uncomfortable, and debated whether she should stay, or go home and change. She was questioning her choice to wear a purple leather one-piece jumpsuit. It was sticking to her like a second skin, and she was starting to sweat. She also felt self-conscious about the bruises that were visible on her arms and wrists. Thank God, the ones on her ankles were hidden. "Crap. I hope I don't have to go to the ladies room! I'll never be able to get this damned thing back on!"

As she rounded a corner, she noticed the sky turning black. Dark clouds formed and hovered over her. It felt like they were following her, alerting her to some impending danger. Her saliva production suddenly stopped, and her mouth went dry. Taking deep breaths, she tried to calm her frayed nerves. She was scared witless, but knew she couldn't back out now. Knowing that Robert, Fredrick, and some of his men would be there watching over her gave her little comfort. Whoever had broken into her house and terrorized her would be there. For all she knew, he, too, was already in there waiting for her.

She reached the main entrance of Bellesto's, and stopped the car by the striped awning. The valet promptly opened her door and gave her a warm smile. Her mind was racing. Could he be the one? Is he connected to the person that's after me? She didn't move, and jumped when the young man cleared his throat.

"Ma'am?" He looked at her, waiting for some movement or response.

"Oh, I'm sorry! I must have the jitters."

Taking her hand, the young man helped her out of the car. He asked, "Are you in the contest this evening?"

"Yes, I am, and I'm feeling rather anxious right now."

"I understand. I'm sure you'll do a great job."

"Thank you."

She watched him get in the car. He stopped before closing the door and said, "Break a leg." Not waiting for a response, he closed the door and vanished around the corner.

☙❧

THE AIR WAS THICK WITH SMOKE, THE lighting dim. Slowly, Charlie made her way to the back of the restaurant where the club was located. The restaurant was packed with patrons enjoying their meals and after-dinner drinks, and she wondered how many were planning on staying for the contest. She had a half hour before curtain time, and she desperately needed a drink to calm her frazzled nerves.

From behind her, she heard her name called, and turned to find Antonio Bellesto walking towards her. His aura emanated power as he strode up to her and grasped her hands tightly in his. He raised them to his lips and brushed them with a light kiss that sent chills down her spine. "You look exquisite this evening, Maria."

Her eyes were transfixed on his slate tie, but when she raised them to meet his, she felt a cold rush of wind flow right through her. Though he smiled at her, his eyes were narrowed, dark, and menacing.

Clearing her throat, she teased, "Thank you, Antonio."

He said nothing. For what seemed like an eternity, he stared into the very depths of her soul. He cocked his head to one side and asked, "Is something wrong, my beautiful?"

Stammering over her words, she replied, "No... no, not at all. Why do you ask?"

"I ask because I see something in your eyes that shouldn't be there."

Wrenching her hand free from his powerful grasp, she took a step back. "And what might that be?"

"Fear, Maria."

She laughed a little too loud for her taste, and knew she had to stay in control. "It's probably just stage fright. I always get nervous when I have to get up in front of a large group of people. I'm sure you know how it is."

His tone was icy when he replied, "No, I don't."

She desperately wanted to end the uneasy conversation. She felt like her chest was going to explode as she silently counted the rapid beats of her pounding heart. She anxiously waited for him to say something. She didn't like the vibes he was sending her. But his bland expression made it clear that he was waiting for her to make the next move.

Sighing, she said, "I think I'll go check in and then get a drink. It was nice seeing you again, Antonio."

As she tried to brush past him, he stopped her with a heavy hand on her bare shoulder. She winced as his fingers dug deep into her silky flesh. When he spoke, it was not a request but a command. "After the contest, you will come upstairs with me to my office so we can celebrate."

She knew better than to argue or decline, so she merely nodded her head in consent.

Satisfied, he bowed, and said, "Until then."

She watched him turn and walk towards the entrance of the restaurant. He stopped every now and then to greet diners and wave acknowledgements to others. He turned back once, and saw her watching him. When their eyes connected, she felt a fear she had never felt before.

A congenial smile formed on his mouth, but the deep rage he was feeling inside gleamed wickedly in his eyes. That look told her he knew. The question was, how much?

She went to the booth, checked in, and handed the disc jockey her music. After he finished cueing it for her, he gave her earphones so she could listen for herself. "Perfect. Thanks, Mario."

"Anytime, Maria. Good luck."

"Thanks."

She headed for the bar to order a drink. Fredrick and Robert were seated at a round table in the middle of the room. Neither acknowledged her presence when she cast a quick glance in their direction. She found a seat at the bar. As she swiveled her chair towards the DJ booth, the lights blinked on and off to alert the patrons and contestants that the contest was ready to begin. Charlie quickly scanned the room for Fredrick's other men. She felt uneasy because she hadn't met them prior to this evening.

Panic swelled in her but she fought to remain calm. She picked up the crystal wine glass by the fragile stem and gulped down more of the crisp liquid than she should have. A burning sensation slid down her throat, forcing her to cough. Her attention was drawn to the booth by the sound of the DJ's voice coming over the PA system.

"Ladies and gentlemen, may I have your attention, please!" Slowly, the murmur of voices came to a halt, and all eyes were riveted on the handsome DJ now commanding the middle of the stage.

"Welcome to Bellesto's lip sync contest! I ask that there be complete silence at the very beginning of the performances. You, the audience, will choose the winner by applause." Cheers were heard and some audience members started to clap. "We have an eager crowd here this evening! I ask that you applaud after the performance is over, not before."

Laughs flowed freely through the room as the DJ waited patiently for the noise to die down again. When it did, he announced the first contestant. "Ladies and gentlemen, let's give a warm welcome to our first contestant, Angelo!"

CHAPTER 53

HER PALMS WERE SWEATY... HER MOUTH bone dry. They were at the end of the contestant roster now, and her name would be called any second. She looked up to see four strobe lights anchored to the ceiling. She was temporarily mesmerized, watching them swirl around and around, emitting colorful rays of psychedelic color across the dance floor and walls.

Charlie nearly jumped out of her skin at the sound of her name blaring out over the speakers. Tentatively, she rose from her seat and made her way to the center of the stage. She didn't dare look in the direction of Fredrick and Robert. She was nervous enough.

Once she got into position, her eyes locked with Bellesto. He blew her a kiss, and she knew it was the kiss of death. She couldn't worry about that now, she had a job to do. She had probably read too much into the conversation, anyway. Shaking off all thoughts of the night before and Bellesto, she bowed her head, and waited for the noise to die down. As the music started, she began what would be the most memorable performance of her life.

At the end of her performance, there wasn't a dry eye in the house. She stood transfixed. Everyone stood and applauded, screaming her name. She glanced at Robert, and instantly, teared up. His eyes glistened as he applauded and screamed out her name. Fredrick kept slapping him on the back, with a wide grin plastered on his face. Charlie made her way back to the bar, accepting compliments along the way from various patrons.

The DJ was going to announce the names of all the contestants again, and through a process of elimination, the winner would be crowned. The selection process took a half hour. She was the last contestant, and the audience went wild. She won hands down, and shuddered as she watched Bellesto make his way onto the stage to present her with the prize. When he stood by her side, he cocked his head and leaned ever so slightly to the side so only she could hear the words he spoke.

"My, you are full of surprises, aren't you, Maria? I hope you like receiving them as much as giving them, because I have one waiting for you in my office."

She trembled at the sound of the ice in his voice. It had a daring and violent undertone to it, and she wondered what he had in store for her. Smiling, he grasped her hand in his, and pulled her into a tight embrace, kissing her much too roughly. The crowd went wild, laughing and clapping. Stunned, she pulled back and gasped. She knew Robert and Fredrick saw everything, and fought to keep her composure.

Bellesto pulled her off the stage to the side of the DJ booth. His eyes bore right through her when he said in a commanding tone, "I'm looking forward to celebrating with you, my beauty. Why don't you go up to my office and wait for me there. I'm going to get a bottle of my best champagne, and then I'll be right up."

Her mind was reeling. Everything was happening too fast. She knew she had to stall for time. Robert had given her a wire to put on herself so they could monitor her location and conversation. It was the latest technology, only a half inch in length, and it served as both a homing device and microphone. Meeting Bellesto's penetrating stare, she coyly replied, "I'd love to, but first, I'm going to make my way to the ladies' room so I can freshen up."

Though there was a smile on his face, the statement he made was a threat. "Of course, but don't take too long, I don't like waiting."

Sweat poured down the sides of her face as she planted the small microphone inside the waistband of her leather jumpsuit. Once she had secured it in place, she silently prayed that Robert and Fredrick were also in position and waiting. The door to the ladies' room flung open, making her jump. Two women entered, bantering back and forth about the contest.

When Charlie emerged from the opened stall door, the two women gasped and instantly rushed to her side. Graciously accepting their compliments, she made her way to the mirror to freshen up her makeup. Her hands were shaking as she pulled the pouch from the bottom of her bag. When she was finished, she inhaled deeply and prayed she would be able to handle whatever was coming her way.

As she exited the ladies' room, she decided to make her way back to the club before going up to Bellesto's office. She wanted to see if Robert and Fredrick had left yet. A huge man, well over six feet tall, approached her. He wore a black suit that appeared tailor made to fit the collection of muscles that bulged out from the fine material. He smelled of death, and instantly she was on alert.

She tried to make her way around him, but he blocked her path and placed a chafed hand on her bare shoulder.

CHAPTER 54

WHEN HE SPOKE, HIS VOICE WAS GRUFF AND low. "Mr. Bellesto would like you to wait in his limo for him, ma'am. Please come with me." She knew if she went, she would be signing her own death certificate.

Lifting her head high, she exclaimed with the last bit of control she could muster, "I just left Mr. Bellesto, and he asked that I wait for him in his office."

Not listening to her words, the man tightened his grip and steered her in the direction of the door towards the back of the club. Once they reached the exit, her fears sprung to life. There, in her lower spine, was cold, hard steel. He pushed it roughly into her delicate skin and said, "If I were you, I'd smile, and not say a word."

He pushed the door open with his free hand, and led her to the long, black car parked by the back alley. Her mind was racing, but no plan of action was coming to her. What should she do? If she tried to fight him off, he would shoot her. They reached the back door of the limo. She never saw the other figure approach from behind.

Before she could react, a hand slammed down over her mouth, and another wrapped around her neck. The man who had led her to the car roughly grabbed her arms, pulled them behind her, and tied them together.

Then it happened for the second time. She felt an impending blackness wash over her as she silently cursed,

"Jesus, not again."

CHAPTER 55

HE WAS PACING BACK AND FORTH LIKE A caged animal. He was on edge, and now regretted the moment he agreed to let Charlie continue on the case. Fredrick stepped out of the van they had parked two blocks down from Bellesto's restaurant. "We got her transmission just fine, Robert. She's still in the club. Dagastino and Lynch are still in there covering her; they said she went into the ladies' room."

Robert turned to look his best friend in the eye. His voice was full of concern when he insisted, "I don't have a good feeling about this. Did they see her come out yet?"

"No."

Exasperated now, and on the brink of exploding, Robert wanted answers, and he wanted them now. "Well, where the hell is she, then?"

Fredrick grabbed Robert by the shoulders and tried to calm him down. Feigning a laugh, he said, "She's probably taking her time--you know how women are. Look, some of my best men are in there with her. As soon as they see her come out, they'll let us know."

Edging Robert towards the door, he said, "Come on, let's get back in the van so we don't miss anything."

Both men had their backs to the steel door of the van, so when it flew open, the two men jumped. Agent Serentino poked his head in. His skin had a chalky hue to it and he was physically trembling. He knew that what he was about to say would put these powerful men over the edge.

Fredrick took a step towards the door and leaned a hand on the side of the cold metal. "What do you have for us?"

When Serentino hesitated, Robert rushed towards him and grabbed the collar of his shirt, pulling the man forward, and causing him to stumble. "Spit it out, damn it!"

Serentino whispered, "She's gone, sir."

Robert thought the ground gave way under him. His legs turned to Jell-o and he couldn't breathe. Fredrick rushed to his friend's side, directing his question at Serentino. "What do you mean, she's gone?"

"Agent Dagastino and Lynch just told me that she was nowhere to be found inside the club. I checked the homing device, and apparently she's in a vehicle headed south towards the warehouse district."

Like bolts of lightning, the men piled into the van and took off in the direction they were just given. A heavy mist was rolling in and it made the moonless night seem that much darker. Once inside, Fredrick radioed Dagastino and Lynch.

"Get the hell out of there, now, and head south towards the warehouse district!" He glanced over at Robert. There was nothing he could say. He knew what was going to happen now. His friend was going to find the sick bastard responsible for this, and make him suffer a cruel and agonizing death.

Silently, Fredrick prayed that when they did find Charlie, she would still be alive. He knew how these men operated. It didn't matter she was a woman. In their eyes, she was the enemy, and no mercy would be shown to her. Just the thought of what might happen made his skin crawl.

Robert stared straight ahead, deep in thought. He silently cursed himself for allowing her to follow through with the plan, and vowed to find her, no matter what it took. His jaw was set, his eyes ablaze as he imagined finding the bastard and showing him no mercy as he killed him. He knew he had to stay in control and utilize his training, experience, and senses to their fullest potential if they were going to find Charlie. He didn't consider himself to be a religious man, but now, he silently prayed and made a pact with God.

I pray you will guide me to her and that I find her in time, alive and well, and if I have to, I'll gladly sacrifice my life for hers. Please protect her; she needs you right now, more than ever.

CHAPTER 56

THE NIGHT HAD AN EERIE SILENCE TO IT. THE only sound came from the crunching of the limo's tires slowly rolling over the grey gravel. The moon, which shone brightly only hours ago, was now mostly hidden by thick misty fog. The long, sleek vehicle looked out of place as it pulled up next to a capacious cement building and stopped by a steel entryway. Two large men wearing muscle shirts and sweatpants exited from the side of the building and rushed to open the back door of the limo. When Darrell emerged, his shoulders were set, his mouth taut.

He slowly raked in his surroundings. He was sure they hadn't been followed, but still felt the need to be cautious. He filled his lungs with the salty air, and cast his gaze upon the Providence River. The waves were slowly crashing up against the stone wall. A storm was brewing, and he knew it was only a matter of time before the soft caresses of the waves turned into violent thrashing. The sky was getting darker by the minute as the moon vanished behind black velvet cloaks.

The driver had gotten out of the car, and waited with the other men for their orders. They knew never to disturb their boss when he was in thought, which was often. Actually, they all secretly discussed the sanity of the man who paid them.

Small pellets of rain drifted down from the heavens. No one moved. No one spoke. Finally, after what seemed an eternity, Darrell turned to face the three men in front of him.

When he spoke, it was with quiet determination.

"Luke, Rock, take her from the car and bring her down to the dungeon. Crow, come with me."

Crow, who was well over six feet tall, felt indebted to his boss, because he had given him this job when he got out of prison, no questions asked. Though he was grateful to him, there was something amiss about him that he couldn't quite put his finger on.

199

Something always seemed out of place.

CHAPTER 57

LUKE AND ROCK HAD THE BODY OUT OF THE car by the time Darrell had reached the entryway. When he heard Rock mumble, "Oh shit," Darrell turned quickly to see what the problem was.

Eager to get on with his plan, he asked, "What is it, Rock?"

Rock looked to Luke and they both knew the shit was going to hit the fan now. Losing patience, Darrell raised his voice and shouted into the darkness, "What the hell is it? I don't have all night!"

Rock cleared his throat, then said, "I felt something in her waistband. She seems to have some type of wire on her, boss." Darrell instantly saw red. He pushed Crow off to the side and hurried back to the car, where Luke and Rock waited. Slowly, Rock pulled out a small, black wire that had a microphone and chip connected to it. He handed it to Darrell, who held it up in the dimness. He knew all too well what it was. He threw the device down onto the gravel and smashed it with the heel of his shoe. As he looked down at the sleeping woman, rage engulfed him, and he snapped. Nothing could have prepared Luke and Rock for the blow that came next. Like lightning, Darrell raised his arm high above his head, made a fist, and slammed down hard into the side of her face. The blow was enough to make Rock and Luke let go of her body. They all watched in silence as she slammed into the hard, unforgiving gravel lifeless. His blood was boiling as he fought to regain control of himself. He didn't want his men to see him totally lose it. Oh, no, that would be just for her. He was going to inflict so much pain on her she'd be begging him to kill her. Inhaling deeply, he plowed his right foot into her side. He turned to make his way back to the door. He never looked back as he said, "Pick her up and throw her down in the dungeon. I'll take care of her later."

Crow reached for the handle and pulled the door open. Luke and

Rock guessed that this woman must have done something awfully wrong to get their boss into such a raging state.

They also knew her time was quickly running out.

CHAPTER 58

BELLESTO SLAMMED THE DOOR TO HIS OFFICE with such force it threatened to fall off its hinges. Pacing back and forth, he tried desperately to control the fury that was boiling up inside him. He turned to his men, who were watching him through half closed eyes. When he spoke, his voice was like steel. "I want to know what happened to her and I want to bloody know now!" Both men were at a loss for words, because they didn't know.

When neither made a reply, Bellesto stormed to his desk and picked up the first thing he saw, a marble paperweight, there mainly for display, and hurled it against the far wall. The heavy object smashed against one of the priceless pieces of artwork that he had had flown in from Italy. The glass shattered into small fragments, sending shrapnel through the air, and causing both men to jump out of the way.

Face red, breath coming in heaves, Bellesto barked, "Get Frankie up here, now!" Both men rushed to the door, anxious to get away from their boss' wrath. They knew someone's head was going to roll, and neither wanted it to be theirs. After the door closed behind them, Bellesto stomped to his desk, pulled out his chair, and sat. He had a sneaking suspicion that he knew who took her. Mumbling to himself, he spoke the man's name, who was now his number one enemy. "Darrell."

As Bellesto clenched and unclenched his fists, his mind raced as how to handle this now delicate situation. His thoughts were interrupted by the sound of the office door opening, and glass crunching under heavy footsteps. Frankie, his right hand man, stood about seven feet tall. He had worked for Bellesto for years now, and was trusted.

He entered the room, and approached Bellesto's desk. His look was hard as he met his boss' gaze. Seconds ticked by as neither man said a word. Frankie knew better than to say anything.

When his boss was ready, he would speak, so he stood at attention and waited. Finally, Bellesto pushed his chair back and rose. He walked around to the front of the desk and extended his hand. Frankie readily grabbed it and gripped it tight. The two men then embraced and kissed each other on both cheeks.

Standing totally erect, Bellesto sighed wearily, and said, "We have a situation on our hands, Frankie. It seems Darrell has taken Maria." Frankie was already aware that Maria was a cover. Charlie was her real name and she was a Private Investigator hired to tail his boss. He also knew that Darrell was a sick son of a bitch and needed to be eliminated, pronto.

Bellesto started to pace the room again. He turned to look at Frankie, and asked, "What can you tell me about this?"

Frankie cleared his throat before filling his boss in on the facts as he knew them. "I don't know much, boss, but what I do know is that the limo and Crow are gone."

Bellesto flinched, not knowing if he had just heard right. "Say that again?"

"Crow and the limo disappeared shortly after the contest. I'll bet that Darrell made him an offer he couldn't refuse."

"I'll bet he did, that son of a bitch. When I get finished with the both of them, they'll wish they were never born!" Just as he was about to continue his tirade, a thought came to him. "Maria, I mean Charlie, said she had to go to the ladies' room. I told her to come up to my office right after that. Crow must have been waiting for her and somehow forced her to go with him instead."

Frankie made no verbal reply--he knew his boss was probably right, so he only nodded in agreement. "Frankie, go see what else you can find out for me. I need some time to think before I make my next move."

"Sure thing, boss."

Bellesto waited until Frankie had closed the door behind him before walking back to his desk. He pulled out the plush leather chair and laid his head back in consternation. He had a very important decision to make now. The question was, would it be the right one? He closed his eyes so he could concentrate better. Silently, he weighed the pros and cons of the idea that was flickering through his brain.

After several moments, he opened his eyes, leaned forward, and grasped the receiver, holding it next to his ear. With his free hand, he reached down to where his hidden compartment was. From under the desk, a drawer slid into view. A small smile curved the corners of his mouth at the irony of the situation.

There, in the drawer, were small index cards with names, phone numbers, and vital information on some of his most formidable opponents. When he found the one he was looking for, he slowly punched in the numbers, and waited. A gruff voice answered on the second ring and Bellesto knew at that moment he had made the right decision.

CHAPTER 59

THE DUNGEON WAS COLD AND DAMP. THERE was nothing in the room but one very small window that allowed only a miniscule amount of light in, and an old, battered grey steel chair. Her limp form lay in a disheveled heap on the hard, unforgiving stone floor. Still falling in and out of consciousness, her wet body shivered violently from the intense chill in the room, forcible waking her to the horror she was in. Slowly, Charlie pried open her dry mouth and gasped for breath. She could taste blood in her mouth as she tried to produce some saliva.

In a futile effort, she tried to lift her hand so she could move a clump of hair matted to her face. Her body felt heavy, and when she tried to move her legs, a muffled cry of pain escaped from her parched throat.

The intensity of her situation slowly took root. Someone had handcuffed her hands behind her back and placed shackles around her ankles.

Trying desperately to stave off a mounting wave of panic, she closed her eyes and took some deep breaths. Her entire body was racked with pain. It felt like someone had beaten the bloody shit out of her. She meditated, hoping to lower her rapid heart rate, and clear her muddled mind. A million questions formed in the recesses of her consciousness.

Softly speaking to herself, she asked the questions that were burning inside her. How long have I been here? Where the hell am I? Who the hell took me? Her head pounded wildly as she fought off the urge to vomit. If she thought she experienced horror in the past, she was in for a big surprise. She lay still, trying to remember exactly what had happened to her once she stepped outside the restaurant. She became more frustrated as her brain wouldn't cooperate with her.

Just as she felt her body relax a fraction, a booming sound came from outside. She hadn't been aware until now, but a major storm was brewing. She listened to the heavy pellets of rain slam against the cement building, and cringed when another bolt of lightning crashed near the structure.

She inhaled deeply as she heard the faint sound of footsteps approaching. Cold sweat poured down the sides of her face as ragged fear engulfed her.

CHAPTER 60

THE CELL IN THE BACK OF THE VAN RANG TWICE. When Serentino answered, the transmission was lost. Robert was livid. Yelling over the din of l thunder, he said to Fredrick, "What do you mean we lost the fucking transmission!"

They had pulled the van over to the side of the road. Visibility was bad and only getting worse, as a thick blanket of fog rolled in. They weren't far from the warehouse district, which was located in downtown Providence.

Inwardly panicking, Fredrick made every effort to remain calm for the sake of his friend. He knew Robert was on the verge of losing it, and wouldn't be able to think clearly from this point forward. Keeping his voice steady, he replied, "The storm may have knocked out the receiver, Robert. All we're getting now is static."

Robert slammed his fists down hard on the steering wheel. Just when Robert felt all hope was lost, he heard a faint chirping noise come from the back of the van. Both Fredrick and Robert froze.

With a sense of insistence, Agent Serentino called to them: "Boss, you have an urgent call!" Fredrick slid open the partition that separated them, and snapped, "Who is it?"

"He won't say who he is, but he did say he just called but got disconnected. He said he knows who took Charlie!" Fredrick and Robert collided as each tried to get to the back first. Fredrick was ready to snatch the small cell from Agent Serentino, but Robert was quicker, and grabbed it out of the agent's hands.

His voice hard and low, Robert inquired, "Who is this?"

As he listened to the answer to his question, his already chalky face went grey. Fredrick had no idea who the person on the other end of the line could be to elicit this sort of reaction from his friend.

Robert reached for a pad that was placed near one of the monitors. He scribbled quickly, asking nothing. Fredrick peered over his friend's shoulder so that he could read what was being written. He sucked in his breath as his brain comprehended the information that was there in black and white.

He thought he was scared for Charlie before, but now an intense foreboding overcame him. A bolt of lightning streaked past the van, rocking it back and forth. Robert dropped the cell and swore. "Fuck!" When he retrieved the small phone and returned it to his ear he yelled, "I lost him! Damn it!" Frantically he tried to get a dial tone, but it was no use.

When he looked deep into his friend's frazzled face, they both knew what the other was thinking. Neither would dare say the words they knew to be true.

Charlie was running out of time...and fast.

CHAPTER 61

BELLESTO SILENTLY PLACED THE PHONE BACK on its cradle. He knew the sudden turn of events was drastically changing the direction of his plan. He had to think fast, and organize a new route to take. He pressed down the button on his intercom and asked for Frankie. While he waited for him, he contemplated all of his options. He had to admit, there were few.

He knew Robert and Fredrick to be fair men, and he also knew at this point they would both be willing to strike a deal with him. It was in his favor Robert's girlfriend was taken hostage. If what he heard about Robert in the past was true, then he knew he would do anything to ensure the safe return of his love.

Bellesto had told Robert what he knew and the general vicinity of where he believed Darrell might have taken Charlie. He also warned Robert of Darrell's obsession with his ex-wife. The kingpin silently cursed himself for allowing Darrell to continue on in his organization. Bellesto didn't misjudge people often, but this time he had, and it was going to cost him dearly.

He gave Robert his word that he would try to locate Charlie, and if he did, he promised to protect her and return her safely to him. Another drastic detour from the plan. His intent had been to do away with her, but now that he'd given his solemn vow, he wouldn't turn back. He knew he dealt in many shady dealings, but when he gave his word, it was as good as being written in his own blood. He embodied what he believed many businessmen lacked: a code of ethics, and following through on what he says. This time would be no exception.

Frankie knocked on the door and poked his large head in. "You called for me, boss?"

"Yes, come in, Frankie." Once Frankie was seated in the oversized burgundy leather chair facing his boss, Bellesto spoke. "There has been another drastic turn of events. Listen carefully, because we don't have much time..."

CHAPTER 62

THE FOOTSTEPS WERE GETTING CLOSER. THE small amount of light that had been filtering in through the small window was even dimmer now. She lay facing the bars and cringed inwardly. She was trapped and caged like some wild animal. She knew she had no way to get out. The footsteps stopped in front of the steel doors as another bolt of lightning and crash of thunder cut savagely through the darkness.

Through the shadows, she could see a figure standing by the iron bars. Whoever it was said nothing. He stood looking in at her, and she thought it best to pretend she was still out cold.

Charlie closed her eyes tightly, and listened as attentively as her sense would allow. She heard a jingling noise, then the sound of a key sliding into the lock. A loud click echoed as it pierced through the blackness. She was holding her breath now, not knowing what to expect.

The large body walked slowly towards her, and stopped no more than an inch from her. The rain splattered onto the side of the cement building as the wind howled threats into the night. She held her breath waiting for the inevitable... her death.

The massive frame bent down and seized her by the arm. His colossal hand dug into her already bruised skin as he brought her to her knees. Involuntary screams escaped from her throat as pain surged through every inch of her mangled body.

His arm held her steady as his free hand formed a fist and slammed it against her head, sending her whirling. She crashed against the cold, cement floor, fighting to stay conscious. She tried to move, but the figure seized her shoulder, and roughly pushed her back down.

He had knocked the wind out of her, and when she could finally inhale again, she glared up at the imposing silhouette through black marble eyes that burned with malice. She fought the panic that threatened to drain her of her last ounce of willpower.

Holding back a rush of tears, she brazenly looked up at the dark figure and hoarsely shouted, "Go to hell, you bastard!"

She recoiled, making herself as small as humanly possibly as the massive shape grabbed one of her arms and dragged her behind him. He approached the solitary steel chair on the far side of the room and threw her roughly onto it. He reached behind her and unclasped the handcuffs. When it was evident that he was not going to leave them off, Charlie let out a wail of desperation.

"Please! Whoever you are, just leave them off!"

Uncontrollable sobs escaped from her dry throat, and inwardly she chastised herself for displaying such weakness. The figure behind her stopped momentarily as if considering her plea.

"I promise I won't fight you or move. I just need the circulation in my arms to start flowing again."

Silently, the ebony cloaked individual counted to ten. When he was finished, he put the handcuffs back on, but didn't lock them into place, ignoring her pleas and protests. He made a wide circle around her until he was standing directly in front of her. Oh, how he loved seeing her like this! She still couldn't see his face, because he had the cloak's hood pulled far down over his features.

The darkness of the cell added just the right touch for him, as the anticipation of what he was about to do continued to build He couldn't wait to see her reaction when he unveiled himself!

Through half slit eyes, he watched her. She was silent now, observing him, and assessing her situation. Too bad she has no options. He studied her facial features, and could faintly make out dark welts forming on her usually glowing skin. She had two black eyes, dried blood caked all over her, and her hair was in total disarray. Still, he concluded she was the most beautiful creature ever created. It was a shame her beauty would quickly dissipate as he tortured her.

Reaching under his robe, he located the small flashlight he had taken with him, tightly curling his fingers around it. He wanted to make sure she could see his face clearly when he was revealed to be the one who had taken her.

CHAPTER 63

THE WINDS WERE SO FIERCE NOW, BELLESTO needed two of his men to close the back door of the new Lincoln he had purchased only a week ago. Once all his crew were safely inside, his driver carefully maneuvered the vehicle out of the lot and headed towards the warehouse district.

Construction was being done on the bridge they had to cross to reach Fox Point. The lanes were narrow and visibility almost nil as the car rocked from side to side.

The radio was on low, but still loud enough for everyone to hear a major hurricane was heading their way, expected to reach full force within the hour. Winds were predicted to reach over one hundred miles per hour, with heavy rains causing severe flooding. The warehouse district, which was located on the waterfront area of Providence, would be especially hard hit.

The hurricane barrier was ready to do its job of protecting several hundred million dollars' worth of property in the downtown area. The barrier, once closed, would be twenty five feet high and stretch for a half mile, from Allens Avenue to India Point. Emergency evacuations were in full force for all those close to the low level water areas. Bellesto mumbled loudly more to himself than his men, "Great, and we're heading right for it."

CHAPTER 64

WHEN HE SPOKE, IT EVOKED PURE EVIL. HIS voice was deep and low, layered with a consuming hatred. For a moment, she thought she was losing it. The voice had a familiar ring to it, but she couldn't place from where. Her mind raced to process the quality of tones she just heard. Then it hit her. Abject terror raced through her entire body. Now she knew all too well whose voice was sending chills down her spine. Never in a million years would she have guessed that it was the devil himself behind this sick scheme.

Darrell saw the puzzled expression spread across the features of her mangled yet beautiful face. She had recognized something about his voice, but still couldn't quite place it yet. He stood, saying nothing further. Yes, he would be patient and wait for the realization to sink in. Anticipation swelled deep inside his loins. This was truly an exciting moment for him.

Oh, how he had waited for this time to come, and now, all he had hoped for was about to unfold, right before him. He slowly lifted the small flashlight out from beneath the protection of his long cloak. Raising it just above his head, he clicked the button, sending luminous rays flaring out into the darkness. What he saw in her eyes was all the aspiration he wanted to see: pure, unadulterated fear and shock. For a split-second, you could have heard a pin drop; a silence was that deadly. The stillness was finally broken by the sound of his derisive laughter that rang and ricocheted off the cement walls of the dungeon.

CHAPTER 65

ROBERT, FEELING COMPLETELY HELPLESS, DIDN'T know what to do now. The warehouse district was spread out across lower Providence. Under normal conditions, it would have taken no time at all to search the area, but with the hurricane imminent, it could take hours or even longer to search all the warehouses.

The three men listened to the weather advisory on the monitor. Winds were being clocked at ninety miles per hour and escalating rapidly. It was getting too dangerous to stay on the roads.

Evacuations had been under way for hours now, and as they made their way along the water line of Fox Point, they were forced to pull over again because the visibility was so poor. Robert, who was driving, couldn't see much past the windshield. Thick, angry pellets of hail slashed down violently onto the van. He turned to Fredrick with a questioning look that asked, Okay, so now what do we do?

Fredrick, his shoulders slouched, offered the only thing he could think of at the moment. "Okay, let's go through everything we know." Serentino and Robert waited for Fredrick to begin. Fredrick, sensing this, plunged quickly ahead with the facts they had.

"Darrell had one of Bellesto's men apprehend Charlie as she exited the ladies' room. Bellesto's limo was parked and waiting at the rear exit of the club. Darrell's man forced Charlie into the car and took off towards Fox Point, which is where we almost are."

Robert, staring straight ahead, mumbled something inaudible. Fredrick couldn't make out what was said and asked, "What was that you just said, Robert?"

Tearing his gaze away from the windshield, Robert turned to look first at his friend, and then Serentino, who was crouched down on both knees, listening intently. "The limo."

Puzzled, Fredrick glanced from Serentino to Robert and asked, "What about it, Robert?"

Like the bolt of lightning that streaked across the front of the van, Robert turned in his seat, put the gear in drive, and took off faster than he should have. When he finally answered, he had to yell above the howling winds and thunder, "We have to look for the limo! The warehouse district is deserted except for the limo and maybe another one of Darrell's cars!"

Fredrick, fearful of ruining his friend's only hope, didn't say what he was thinking. What if they hid the vehicles, Robert? What if they hid the vehicles...?

CHAPTER 66

BELLESTO'S MAN DROVE CAUTIOUSLY OVER THE Wickenden Street Bridge. Once they made it safely to the other side, all the men inside the car exhaled. Bellesto sat with his eyes closed, head back in silent consternation. His gut told him where Darrell had taken the beautiful Charlie. He directed his driver to go straight down Wickenden Street and then follow the Fox Point Trail. If his instinct was correct, and it usually was, he knew exactly where to find them.

CHAPTER 67

SCREAMS OF RAGE, NOT FEAR, BELLOWED OUT from her parched throat and echoed off the cement walls of the dungeon.

"You filthy bastard!"

In the gloom of the darkness, she thought she saw his face turn red. Charlie knew all too well about Darrell's weak points, and planned on pushing all the right buttons. The only chance she had was to stall for time... that was, if he didn't kill her first. She knew he could explode at any moment, but she knew her options were limited.. She had to keep him talking so she could think.

"You make me sick! You're still nothing but a deranged man!"

He couldn't take anymore. Who the bloody hell did she think she was! She never respected him when they were married and still didn't now. He would show her who was boss. In one swift movement, he was in her face, breathing hard. Her dark eyes gleamed with hatred, and he had to give her credit that she didn't flinch.

When he spoke, his voice was hard and low. "You should thank me that I didn't finish you off yet, my lovely. My, my..." He stood straight and began to slowly pace around the darkened room. "I believe you think because you're a big private investigator now, you are smarter than me. You also seem to think you're stronger than me. You're right about one thing, my dear. This is not a fair situation for you since you are bound to a chair and cannot defend yourself against me. So I'll make a deal with you. I'll undo the handcuffs and shackles and let you defend yourself against me."

He stopped in the middle of the room, looking straight into her black marbles. Her face was blank as she sat totally erect now. "Well, what do you think? Are you up to the challenge?"

Her mind reeled. She knew she was too weak from exhaustion, and the beatings she had taken thus far had diminished any amount of strength she had. But again, she had no choice. She prayed her angels were watching over her now. Clearing her throat, she replied, "You're on."

Darrell walked slowly towards her. When he reached the back of her chair, he stopped. He circled back to in front of her so he could see her expression when he told her the last caveat. Placing his hand under her chin, he slowly eased her swollen face up so she was looking up at him.

"The last rule, my love, is this, and just so you know, once you agree to it, there will be no going back."

She was silently waiting for it. It...being the last hitch to her freedom, or her death. When she made no reply, he continued on.

"The last rule, my love, is that once we begin our tryst together, there will be no mercy shown towards the other person, and our contest will only end when one of us is dead. Do you understand?"

She could feel his hot breath on her face as her mind scrambled to think of what she should do. If she didn't agree to this showdown, he would probably kill her right then and there. She knew she had no other alternative in the matter, so she did what she had done her whole life: prepared to fight.

She looked directly into his maddened eyes and softly replied, "I agree, we fight to the end."

CHAPTER 68

YOU COULD HEAR A PIN DROP INSIDE THE limousine. No one uttered a word; there was no need to. Each of the four men would rather face a horrific death than admit that they were scared witless right now, Bellesto included.

The winds were steadily increasing. The rain was so heavy the streets were flooded as the limo strained to navigate the high levels of water.

Bellesto cleared his throat before speaking. "Frankie, how close are we?"

Bellesto's mind was working in overdrive. He had finally figured out which of the warehouses Darrell had taken Charlie to. He berated himself for not figuring it out sooner, but alas, there were extenuating circumstances. Darrell only had access to one warehouse. Bellesto himself had given him the key months ago.

Shipments were sometimes brought there, checked over, and then transported to their next drop-off spot. Bellesto was sure Darrell was deep inside the confines of that particular building. It would suit his needs well, since the building was ancient and had many maze-like corridors and cells planted in the underground structure.

Frankie's hands gripped the steering wheel tightly for fear of losing control of the vehicle, and he dared not turn to answer his boss. Instead, he raised his voice so he could be heard clearly in the backseat.

"We're there now, boss. What do you want me to do?" Bellesto bellowed, "Jesus! I can't see a friggin' thing!" Silently, Bellesto cursed himself for being such a man of honor. He hoped it was not his fate to be killed in this blasted hurricane. But since he was a man of his word, he knew what he and his men had to do. His thoughts were interrupted by Frankie's loud yell.

"Boss! I found it! I see the back of your limo!" Squinting through the thick sheets of rain, Bellesto could faintly make out the shape of his car. It was parked on the side of one of his warehouses. There was one other car parked right beside it. Bellesto had to admit the bastard was resourceful. He used everything and everyone around him... at no cost to him. But that would all end now--Bellesto would make sure that Darrell paid.... and dearly.

Clearing his throat, he said, "All right, Frankie, cut the lights and pull off to the side. Men, it looks like we go on foot now."

Hesitantly, the four men exited the car. They had to struggle to close the doors, because the wind was so fierce. Bolts of lightning and thunder struck not far off in the distance, and all the men jumped, wondering just what destiny had in store for them on this particularly dreadful night.

Frankie opened the trunk of the car and removed all the items they would need to do battle with Darrell and his men. After dispensing the ammo, guns, and backpacks, they all locked arms, trying to create a barrier against the harsh elements.

Slowly they made their way into the impending darkness to finally put an end to their number one enemy.

CHAPTER 69

ROBERT'S EYES WERE DRY AND RED. His hands ached from gripping the steering wheel too tightly. He desperately tried to clear his weary mind. He made it over the Wickenden Street Bridge, then followed the Fox Point Trail. He didn't know how much further away the warehouse was, but knew he was in the right vicinity.

Before they lost all power, Lynch and Dagastino had called in to report they were on their way. Robert eased around a sharp bend, and slowly maneuvered the van down the gravel road, or rather what was left of it. Straining to see through the fogged windshield, Robert saw a car parked along the side of one of the warehouses. He knew right away it was Bellesto's, and felt a wave of relief to know that so far, he was keeping his word.

Robert cut the lights, and eased the van up behind the parked car. Fredrick sat upright in his seat, and when he spoke, his voice was full of excitement. He pointed straight ahead and yelled, "Look! It's Bellesto and his men."

Without thinking, Robert opened his door and leaped out from the safety of the van and into the storm. He yelled to no avail to the men in front of him. The heavy winds and rain drowned out the sound of his voice. Turning around, he ran as fast as he could back to the van, and turned the lights on and off a couple of times to attract the men's attention. Robert let out a scream as he saw the men one by one stop dead in their tracks.

CHAPTER 70

A LOUD BOOM RANG IN THE DISTANCE, sending even him jumping in his skin. He slid the key into the lock, causing a loud click. Charlie felt the handcuffs loosen around her wrists and tried to wiggle her hands to get the circulation going again.

He was just about to take off the cuffs that bound her aching wrists together when he heard heavy footsteps. Stopping in mid-motion, he strained to discern what the episode was. Standing at attention, he closed his eyes and tried to concentrate. It was difficult to focus with the rain wailing and the constant roar of thunder screaming right outside. The footsteps were more frantic now, and getting closer.

Curious to see what was happening, Darrell started towards the cell's doors. A heavy strain came from the opening above him, and he turned to look up in the direction of the commotion. He heard loud pants as an out of breath Luke and Rock came bounding down the stairs, and hightailed with all their might along the narrowed, darkened corridor. Darrell was frozen, and waited until they were standing right in front of the cell block to ask what the bloody hell was going on.

When they were standing in front of the iron structure, Luke bent over, trying to catch his breath, while Rock grasped the cell's bars as if holding on for dear life. Losing patience, Darrell's voice screeched out into the darkness.

"What the hell is going on?"

Rock, sensing that Luke was not going to be the one to break the news to the boss, took a step back from the bars. He wanted to create as much distance as possible from this irate man when he told him what was transpiring now.

Darrell's dark eyes penetrated into Rock's, waiting for an answer. Luke was still bent over, breathing hard. Darrell told himself that when this was over, he would have to dispose of these two useless Americans!

CHAPTER 71

THEY ALL STOPPED AND TOOK A DEEP breath. The worst thing that could happen was to have your enemy at your back. Vicious winds blew as angry hail pummeled them. Bellesto knew it was his responsibility to face whoever it was behind them. Unlocking his arms, he slowly turned around.

He never thought he would feel relief at seeing this group of men, but under these extraordinary circumstances, relief is exactly what he felt. He managed to lift his arm and wave in recognition as he watched the three men inch their way towards him.

He turned back to look at his men, and immediately detected the apprehension on their faces. He tilted his head to the side and gave a slight nod, letting them know it was alright. Robert reached Bellesto first, and tightly grasped his hand. Fredrick and Serentino nodded to the other men and waited their turns to show respect to the all too powerful man that stood before them.

Once the formalities were over, they joined the others waiting patiently for their next orders. They all made their way to the side of the building where an awning, miraculously still intact, jutted out just enough to give them minimal protection from the harsh elements.

Bellesto was the only one who had knowledge of the underground structure, which contained a crazed mazes of ancient cells, which ran throughout the length of the building. He also knew the location of all the surveillance cameras and sensors that were strategically placed on the outer walls of the warehouse.

He felt all eyes on him as the men waited for their boss to indicate everything was a "go." Speaking rapidly, Bellesto outlined the orders and they all dispersed into the darkness of the night.

CHAPTER 72

RELIEF SURGED THROUGH EVERY NERVE IN her body. She knew what the commotion was; she didn't need these two idiots to say it. Robert and Fredrick were here; she could feel it. Though she was physically drained and severely battered, her body now was energized with a renewed power and vigor. Charlie sat perfectly still and stared down at the barely visible movements circling around on the cement floor.

But then as fast as hope had come, it vanished. She realized all too well what could happen now. Darrell was a loose cannon, ready to blow. Once the two jackasses revealed not only what, but who, the commotion was, he could decide to kill her on the spot. She knew any amount of restraint he had would vanish as soon as he found out the cavalry had arrived.

She tightly grasped the handcuffs that were now dangling in midair, and prayed Darrell would not remember he had unlocked them. Even if they didn't actually see who the intruders were, Darrell would know. She found herself holding her breath as Rock mumbled something inaudible to Darrell.

Darrell, totally exasperated now, struggled to open the heavy iron door of the cell. Rock stumbled backwards as the hinges screeched, echoing through the dimness. Darrell, once out of the cell's confines, took two steps forward and grabbed Rock's throat.

His voice was menacing when he growled, "If you know what's good for you, you blasted idiot, you'll speak up and tell me exactly what the hell is going on!"

Rock, his face ashen with fear, knew he had no choice in the matter; he just hoped his boss wouldn't exact his wrath out on him. Releasing Rock's neck, Darrell inhaled sharply and fought to get control. Now was not the time for him to lose it. No...he would save that for her, and her alone.

Through clenched teeth he demanded, "Okay, Rock, one more time now. What is it, exactly is so important that you had to interrupt the time I was spending with my beautiful wife here?"

Rock's eyes darted from Darrell to Charlie, who was still staring down at the floor. Confusion passed over his weary features as he thought to ask his boss why he referred to his ex-wife as his wife, but he quickly decided against such a question. Taking a deep breath, Rock forged ahead, speaking rapidly.

"We have a situation, boss. It seems there are some intruders outside. I tried to make out who they were on the monitors, but there's way too much static. I couldn't count how many of them there are, but they're out there."

Everything seemed to stop. His body went rigid as fury flooded his very being. He knew who the intruders were and what they wanted. He would make sure they didn't succeed in their endeavor. Failure was not an option for him... no way. He had come this far and he wouldn't allow any interference from anyone, no matter how powerful they thought they were.

Darrell waited for his breathing to slow down before he spoke. Luke and Rock stood like two ancient statues, waiting. When Darrell was ready to continue, he slowly turned and faced his exotic prisoner. Charlie watched in silent horror as his features started to contort.

"What to do now."

His mind weighed what options he had. He could kill her right then and there and be done with it, but that would make it too easy. He always thrived on a hearty challenge, and this certainly qualified as one. He could leave her here and go up and assess the situation himself, which he knew was top priority. Yes, he would leave her here for now, and when he had them all right there with her, he would give them a show like they'd never seen before.

He actually started getting aroused at the plan that was taking shape inside his magnificent mind. He couldn't wait to see her lover's face when he, Darrell, the invincible one, took her right there in front of him! That would be worse than killing her.... Oh, yes, he will suffer more watching me savagely take her, and the final blow for him will be when he sees how much she enjoys it! She probably came off as all innocent and demure with the old geezer! Well, he would pull back the curtain and show the old man how she really liked it! He had to fight off the urge to caress himself. He could feel the bulge in his crotch growing bigger and harder.

A shuffling sound snapped him back to the present. He whirled around, the only sound now coming from the slight swishing of his cape. Rock and Luke were quickly barreling towards the staircase. The two men sensed their boss' stare on the back of their necks and stopped dead in their tracks. This was just too much for him to bear.

These two blubbering idiots needed to learn to respect their master. How dare they try to sneak away from him! They were showing his beloved wife they had no regard for him! No one made a fool out of him--no one. Now he would make an example out of one of them. Charlie would have to have adoration for him after this. She would finally realize no one disrespected him, and if they did, they would pay the ultimate price....death.

In one swift movement, Darrell pulled out the revolver that was camouflaged beneath the folds of his cape. Now he had to choose which one to eliminate. Unfortunately, neither was more valuable than the other, so he simply shot them both. The sound of the two bullets echoed off the walls as euphoria flowed through Darrell.

Charlie, unable to hold back the dread and horror that ripped through her, inhaled so deeply she felt her lungs would explode. She knew she needed to keep silent, for fear Darrell would remember her unlocked handcuffs.

Darrell, satisfied he had made his point to his beautiful wife, did not turn around or a say a word to her. In certain instances, silence said so much more than any words could. Purposefully, he strode to where the two bodies lay and simply shoved them aside with his foot as if they were no more than mere sacks of flour.

Charlie, unable to see in the darkness, listened to Darrell's footsteps become more and more faint. The last sound she heard was the reverberation of a door being shut.

CHAPTER 73

THE MEN SPLIT UP INTO THREE TEAMS IN order to cover all the entrances. Robert made sure he paired off with Bellesto. Though Bellesto had given Robert his word, Robert still didn't trust him. Serentino went with two of Bellesto's men, Frankie and Louie, so they were covered. Finally, Fredrick paired off with Bellesto's last man, Giovanni. Robert knew Lynch and Dagastino were on their way and when, and if, they showed, they would know what to do.

He told himself he had no time to worry about them, and felt secure in the fact they were highly trained and competent enough to handle anything that developed.

Bellesto handed out keys for the entrances and last minute instructions to the men. When he had finished, each team went their separate ways into the foreboding darkness of the night.

CHAPTER 74

INSIDE THE BUILDING, DARRELL AND HIS FINAL man Crow were huddled together, quickly discussing their own plan of attack. They decided to cover what they believed to be the only two entrances. Having no knowledge of the third entrance would later prove to be Darrell's downfall.

Darrell noticed all the monitors and sensors were completely blown out from the ferociousness of the storm raging outside. Shrugging noncommittally, he assured himself that he didn't need them anyway...after all, he was infallible.

Darrell headed towards the back entrance, knowing his formidable opponents would go there, rather than to the side where the cars were parked. Anticipation swelled as he contemplated his enemy's next move.

As he made his way effortlessly through the complex maze- like structure, he praised himself for memorizing every path. It took extreme patience and diligence for him to learn each twist and turn of Bellesto's labyrinth, but he had done it, and knew this was an advantage to him now in this cat and mouse hunt he was on.

In a short matter of time, he successfully reached his destination, and time seemed to stop for him. He stood perfectly still--eyes closed, inhaling deeply--so his senses would be heightened to their fullest potential. Gripping the small compact revolver in the palm of his hand, he waited like a lone cougar ready to pounce on his unsuspecting prey.

CHAPTER 75

THE RAIN HAD SUBSIDED SOMEWHAT, WHICH WAS A godsend for them. Bellesto led Robert to the entrance on the Northeast side of the building, of which he hoped Darrell had no knowledge. The winds were still vicious as the two men struggled to make their way to the hidden entrance. Bellesto suddenly stopped, causing Robert to bump into him. When Bellesto said nothing, Robert directed his line of vision to where Bellesto was intently staring.

"We're here."

Robert, not fully understanding, asked, "What do you mean by 'we're here?'"

Bellesto turned to face Robert and informed him that the entrance they were searching for was right where they now stood. Robert, not wanting to appear stupid in front of one of the most powerful organized crime men, merely nodded in agreement.

"This is good news for us, my friend."

"Why is that?" Robert asked.

Bellesto let out a long sigh and then patiently explained, "Because none of the earth has been disturbed." He pointed to a mound of grass and mud directly at their feet.

"This is a good sign. It tells us Darrell has no idea this door exists. We will be able to enter unsuspected and have the element of surprise on our side."

Robert was more than ready to go to battle now, and when he spoke, the excitement that had been building up within him rang out loud and clear into the darkness.

"Let's do this."

Both men fell to their knees and took off the backpacks they had been carrying. They each took out the tools they needed to expedite the process of clearing the entrance. Together, they worked quickly and methodically, and within a short period of time they had the door open. They put away the tools then put their packs back on. Each man brandished his own powerful revolver and prepared to face the devil as they silently made their way down into the underground structure.

CHAPTER 76

SERENTINO, FRANKIE AND LOUIE STOOD WITH their backs pressed against the wall of the southwest side of the building. Frankie gave the orders, and as Serentino listened, he decided it was just as well to concede, since he had no knowledge of the interior layout of the warehouse. Frankie, unsure if the monitors and speakers that were strategically placed along the outer structure were still operational, whispered into the eeriness of the night.

"All right, Louie, you cover me once we make our way in. Serentino, you stand off to the side and then follow Lou...any questions?"

Both men shook their heads no. Each got into position, not sure what they would find once they made their initial move. From what they gathered, Darrell had at least three men with him, maybe more. Frankie quietly inserted the key into the lock and turned. He felt the bolt give and slowly turned the knob. He gave one last glance back at the two men as he prepared to pull the door open.

Crow was on the other side, waiting with anticipation for his marks to enter. He briefly considered covering the array of windows that lined the side wall, but thought better of it. In better conditions, his marks might have considered them as a point of entry. Of course, a ladder would be needed to reach the opening, but with winds gusting at over 100 miles per hour, there was no way it would stay against the building. His gut told him these goons wouldn't be stupid enough to try that now. No most likely they had a key. What fools, he thought.

He puffed out his chest like a robin who had found a tasty worm for its dinner as he lifted his revolver and aimed at the opening. He was hidden off to the side, away from the door, when the sound of a key turning in the lock played like music to his ears. They would have no time to react, because he had the element of surprise on his side.

Inhaling deeply, he watched as the door slowly opened. He didn't bother to wait for the large figure to fully enter. As soon as Crow saw its shadow on the wall he fired off three shots, all of which were direct hits on his unsuspecting target. Frankie's anguished screams ricocheted off the walls, and then died within the wailing winds of the night. Serentino and Louie were momentarily frozen, watching the horror unfold before them. Like a movie playing in slow motion, Frankie fell face first onto the concrete.

Louie's reflexes finally kicked into high gear, and he scurried away from the entrance. He blindly opened fire in the direction of the shots. Nothing but a stone cold silence settled in the now empty room as the two men bolted inside, their pistols at the ready, looking for any sign of movement. The winds howled as the two men assessed their situation.

There were three hallways leading to God knows where and only two of them left. Serentino leaned down to check the pulse in Frankie's neck while Louie scoured the room. When Louie felt sure they were safe for the moment, he hurried over to where Frankie had fallen. Both men rolled Frankie onto his back, with as much care as possible. Frankie had taken three in the chest. Blood gushed rapidly from the wounds, and the two men knew there was no way to stop it and save their newly minted comrade.

Serentino choked on his saliva as he tried to speak. His voice was a harsh whisper when he asked Louie, "So what do we do now? Frankie knows the layout of this place."

When Louie responded, his words cut the air like cold steel, "We find the mother and return the favor, that's what we do."

Frankie uttered his last words while his lifelong friend cradled his mangled body in his arms. Louie took no notice of his friend's blood staining his drenched clothes. The smell of death permeated the air, and Serentino had to look away as Frankie's "pisano" choked on his tears. "I want you to find the bastards and show them no mercy. I'll hang on for as long as I can. Now get the fuck outta here."

Both men could only nod in agreement to Frankie's last request, knowing they had to move before the enemy targeted them next. Both men stood and listened intently for any sound coming from within the facility. Silently, they gestured to one another as each chose a hallway, and ventured into the unknown abyss of the complex structure.

CHAPTER 77

FREDRICK AND GIOVANNI ENTERED AT THE northwest side of the building. There were no lights on and both men's senses kicked into high gear. Giovanni took a miniature flashlight out of his coat pocket. Though the light was small, it illuminated the room enough for them to see that it was no more than nine square feet, but had four openings leading to the internal sector of the building.

Bellesto told them which opening to enter, after which, they were to follow the long corridor into the main hub of the building. There they would find a heavy steel door at the southwest corner of the room. The door was hidden by a fake wall, and they would need to feel along the side of the structure to find a lever. They were to pull the lever down and to the right to activate the fake panel. Once that was taken care of, they were to descend into the ancient dungeon where he suspected Charlie was hidden.

Sweat poured down the sides of the two men's faces as they made their way to the opening. Fredrick led the way with Giovanni right behind. As they navigated through the tunnel, neither man articulated their thoughts. If they had, they would have been surprised to discover they were thinking the same thing: now that they had entered the long narrow corridor, they were easy targets for anyone waiting on either side.

CHAPTER 78

DAGASTINO AND LYNCH WERE ON THEIR WAY to the warehouse district when the winds swelled to over one hundred miles per hour. When they finally reached the entry point of the Wickenden Street Bridge, they had to stop. Looking at each other with trepidation, they knew there was no way they could cross over. The bridge had become an obstacle course of sorts, blocked in places by large pieces of debris, not to mention the car was being tossed about so alarmingly, both men feared it would be picked up and blown away. Dagastino, speaking more to himself than Lynch, griped, "Fuck, I feel like I'm Dorothy in the Wizard of Oz right now!"

Lynch laughed nervously and replied, "Okay, Dorothy, so what do we do?"

Pondering their options, which were nil at the moment, Dagastino turned to Lynch and declared, "Look, there's no way we can make it over the bridge without us getting killed. We have to find shelter, and now. We have no choice but to turn around." Lynch merely nodded in agreement. There was else nothing to say.

CHAPTER 79

CHARLIE STARTED TO HYPERVENTILATE AS the cell closed in on her. She was gasping for air, trying to stay calm. Outside, the winds tore angrily at the cement compound. She could feel the warmth of her blood oozing slowly down her wrists, collecting in a pool in the palms of her hands. She could feel her ankles swell as the bindings bit savagely into her flesh. Starting to feel faint, she desperately fought off the urge to pass out.

Unfortunately, a lack of sleep and the fierce beatings she had endured had taken their toll. As she slid further into a dark abyss, her mind's final thoughts were an admonishment for lacking such common sense. Earlier, she had wondered how Darrell knew everything he did. Much too late for her, the light bulb finally went on and the realization hit her like a hard fist to the gut. She had never changed the locks on any of her doors. It had never occurred to her to do that. Something so incredibly simple. But she was too preoccupied with trying to keep her head above water and start her life over again.

As her thoughts became more muddled, her head drooped, and she passed out floating into oblivion, knowing full well that her stupidity had led to her own demise.

CHAPTER 80

THEY SILENTLY CREPT DOWN THE FLIGHT OF steel steps into the depths of hell. Each man was lost in his own thoughts as they pondered where the devil was hiding. Their thoughts were interrupted by savage winds reeling around, only one flight away from where they stood. Both men nearly tumbled down the flight of stairs from the unexpected booming sounds raging outside. Inhaling deeply, both men stopped. After regaining their composure, they descended the last steps.

Once they reached the bottom, Robert reached out to Bellesto and pulled him closer. He whispered into his ear, "What do we do now? Should we chance it and put our flashlights on?"

Uncertain of what to do, Bellesto whispered back into the darkness, "No, not just yet. Let me get my bearings first. Hold on to the back of my coat and stay close."

Taking baby steps, they silently crept into the unknown. After what seemed like an eternity, Bellesto finally stopped and spoke.

"We should be nearing the door that leads into the main area of the underground dungeons. If I were Darrell, this is where I would have brought Charlie."

Eagerness rang through Robert's voice as he replied, "That's great! Charlie shouldn't be too far from us, then."

Bellesto didn't want to delude Robert, but he also didn't want to take away his hope either. Tactfully he found a happy medium, suggesting, "I'm sure she is, Robert, but we'll have to negotiate through a series of mazes first to find her."

Momentarily confused, Robert's question echoed off the cement walls. "Mazes?"

"Yes. Don't you remember me telling you the underground structure was practically ancient? This is where alcohol was hidden during prohibition, not to mention, some of the most notorious crime families in Rhode Island and our neighboring states have used these cells."

Before Robert could interject, Bellesto spoke on. "The family would apprehend the underlings of their competition and bring them here, where they were questioned and tortured. After they were no longer of use, they would be disposed of."

Too stunned to speak, Robert merely gasped. After a moment, he asked Bellesto, "What was it used for before prohibition, and who built it in the first place?"

"My dear friend, to adequately answer your question I would need a fine wine and time, neither of which I have right now, so if you don't mind, you'll have to table your curiosity for the time being."

Slightly deflated, Robert acquiesced , "Right."

"I think it's okay to take out the flashlights now and put some light on the subject. What do you say, my friend?"

Not answering, Robert quickly took his backpack off and pulled out his flashlight. He pressed the button and light seared through the intense darkness. Once their eyes adjusted, they surveyed the room. Not far off in the distance was a huge metal door. Eyeing it, Bellesto let out a sigh.

"Yes, I believe this is what we are looking for."

Not waiting for him to answer, Bellesto strode to the door, with Robert following quickly behind. Once they reached the door, Bellesto pulled a key out of his side pocket. He inserted it into the lock and turned. A slight click was heard as a smile spread across his face. He yanked hard, straining to get the door open. Finally, the massive portal gave way, and Bellesto gasped at what appeared before him. The intricacy of the maze never ceased to amaze him.

Robert stood perfectly still, eyes wide, mouth open. "My God! Whoever designed this was either a genius or a madman!"

Stifling a small laugh, Bellesto concurred, "A little of both, I would think. Yes, I believe I'm right about that. No one can be that intelligent without also being a little whacked, so to speak, don't you think?"

Robert really didn't catch what Bellesto said, because he was mesmerized by the room's many openings. Bellesto cleared his throat to grab Robert's attention, and advised, "We're going to have to split up now. You go to the right and I'll go to the left."

Alarm instantly put Robert on edge. He still didn't trust Bellesto.

He definitely didn't feel comfortable splitting up and being abandoned on Bellesto's turf. His thoughts raced. What if Bellesto has set me up--or worse, set Charlie up? He knows the layout of the underground better than anyone. Why does he want me to go to the right?

Losing patience, Bellesto spoke respectfully, but sternly. "Robert, we have to go now. Time is of the essence if we want to get Charlie back alive!"

Robert acted on instinct, and made a split second decision. "I'll take left and you take the right."

Confusion was etched over Bellesto's taut features. His voice took on an icy quality when he asked, "May I inquire why you prefer to go right, Robert?" For what seemed like an eternity, the men glared at each other in the dimness.

Robert knew he had to be careful. The last thing he wanted to do was turn Bellesto against him. Letting out a nervous laugh, he replied, "Simply because I'm superstitious, my friend. Growing up, my father taught me to always go to the right. Something about it being good luck and all."

Bellesto took in Robert's words but knew he was being fed a line of crap, but since he, too, was raised with ceremonial superstitions, he didn't push the issue. Besides, he was doing exactly what he wanted him to do. The problem with cops was that they were all so damned predictable! Lightly slapping Robert's shoulder to show there were no ill feelings, Bellesto reassured, "I understand, my friend. I, also, was raised with certain beliefs. Good luck."

Bellesto headed for the right opening, not giving Robert enough time to react, let alone answer him. Something nagged at him deep down. Why did he feel like he had just been played for a fool? For Charlie's sake, he hoped he was wrong. Robert set off to the left with a fierce determination. He had to be the one to find Charlie first.

Her life depended on it.

CHAPTER 81

CHARLIE AWOKE SHIVERING IN THE DARKNESS of the cell. Jutting her tongue out, she tried in vain to moisten her parched lips. Moving her head slowly in small circles, she tried to work out the kinks. From what she could feel, she surmised one of her eyes was swollen nearly shut.

Then she felt it-- the cool hard metal in her hand. She must have passed out grasping the opening of the handcuff. Placing the cuffs on the floor, she shook and wiggled her hands to increase the blood flow. She examined her ankles and realized there was no way she was going to get the shackles off. Gingerly she stood, testing the strength of her legs. As soon as she was erect, she had to sit again. A wave of dizziness swept over her, and she felt lightheaded.

Thinking aloud, she weighed her options. Okay. This is good. I can use my hands and take baby steps. I just have to get up and walk to the cell door.

Standing again, she waited for the fuzziness to subside before she started the seemingly endless task of reaching the opening. The trek was slow going because the shackles restricted her from taking anything but the smallest of steps. But once she reached her goal, she inhaled and offered a small prayer of thanks. With both hands, she gripped the cold steel and pushed. The hinges let out a shrill sound that pierced the stillness of the dark underground. Charlie cringed at the noise, and prayed it hadn't been heard on the upper level.

Now that the door was open, she had no bloody idea what to do next. She stood in silent consternation, debating her next move. She didn't know how far she would be able to get, because the shackles were weighing her down and continued to bite into her already torn flesh. But she recognized she had no choice in the matter. She could not, and would not, be a sitting duck any longer. She'd have to rely solely on her instincts and training.

A wistful smile formed on the corners of her mouth as thoughts of Robert flooded through her mind. Whispering into the darkness, she lamented, "Well love, I was trained by the best. Now we'll see how much I really learned. Stay close by me and guide me. I need you now more than ever."

With that little prayer said, she focused on what she could detect in the prevailing darkness of the underground structure. She knew it was futile for her to even consider taking the steps that led to the upper level. She decided instead to head right towards what appeared to be a long narrow corridor. She hoped to find a door that would lead to the outside. Though the storm continued to rage, she knew she would be far safer in the harsh elements than alone and unarmed in the enemy's territory.

Inhaling a dose of courage, Charlie began the slow trek into what she prayed would be the path to her safety.

CHAPTER 82

HE WAITED FOR HIS PREY. HE COULD SMELL HIM NOW. He wondered if there would be more than one. His gut told him that was a definite probability. They, whoever "they" were, were close... he could feel them. The winds were picking up again, forcing him to strain to hear any other sounds. Finally, he heard what he was waiting for... a slight click. Someone on the other side was trying to open the door. He purposely positioned himself in a hidden nook at the far corner of the room. The chamber he was in was nothing but a shroud of blackness. There were no windows, no cracks, nothing that even a sliver of light could sneak through. When his opponents entered, he would quickly flash on his light, supplying just enough radiance for him to see his targets. He had yet another advantage over his prey; he knew the layout. Once he took care of his marks, if there was indeed more than one, it would take only a matter of microseconds for him to disappear into the structure.

He already had the fake panel open. All he had to do was take one step back and pull the lever--and presto, he would vanish! His senses kicked into overdrive when he heard muffled sounds coming from the narrow corridor. It was show time. A demented smile formed on his ghostly features.

He raised his arm, aimed, and waited for his unsuspecting targets.

❧

FREDRICK AND GIOVANNI WERE SOAKED TO the bones by the time they reached the entrance they were looking for. Fredrick swiped a hand across his brow, and whispered to Giovanni, "All right, we're nearing the end of the corridor."

Bellesto had given them the layout of the room, including the particulars of the hidden panel. Both men knew that if anyone was lurking inside, it would be in close proximity to the panel. Their plan was that Fredrick would roll into the room and open fire in the direction of the panel and Giovanni would cover him. Not much of a strategy, but it was all they could think to do, considering the circumference of the area they were dealing with.

Frazzled by nerves, they waited. Then all too fast, it happened, and as quickly as it started, it was over. Fredrick lunged into the room, doing a somersault. Giovanni, only halfway in the opening, was positioned perfectly for Darrell.

That was all Darrell needed. Holding the compact flashlight in one hand and a gun in the other, he quickly streamed the light in the direction of the corridor and fired, not giving Giovanni enough time to react. By the time Fredrick rolled out of his somersault and returned fired, it was at an empty wall--the panel was closed. Whoever had been there was gone. Fredrick rushed to Giovanni's side and felt for his pulse. It was weak. Fredrick gently rolled Giovanni from his side onto his back.

When Giovanni spoke, his voice was strained.

"He clipped me twice, but I'll be all right. You just go and get the bastard." Fredrick, unsure of what to do, hesitated. Giovanni knew what Fredrick was thinking and made the decision for him. "Fredrick, Charlie is our top priority! Your friend would never forgive you if you sat here babysitting me! Now get the fuck outta here, I'll be alright."

Fredrick quickly removed his coat. He then took his shirt off and put pressure on the wounds as best he could. In all his years on the job, he could never tolerate the sight of flowing blood, and from the little he could see oozing from Giovanni, tonight would be no exception. As he pressed into Giovanni's flesh, his hand quickly became soaked with blood.

"I need you to keep pressure on these wounds. I don't know how long you'll be able to do it, but it'll help. I'm going to help move you away from the door before I go. Keep your gun close, just in case our friend decides to come back. And don't hesitate to kill the mother. Understood?"

A brave smile curved on Giovanni's face when he answered, "I'm looking forward to it."

Fredrick hastily wiped his hands on his coat to get as much blood off them as possible. He then turned it inside out, rolled it into a ball, and placed it under Giovanni's head. He got up shivering, as the damp cool air of the cell began to seep deeply into the warmth of his blood. Too much time had passed for him to catch whoever it was; he had to do double time now.

Rushing to the panel, he pulled on the lever to access the secret room. Once inside, he pulled it again, but as the door closed, he realized he had no bloody idea where the hell he was going.

CHAPTER 83

PERSPIRATION SOAKED THROUGH HIS clothes; water oozed from every pore. He looked like he had gone for a refreshing swim, but felt anything but refreshed. He stopped momentarily to wipe his brow in an attempt to cease the moisture from running into his already burning eyes.

Never had he been in a situation like this before. He was in total darkness, feeling his way down a narrow opening. His arms felt like lead weights, fatigued from feeling the walls, searching for break off points, and to his dismay, there were many. He offered continuous silent prayers for Charlie, speculating if anything happened to her, he wouldn't be able to go on. Never in his lifetime did he think he'd be blessed to find not one, but two, extraordinary women. This time, though, he was determined not to lose her.

Switching gears, he tried to recall the directions Bellesto had given him as to which break off point to enter. Unfortunately those important details appeared to have been erased from his memory. He was feeling stifled and hot in the narrow corridor, finding it more difficult to concentrate. When he got out of here and this nightmare was over, he wanted to remind Bellesto to tell him more about the history of this building and the infamous prohibition period.

He started walking again. He had a feeling he was close to reaching the point he was looking for. He could feel it deep down knew that not finding his beloved was not an option. Unexpectedly his senses reignited, something he didn't question. After all his years on the job, he realized that the subconscious mind recognized when to dictate what needed to be done, and if one was smart enough, one listened. Thinking back now, he realized the only time he screwed up on a case was when he didn't surrender to that nagging feeling in his gut, or address the thoughts that kept racking his brain.

His body stopped walking. He had reached it, he was sure of it.

This was where he had to turn. He bloody wished he had time to go back and get his infrared goggles, but who would have known that he would be enmeshed in an intricate, maze-like structure in near total darkness? Robert turned and picked up his pace.

From this point on, it would be a guessing game as to where Darrell had hidden Charlie.

CHAPTER 84

HE FLEW DOWN THE FLIGHT OF STAIRS WITH ease as his cape billowed out around him. He knew Fredrick would waste precious time making sure Bellesto's man was okay. A pleased smirk flickered across his taut features; he found the situation quite amusing. Never in a million years would he have thought Bellesto would team up with her lover and the precious FBI!

Excitement percolated as he made a split-second decision. It would take Fredrick some time to find the right pathway to where his lovely prisoner was, so he decided to pay her a quick visit and fill her in on the latest developments. He couldn't wait to see the expression on her face when he told her he had eliminated her lover!

"I think this little theatrical production could use some added drama, if I do say so myself!" He rounded the bend to where the cell was and stopped dead in his tracks. At first he thought he wasn't seeing correctly, and blinked a few times. He stumbled to the now-open cell door and peered inside. She was gone! The cell was empty except for the battered steel chair at the far side of the small room. The handcuffs had been set neatly on the cement floor. Fury rose up. His eyes bulged out of their sockets in disbelief at what he was seeing. His heart pounded wildly as his breath became hard and ragged. This was the breaking point for him. Any self- restraint and control he had retained now dissipated into thin air. Imploding, he bellowed a primal scream out into the dark cell... like a man who had gone completely mad. And then he did...

❧❧

SHE HEARD SOMETHING, A DEMENTED SOUND echoed off the cement walls of the underground. She picked up her pace, knowing it was Darrell's reaction to finding the cell empty. Off in the distance, not far from where she stood, she heard a shuffle, but knew it couldn't possibly be Darrell, because the screams of rage she had just heard had come from the opposite direction.

Charlie pushed her body up against the cool cement, trying to make herself as small as possible. She couldn't take any chances at this point. Whoever was headed towards her could be working for the devil himself.

The steps were getting closer as she held her breath, waiting. She wouldn't be able to tell who it was until they literally came by her, and even then, it would be just a shadow. Her nerves were frayed, but the anxiety building inside her would be converted into adrenaline and used to her advantage.

She was ready to fight for her life, and prepared herself to strike out.

⌘

ROBERT HEADED IN THE DIRECTION OF THE screams he had just heard. He assumed it was Darrell, and was more frightened than ever for Charlie. Panicked thoughts raced through his brain as he charged through the narrow opening. Was Charlie with him? Had he hurt her, or worse yet, killed her? Why was he yelling? He sounded like an insane man. Robert whipped around the bend, not noticing the figure pressed tightly up against the stone wall.

Two fists came out of nowhere and made contact with his gut, throwing him off balance. Stifling a scream, he sucked in and reached out into the darkness. As his fist made contact with the stone wall, his groin was bashed. Biting down hard on the inside of his cheek, he inadvertently bent over in the cramped space and felt something soft and fleshy.

His mind reeled, knowing he had only a fraction of a second to decide to strike out with all might, or speak the name that was on his lips. It had to be her, he convinced himself, it just had to be.

Taking a chance, he whispered out into the gloom, "Charlie? Is that you?"

WHOEVER IT WAS WAS COMING CLOSER, SHE could faintly make out the labored breaths in the dimness. Her options were extremely limited as she quickly thought of what she could do to protect herself from this assailant. What she couldn't do was just stand there and do nothing. Whoever it was would be right on top of her in a matter of seconds.

Mustering all the strength she could, Charlie put her two hands together and struck out. Not waiting for whoever it was to react, she crouched lower and again struck out, this time into what she hoped was the groin area. As she rose to stand, her breasts made contact with the person's face. She froze, not knowing what to do next.

It was then that everything stopped for her. Time stood perfectly still as she heard the voice she thought she would never hear again. Charlie whispered back into the darkness, "Robert, oh, my God!"

She lunged forward in the too small space, gasping for breath. Robert reached out, too stunned to say anything, and wrapped his arms tightly around her. Typically he was not a man who cried. But as he felt the reality of her in his arms, the gates opened and all the tears he had been holding in came rushing forth. He held her so tightly, he was practically crushing her. She didn't say anything because being crushed by him right now was what she wanted most. They held each other crying tears of relief that each was safe. After what seemed like an eternity, they released their hold on one another just a fraction.

Robert, overwhelmed with emotion, found it hard to speak. With difficulty, they could slightly make out each other's features, and each saw a love and tenderness that ran so deep nothing, and no one, could shatter it. Robert cupped her face in his hands and gently wiped the free flowing stream of tears away with his thumbs. His voice was choked with emotion when he spoke.

"I think we better get out of here, and fast. It's awfully quiet now, and I'm sure Darrell is headed in this direction. Hold my hand, and whatever you do, don't let go. Just follow my lead and you'll be fine."

The words he said brought a new wave of tears from her. She remembered in the beginning he had said the same thing to her--Just follow my lead...

Overcome with emotion, her words came out all jumbled,

"Robert ... I can't move very fast... I... my... ankles are bound... with shackles. For the first time he looked down, and could faintly make out steel bindings around the bottom of her legs. His anger mounted as he bent down, trying to remove the leg irons. It was a futile effort and he knew he was wasting precious time now.

He stood up in the small confines and asked Charlie, "Can you walk alright?"

"Yes, I just can't take big steps."

"Look, Love, you just hold onto me. When we reach the main room up ahead, there's a door that I'm hoping will lead to the outside. I'll carry you then."

Trying to be brave, she laughed nervously and replied, "Oh... always the romantic!" She didn't dare ask the questions that seared in her mind. What if the door doesn't lead to the outside? What then? Pushing away such thoughts, she gripped Robert's hand for dear life as they started making the slow hike back through the narrow passageway.

Unbeknownst to them, the devil himself was right behind them and he had heard everything.

CHAPTER 85

FREDRICK MADE HIS WAY DOWN THE darkened stairwell. Once he reached the last step, he pulled the lever to the right and the fake panel slid open with ease. He had no idea where to go. Before him was yet another maze. He could go straight, to the right, or to the left.

"Damn it! Which way now?"

He opted to go left. He walked for about ten minutes, only to run into a dead end. "Fake passageway, fuck!"

He quickly retraced his footsteps, and once back at his point of origin, went straight this time, only to find the same thing... another dead end. Impatience surged through him as he frantically returned to the beginning yet again. He started to feel stifled in the slim opening, and though he knew the underground was frigid, he found himself sweating profusely.

Once back at the same starting point, he proceeded down the only way remaining...to the right. Just as he was about to take his first step into the narrow passageway, he heard a demented scream, and froze in mid stride.

As soon as the shock of what he heard wore off, his adrenaline kicked in, and he took off running into the passageway towards the loud screeches he had just heard.

❧

BELLESTO, HAVING GONE RIGHT, knew he had to follow the outer mazes of the structure in order to reach the cell where he believed Darrell had Charlie. Robert should have reached her already, if he hadn't made a mistake. He considered himself to be making good time considering he had not been in the underground structure for some time. Even being in the blasted dark during a major hurricane had only proven to be a stumbling block not a road block.

As he navigated through the last passage, his movement was halted by screams of rage off in the distance. There was no doubt who those screams belonged to, and he hoped Robert hadn't been too late. Gripping his pistol, Bellesto made sure the silencer was in place. He took off like a bolt of lightning around the last bend, and hoped he would be the one to have the honor of putting the bullet right between the devil's eyes.

CHAPTER 86

CROW HAD TO MAKE HIS MOVE! THEY WERE HEADED right towards him! They didn't know he was right there at the end, waiting for them. He started counting to ease the excitement that now rippled through him. "One...two...three..." His boss was going to be very happy with him. Maybe he would get a promotion after he learned that he, the Crow Man, single handedly took out three of their arch enemies!

Serentino and Louie were finally approaching what they hoped would be the end of the maze. After encountering a few dead ends that required them to retrace their steps, they finally made it to the area where they believed the cellblock was located. Neither man saw Crow lurking in the darkness, crouched down, pistol aimed right at them. They had no time to react to his presence, let alone fire their weapons at him. Two clean shots rang through the cellblock, reverberating off the cement structure. Both men dropped simultaneously to the unforgiving floor, shocked expressions on their faces. Crow walked over to where they lay and gave each man a hard kick in the side. When no screams or movements were made by either man, Crow was satisfied that both were no longer an issue.

Crow turned and went on his merry way, humming a little tune, ready to find his next unsuspecting target.

CHAPTER 87

HE COULDN'T BELIEVE HIS GOOD LUCK! HE had both his targets together like two sitting ducks. Though elated, a sick feeling took up residence in the pit of his stomach as he listened to their declarations of love for each other. He bit down hard on his lower lip, drawing blood. His hand gripped the pistol so hard his knuckles turned white. He was taking his time. There was no rush, now that he had them right where he wanted them.

He had to give her credit, though, she was one tough cookie. He never would have thought she had it in her. He reprimanded himself for not remembering to re-lock the handcuffs. But she would pay dearly for his little misstep. It was her fault, anyway, that he had gotten sidetracked.

Darrell stopped his plotting when he again heard them whisper to each other. She was having a hard time walking with the shackles bound to her ankles. "Poor baby, you just keep going. I'm going to take care of the pain for you so you won't ever feel anything again!"

He wanted to regurgitate, his ears assaulted by the words her pathetic lover was saying to her. He was coaxing her like a child being promised a fucking prize if they did what they were told.

Well, he had the prize and he was going to give it to both of them, all right.

CHAPTER 88

HE WAS EXHAUSTED, MORE MENTALLY THAN physically, though his limbs felt like they had been torn from his body and then haphazardly put back on. He reached the empty cell and took in the sparse surroundings. He noticed the battered steel chair at the far end of the room and walked towards it. He noted the cuffs, stained with blood hanging from the back of the chair, dangling ever so slightly. He cringed, his body stiff, when he looked down in front of the chair and saw stains of what he knew was more blood--Charlie's blood. He wondered what the bastard had done to her, and how much the poor thing had endured.

Shifting gears, he focused on the positive. The empty cell was definitely a good sign, and he breathed a sigh of relief. The screams must have been Darrell's rage at finding his victim gone, so somehow Charlie had gotten away. Suddenly a cold chill swept through him, and the hair on the back of his neck began to prickle. He sensed something, or rather, someone, behind him. He knew he better draw his gun, and quick. Just as he was poised to make a move, the voice spoke.

"I wouldn't do that if I were you." Fredrick didn't recognize the voice, so he knew it had to be one of Darrell's men. "Put your hands in the air, and turn around slowly."

Fredrick did as he was told, but knew he had to try and buy some time, precious time. He had to keep this bastard talking so he could weigh his options. From where the large figure stood, Fredrick could only make out the outline of the man's face. Whoever this man was, he was a big boy, that was for sure. He stood over six feet tall and was bald. Baggy sweat pants, which used to be white, were now stained with what Fredrick assumed to be blood.

His opponent slowly walked towards the cell's opening. Fredrick's mind reeled, "Keep coming... that's it... closer now, so I can see that ugly mug of yours." The room was silent as the men assessed each other. Fredrick, trying to find humor in the situation, thought, See, I knew you'd be damned ugly. No one, not even a mother, could love a face like that.

Crow was considering his choices at this point. He knew who Fredrick was. It was one thing to kill a cop, but to kill a biggie from the FBI... well, that was something else entirely. He was taking too much time trying to decide what to do. This guy wasn't leaving here alive, anyway, so he might as well just do him in like the others. The more Crow thought about it, this guy was worse than the others. He was the fucking big pig of the FBI!

A small stone thrown against the side of the cement wall stunned both Crow and Fredrick. Instinctively, they turned to see where the sound had come from. One bullet was fired and hit Crow square between the eyes. He dropped to the floor in a heavy heap, falling face down. Fredrick tried to find cover, but where the hell did one find cover in an open cell, so he did the next best thing...just stood there. He figured since Crow was the one who was dead, it was meant for him to be alive. He waited for the shooter to reveal himself and prayed it was one of his men.

Fredrick held his breath, and continued to wait. Well, the man wasn't exactly one of his, but close enough at this point. Bellesto came through the door with a slick smile on his face. Frederick exhaled. He approached Fredrick, and when standing not more than a foot away, took Fredrick totally by surprise by giving him a hearty slap on the back.

"Good to see you, man! I was growing tired of the lack of interesting conversation, so I thought it was time for all good things to come to an end, so to speak. What do you think?"

Fredrick just stared straight ahead with his mouth hanging open. He didn't know what to say. It wasn't that he didn't appreciate Bellesto's effort at injecting some humor into the situation, but-- actually, he didn't know what the hell the "but" was. When he finally found his tongue, he asked the question that had nagged him for some time.

"Do you mind if I ask you a question?"

"No, not at all. Fire away, my friend."

"You are one strange mother. I mean, you really are eccentric."

It was the first time Fredrick saw Bellesto laugh. "My dear friend, first off, you blurted out two things, not one, and actually neither was a question, they were statements, don't you think?"

Before Fredrick could reply, Bellesto waved a hand in midair and continued on.

"Now I will clarify your statements. The business I'm in requires one to be quite serious and stringent at all times, so when I have the opportunity to inject a little humor, I do so. It helps sustain the equilibrium, if you know what I mean."

Fredrick's tone suggested residual confusion, "Not exactly, but when we have more time, I'll let you explain it to me."

Still smiling, Bellesto said, "Well, in that case, I think we'd better make double time."

"I don't know where to go from here, do you?"

"Yes, as a matter of fact, I do. You see, I came from the east, and you the west, we can't go south, so that leaves north! Elementary, my dear friend!"

Fredrick, having had enough of Bellesto's humor, returned a slap to the back and coaxed, "Then let's go--Darrell is still around here somewhere."

Once Fredrick said Darrell's name, he noticed a drastic change in Bellesto's manner. It was like he had two distinct personas. Bellesto's features grew hard, his eyes mere slits, and his voice thick when he replied, "Yes, it's time to get our friend and end this once and for all. Just be forewarned that no mercy will be shown towards him."

With that said, he turned on his heel and bolted out of the cell. Fredrick had to run to keep pace with him, and before he knew it, they had entered another long narrow passageway into the darkness of hell.

CHAPTER 89

CHARLIE AND ROBERT FINALLY REACHED THE door they were looking for. The silence in the hallway was deafening as they looked at each other. Robert put his finger up to his lips, instructing her to keep quiet. Darrell was in close proximity to them, of that he was sure. Robert bent down to take a closer look at the shackles that ravaged Charlie's delicate skin. Blood continued to ooze out and he wondered, with all her wounds, how much blood she had lost.

He stood up and brought her closer so he could whisper into her ear. "I have to get this door open. Once we're outside, I have an idea how to get the shackles off."

Charlie said nothing, just nodded her head up and down in acknowledgement. Robert slowly placed his hand on the knob as a thought rushed through his already frazzled mind: What if the bloody door was locked? He would have no choice but to shoot at it. Hesitating for just a fraction, he said a quick prayer, Please, Lord, let this door open....please. His hand squeezed the knob tightly, secretly hoping for a miracle, willing it to turn. When he met no resistance, he continued rotating the knob until it could go no further, and then he pushed with all his might to thrust the heavy door open, making as little noise as possible.

His efforts were met by strong surges of air and rain that blew towards them, instantly soaking them to the core.

Robert gently took Charlie's arm and led her outside, closing the door behind them. He didn't give her time to say anything as he swept her up in his arms and ran as fast as he could away from the building. Once at a safe distance, he put her down and explained what it was he had to do, hoping she trusted him enough.

"Charlie I need you to trust me, okay?"

Looking deep into her swollen eyes, he searched for what he

260

hoped would be a sign that she did trust him. Rain continued to pound down on them. Flashes of lightning off in the distance illuminated the dark sky, making the situation feel that much more eerie. Robert assessed damage to her face vowing to kill the mother. For the second time in his life, he had the urge to kill and he knew this time he wouldn't stop until he exterminated Darrell in cold blood.

Charlie stared back, not blinking, and squeezed his hand tightly. That was all the assurance he required. Clearing his throat, he said, "I need you to spread your feet as wide apart as you possibly can. Can you do that for me?"

Still not saying a word, and looking frightened, she bravely nodded in assent to his request. Charlie spread her feet as far apart as the shackles would allow. She knew what Robert had to do, and trusted that his aim would be on target the first time, because her nerves would get the better of her if it wasn't. He couldn't see that well. The rain's brute force kept throwing their bodies off kilter.

Trying to stay calm, Robert lifted his gun and aimed between the shackles. His pistol was loaded with titanium bullets, thank God. Regular ones wouldn't have the power to blast the shackles apart, but titanium ones did. He just had to make sure he didn't miss. He had to get it just right so she could at least walk with no restraint. Of course, he didn't tell her that fragments of the metal would probably penetrate her already damaged body, but he thought best not to share that information with her.

She was in shock, and Robert knew she most likely wouldn't feel the additional pain, since she was already clearly on the edge of passing out. Slowly he pulled back on the trigger, firing a single shot into the ground. Fragments of shrapnel could be heard pinging off the rocks that littered the surrounding ground.

Charlie, who had been holding her breath, let out a loud whooshing sound as she hesitantly took a step.

CHAPTER 90

DARRELL OPENED THE DOOR AND STEPPED out into the raging storm. He couldn't see beyond his own feet. Unsure of which way they went, he closed his eyes as the rain further drenched his already soaked clothes. Lightning and thunder boomed, as he strained to hear anything that might tip him off as to which direction they had taken.

Then he heard it. A gunshot. He was sure of it. The sound was muffled by the cacophony of noises from the storm, but he was certain it was a gunshot, and relatively close by. He took off running, eager to take them both by surprise.

CHAPTER 91

CHARLIE LET OUT A DEEP GROAN AS SHE tried to walk. "I can't do it, Robert. I can't walk." Robert knelt down to inspect her ankles. From what he could tell, her ankles were bleeding badly and quite swollen. From the angry sky, a quick flash of light illuminated her pale face. She was exhausted and at the end of her rope.... she couldn't go any further.

He needed to get her to a hospital, and quick. Robert made a difficult decision, and tried to sound confident when he shared his thoughts with her. "Charlie, listen to me. I need you to stay here and wait for me."

Panic surged as she listened to his words. He was going to leave her there all by herself, with Darrell God knows where. Robert detected the flash of alarm that raced across her pale features and raised his voice a fraction, "Charlie! Listen to me, you can't walk another step. The truck is around the other side of the building."

Seeing the intense fear in her eyes, Robert frantically searched his surroundings. Finally, he noticed the archway that curved around the bend of the building. "Okay, Charlie, I'll carry you over there," nodding his head in the direction, "so you won't be seen. Just lay low, and I'll hurry as fast as I can okay?"

She nodded; it was all she could do. Why did she feel so tired and weak? All she managed to do was mumble a quick

"Okay." Robert lifted her effortlessly into his arms and brought her to the archway. He placed her as gently as he could on the ground, and his heart ached when he took in her drawn face and the bruises that had formed a racetrack around her usually radiant features. Her skin no longer had the Mediterranean olive color--now it was shades of blacks and purples melding together to form a new color he had had never seen before.

The ancient boulders formed a somewhat protective barrier for them. Charlie lifted her head, gazed at the shapes of the stones, and noticed how they all glistened in the darkness. Small bushes that usually lined the outer perimeter now revolted against the strain of the fierce winds. Before Robert left, he reached deep into his coat pocket and pulled out a small revolver. He handed it to her, saying nothing; words were not necessary. He was confident she would know what do with it; after all, he had trained her.

Bending one last time, he kissed her forehead with the utmost care, and then in an instant, he was gone. Charlie peaked around the corner of the arch and watched his back depart, as she fought to stay awake. She allowed her body to mold into the wet, cool ground. She inhaled the chilled, crisp air, thankful to be out of the dungeon where the smells had been stifling. Wearily she closed her eyes--not that there was much left to close, for both of them were already swollen half shut. She reasoned with herself she only needed a quick moment to catch her breath and relax. Yes, that's what the doctor ordered. Then her batteries would be recharged and she would be fine. That's what she told herself, but part of her didn't believe a word of these assurances.

Her eyes were closed when she heard the splashing of footsteps. Immediately, her senses were on high alert. All she did was close them for a split second. When she opened them, she couldn't believe what she saw: a figure dressed in black, heading straight for the archway. It was the devil himself. He was totally oblivious to the winds raging around him. His body was being thrown off balance, but that didn't deter him from making progress to his destination. He moved with slow deliberate strides, not seeing her.

She watched his line of vision switch to the headlights that suddenly appeared. Robert had just pulled the van up to the archway and hadn't yet seen the figure approaching. She didn't know what to do. She was, for the moment, frozen to the hard gravel that only a moments ago had provided soothing comfort. Now the gravel tore into her sore behind, making her bolt upright. She pressed her body against the rough stones, and maneuvered herself around the archway.

Then a slow motion movie began to play out. She didn't have the luxury of viewing it in color--no, this movie mimicked the era of black and grey. Death was coming quickly, and she'd be damned if she let the devil win. She knew what she had to do. It was a long shot, but she had no other options.

From this point on, everything that happened did so in the blink of an eye.

SHE GRIPPED HER GUN SO TIGHTLY HER already white knuckles turned even whiter. She closed her eyes to heighten her senses. She inhaled deeply, then exhaled to slow down her heart rate. She felt her surroundings, and waited. She made a split-second

decision, and broke into a full run. How Charlie was going to pull off what needed to be done, she didn't know, but had to at least try, or else Robert would die.

Charlie hurtled towards the man who had given her his heart while flashbacks played in her mind. Because of Robert, she had finally grown into her own skin and was at peace with herself. Now she could accomplish whatever she desired in this life, and it was all because of him, his faith, and his unwavering love for her.

She wanted - and needed - to show her gratitude to Robert. If the price to pay was sacrificing her own life, then so be it. To Charlie it was indeed a small penance, for through Robert she had truly learned to love and give freely of herself, and in return, she was enveloped in the beautiful and sensual kind of passion she had only read about in romance novels. She couldn't lose him, she just couldn't.

What Charlie didn't realize was Darrell had stopped. He saw her running towards Robert and allowed her plenty of time to get in front of him.

When she mustered the courage to glance out of the corner of her eye, she saw Darrell crouched down on the muddy pavement, gun drawn, waiting for the right moment to fire at his unsuspecting target.

The last thing she remembered was ambushing Robert while firing shots at Darrell, then being hit, not once, but twice.

ROBERT PULLED THE VAN UP TO THE SIDE OF THE archway. He saw Charlie sitting on the wet gravel, eyes closed. Heart racing, he jumped out of the van and made his way to the passenger door. He wanted the door opened so he wouldn't have to fight with it while he had her in his arms. It was a godsend that at the moment, the raging winds had quieted down enough so he wasn't worried the open door would slam shut on him.

In the blink of an eye, the rains ceased, the winds stopped, and all that remained was the silent eeriness of the night. As he raced to the front of the van he was body slammed. He tumbled to the ground as shots rang out into the darkness, followed by the screams of the woman he loved with his whole heart and soul.

CHAPTER 92

THE PAIN WAS UNBEARABLE. SHE WAS thrown from the pressure of the gunfire. Her body crashed down hard onto the pavement. Before passing out, she placed her hand on her shoulder, then moved it to feel the burning spot in the middle of her stomach. When she examined her hand, it was dripping with what she knew was blood. She felt the warmth drain from her chilled body, and gave thanks that she was the one hit, not Robert.

She was sliding into an unconscious abyss. She fought with all her might to stay awake. She heard more shots being fired. Her vision was blurred; she couldn't see. She fumbled for the pistol on the slick pavement, but her efforts were futile.

The last thing she saw, or rather thought she saw, was Darrell jumping off the side of the embankment into the icy waters of Narragansett Bay. After that, her head dropped, her eyes closed, and she realized she was finally going to be able to sleep now.

❧❦

IT TOOK ROBERT A SPLIT SECOND FOR THE events to sink in. He had been rushing to the front of the van to get Charlie from under the archway when she body slammed him. They both tumbled to the ground, but not before Charlie fired off shots at Darrell. The devil used her positioning to his advantage, shooting her directly in the middle of her stomach, before clipping her right shoulder as she turned to block Robert.

When he looked up from the pavement, Robert saw Darrell was running towards the embankment at full speed while still firing haphazardly. Robert didn't know if his beloved had hit her intended

target, and at the moment he really didn't care.
    He had to help Charlie.

CHAPTER 93

ROCK WAS SHIMMYING DOWN A PIPE on the side of the building. He had witnessed everything and was ready to finish the job for his boss.

Unbeknown to Rock, two figures had just rounded the bend of the building and had stopped when they heard Rock's movements on the pipe. They ducked down, watching his every move. In a matter of seconds, Rock would be on the ground.

In one swift motion, his feet hit the pavement and his gun was drawn. Just as he was preparing to take aim at his unsuspecting targets, shots pierced the thick fog that was now rolling in. Rock fell face first onto the wet gravel. A loud crack echoed out into the stillness of the night. It was obvious to the shooter Rock's nose had broken when his face crashed onto the pavement. Blackish red blood gushed out forming a puddle that slowly inched its way across the gravel towards the sea.

The two figures glanced down at the dead man, trying to decide what they should do next. As if reading each other's minds, they both crouched down in unison, neither man uttering a word. One took hold of Rock's shoulders and the other grabbed his feet. They walked silently in sync to the edge of the embankment and tossed the dead body over the edge.

Neither man glanced back as they headed over to the van where their trembling friend suddenly let out a scream.

CHAPTER 94

ROBERT FELT FOR CHARLIE'S PULSE. IT WAS very weak but at least she had one. He screamed.

"NO! NO, CHARLIE! OH, MY GOD, PLEASE! NO, CHARLIE! Come on, wake up, babe, it's me! WAKE UP, DAMN IT, WAKE UP!"

Tears streamed down his face as he looked up to find Bellesto and Fredrick approaching. "We've got to get her to the hospital, and fast! Her pulse is too weak, oh, my God, no, please, dear God, NO!"

Fredrick grabbed Robert by the collar of his soaked shirt. He tried to keep his voice even. "Robert, get Charlie and sit with her in the back of the van. We'll get her to the hospital as quickly as we can."

Robert was frozen; his body paralyzed with fear. He just stared at his friend, mouth open, tears streaming down his fatigued face. When he made no motion to move, Bellesto stepped forward, and in one swift movement picked Charlie up and carried her to the back seat of the van. Fredrick practically had to pick up Robert because the man had no feeling in his limbs. Fredrick situated Robert next to Charlie and closed the door. When Fredrick got in on the passenger side, Bellesto was already seated behind the steering wheel, the van idling. As soon as Fredrick was safely in, Bellesto peeled out, the gravel ricocheting off the metal, causing everyone except the unresponsive Charlie to jump in their seats.

CHAPTER 95

THE DOCTORS PERFORMED EMERGENCY SURGERY ON Charlie. She had lost a lot of blood, and was in shock. The doctors were concerned about possible brain damage. When the surgeon entered the waiting room, Robert, Fredrick, and Bellesto were standing with their backs to the door.

Robert pressed both hands on the window as he lowered his head. He sobbed for all the losses he had suffered in his life, but most of all, he cried for Charlie. "Dear God, please don't let her die! Please don't take her away from me. Why the hell did you let her suffer? It should have been me! She's too young and has so much to offer; you know that, damn it!"

"Mr. Fordes?" The 3 men quickly turned around, taking quick steps towards the doctor. But this motley crew stopped dead in their tracks when they saw the look on the surgeon's face. No words were needed. They knew Charlie was dead.

"Mr. Fordes, I don't know how to tell you this, but.... We did everything we could. She lost too much blood and couldn't hold on. She flat-lined about five minutes ago."

Robert collapsed onto the stained linoleum floor and cried the tears of a man who had just lost his will to live. He yelled at the doctor, "LEAVE ME ALONE! JUST LEAVE ME THE HELL ALONE! Everyone get out!"

Tears streamed down the hard lines of his face as his eyes tried to focus on the two men who were watching helplessly as their friend was consumed by grief. He had finally broken...

Fredrick and Bellesto quietly left the room, knowing Robert needed to be alone for the moment, for he was surely in shock. The door to the waiting room closed silently behind them. Fredrick and Bellesto turned their backs, not wanting to go too far, yet wanting to give Robert some much needed privacy.

Fredrick couldn't stand feeling so powerless, unable to do something, anything, to help his most cherished friend. His heart broke as he stole a glance into the room and watched as Robert curled up on the cold tile floor, hugging his body into a fetal position. What he witnessed next, he would never would be able to explain to anyone.

CHAPTER 96

THERE WAS A LIGHT SO BRIGHT ROBERT covered his eyes momentarily for fear of being blinded by its brilliance. The illumination totally enveloped him. He appeared to be captivated where he lay on the tile floor. Shocked by what he was seeing, the most Fredrick could muster was to tug on Bellesto's sleeve, silently nodding in Robert's direction. Bellesto turned to see what Fredrick was staring at, and he too froze....

After Charlie had flat-lined, what most people would believe to be inconceivable was now happening... she was visible right here before Robert. His body was shaking uncontrollably. "My heart holds you just one beat away, Robert. You are mine forever, my love. I'm watching you right now. Can you see me, sweetheart; can you hear my thoughts? I'm in a different place right now, but I'm coming back to you, do you hear me? I'm fighting to come back to you. I need you to believe; just hold on. I'm watching you from up above. Our love will live on! Have faith that our time together isn't over."

Robert froze as if he had just seen a ghost. In actuality he had. "Charlie? Charlie? I can feel you. Please, Charlie, let it be real what I'm feeling."

"It is real, Robert. You must believe. Don't doubt it!"

Robert jumped up, bolted out the door past a transfixed Bellesto and Fredrick, and ran down the corridor. He bellowed for the doctor. A nurse interrupted him.

Sir, what's wrong?"

"Where's Doctor Martano? I need to SPEAK TO HIM NOW! Where is he, damn it?"

"Sir, I think it would be best if you tried to calm down."

"Don't tell me to fucking calm down, I need to see the DOCTOR NOW!"

The nurse went to the desk, picked up the phone and dialed

security. "I've got one that has lost control big time. I think he may even need to be sedated." She placed the phone back on its cradle, and gave Robert a sympathetic look. Trying to sound more confident than she was, the nurse replied, "The doctor is on his way, sir."

But Robert had no intention of waiting. He hustled to the operating room where he knew Charlie was. He burst through the doors with the force of a tornado. Fredrick and Bellesto tried to calm down the nurse who was now running after Robert. Bellesto caught her by the arm trying to stall her; he had no idea why, but knew he should. Fredrick followed his lead.

⤦⤧

ROBERT SAW CHARLIE LYING ON THE operating table, a white sheet completely covering her body. There were two other people in the room, a doctor and a nurse. The doctor addressed Robert, "Sir, you're not supposed to be in here."

He was in a daze. He walked to the table where the love of his life lay and slowly pulled the sheet away from her face. He neatly folded it across her shoulders. The doctor and nurse approached him with caution.

"We're sorry for your loss, but I'm afraid we have to ask you to leave."

When Robert spoke it was a desperate plea, "Do me a favor, please? Don't cover her face with the sheet. Just leave her like this. She needs to be able to breathe." The doctor and nurse may have thought they had heard it all, but this one definitely topped the cake.

"Promise me, please." Robert raised his hand and wiped his tear streaked face. The nurse's eyes filled. She had just lost a loved one, too.

"Sir, I promise to leave the sheet this way for you."

"Thank you. I'll be waiting right outside this door when she comes to." With that said, Robert turned and exited the room. When the doors closed, he stood looking through the glass opening. He felt a hand on his shoulder. It was Fredrick.

"Robert, I..." Robert grabbed hold of Fredrick. The two men who had shared so much through the years now wept over the loss of someone they both had grown to love. Fredrick was at war with himself for having allowed Charlie to continue on the case. Robert was fighting with the reality: it should have been him on that cold slab, not Charlie. When the two friends finally separated, they could only bow their heads in grief.

"She was too torn up, Fredrick. I never should have kept her on the case..." Anguished sobs escaped from the depths of his soul as his body slid to the floor. Repeatedly he banged the wall with his fist. "NO, SHE KNEW! SHE KNEW, FREDRICK!"

"Come on, Robert, let's get you up. Come on, that's right. Don't worry, I'm here for you."

Fredrick helped Robert up from the floor. Almost carrying him, Fredrick led his dear friend slowly down the hall as Robert repeated over and over, "I'm dead, Fredrick. I'm dead."

❦❧

BACK IN THE OPERATING ROOM, THE NURSE, for some reason, stood over Charlie. The doctor had already exited the room to make sure the man who had just left was all right. Following close behind, he felt a slight tug at his heart as he watched the man's friend help him get up from the floor. Meanwhile, back in the operating room, the nurse kept her promise to Robert. She left the sheet folded across Charlie's bruised and battered shoulders.

Charlie could see the nurse watching her, but more importantly, she could feel what the caregiver was feeling. Not so long ago, Brenda, the nurse, had lost her husband of fourteen years. They had shared a good life together, and she missed him something fierce. Brenda knew first-hand the pain that anguished man was feeling, and made a silent wish he could be spared the awful agony he was going through.

Charlie had been given a magical gift. In the heavenly realm she was told her selflessness, love, and devotion to not only Robert, but also all those she had come in contact with, was deserving of life— hers; a life to be shared with the man she loved.

As the nurse started to walk away, she heard a gasping sound behind her, and turned.

CHARLIE WAS GAGGING; SHE COULDN'T GET enough air into her lungs. It felt like they were being crushed. At the last possible moment, the pressure eased, her lungs inflated, and she breathed deep gulps of stagnant air into her windpipe.

The nurse let out a scream which intensified as she watched Charlie's eyelashes slowly flutter open.

CHAPTER 97

FREDRICK WAS MAKING HIS WAY SLOWLY down the hall with Robert when they heard the nurse's screams. They stopped and looked in the direction of the outburst. Two doctors who were conferring in the next room stopped what they were doing and ran to investigate the commotion.

Robert pulled away from Fredrick and took off down the corridor faster than the speed of lightning. He pushed the two doctors out of his way and charged into the operating room. There he saw Charlie on the table looking up at the ceiling. He wished he knew what she was thinking at that precise moment, because he had never seen anyone look so serene. Oblivious to the chaos around her, Charlie was giving thanks for the blessing she had received.

Robert rushed to her side, looking down at her in disbelief. Fresh tears streamed down his face. He dared to utter her name for fear he was hallucinating.

"Charlie?"

Ever so slowly, she turned her head and gazed into the eyes she had grown to love. She offered a small smile to the man she knew she would now have a life with and whispered, "Hey, how are you doing? You okay?"

At the sound of her feeble voice, Robert collapsed and slid down on both knees by the side of the table. He lowered his head and wept uncontrollably. Finally he lifted his face to hers, trying to connect with her heart and soul. A smile curved on his perfectly formed mouth.

"Mrs. Fordes, when you get out of here I'm going to KILL YOU!" Charlie didn't think Robert realized the irony of what he'd just said. After miraculously coming back from the dead, her future husband was already threatening to kill her. She was the luckiest woman alive....

CHAPTER 98

"I CAN DO IT, HONEY!"

Robert had been trying to help Charlie out of the hospital bed. "I'm just trying to help, Love! My, my... are we a little cranky today?"

"How would you feel if you'd been sleeping in a hospital bed for a month? Do you know how uncomfortable these blasted mattresses are? Let me tell you something, Mr. Fordes, I am well enough to kick that shapely ass of yours, so watch it!"

Her eyes gleamed wickedly as laughter bubbled up inside her. Secretly, she loved all the attention and couldn't wait to get home and be showered with more. It had been a long agonizing month, and she still wasn't finished with her physical therapy, but at least she would be free!

Robert had slept on the chair next to her bed the entire time. He refused to leave her side. He only left his "post" for the funerals, (which sadly, she was unable to attend), and to check on things at the agency. All the guys from the office came to visit her, and she finally felt like one of them...one of the family.

CHAPTER 99

ONCE HOME, ALL CHARLIE WANTED TO DO was go and relax on the back patio and watch the crest of waves. She had been fairly silent during the ride home, and Robert seemed to understand her need for reflection, and gave her space. She needed to think and mull over everything that had happened. The bruises on her body, for the most part, had healed, but the nightmares continued as a relentless onslaught of nightly sweats and her thrashing out into the darkness. When they arrived at the house, Robert insisted on carrying Charlie over the threshold. Tilting her head back, she laughed as she teased, "Are you trying to tell me something, Mr. Fordes?"

He didn't answer her right away. But once inside, he gently placed her on her feet and embraced her lightly. Robert breathed in the smell of her fragrant shampoo and considered how lucky he was. Pulling back, he gazed long and hard into those eyes he had come to love, still amazed she had the power to hypnotize him with them. "Finally, he asked, "Do you think I'm trying to tell you anything, Charlie?"

Although fully aware of what he was doing, she merely shook her head from side to side and proclaimed, "No."

Robert bit down on his lower lip, trying to conceal the smile that threatened to spread across his entire face. There was no question, he was planning on asking Charlie to marry him, but he was waiting for the perfect time and a plan. Now definitely was not it, so he acted nonchalant as he turned to close the door, merely responding with an, "Okay."

Charlie changed into some sweatpants and a tee shirt. She grabbed a sweater, as summer was coming to a close and a cool breeze was drifting in from the shore. She informed Robert she was going to sit outside. Walking out the door, he yelled back to her, "That's fine, love, I have to finish bringing in the luggage, plus I have some calls to make. You just relax and take it easy."

Before heading outside, Charlie went to the kitchen she had grown to love and made two cups of hot chocolate with real cream-- none of the fake stuff for her. She was living it up big time now. She added a handful of mini marshmallows, stirring them into the thick, creamy cocoa.

Absentmindedly, she began to think. She had done a lot of that over the past month... think, that is, and she couldn't seem to stop. She covered Robert's mug with a small dish to keep it warm for him, and then took her cup out to the patio. As soon as she opened the door, the crisp air hit her hard, and her body shuddered. She sat on one of the chairs and stretched her legs out, all the while hypnotized by the waves that seemed to be speaking to her. She watched as whitecaps formed and clung to the tops of the jagged edges of the water, then marveled as they disappeared into foamy swirls. She let out a sigh and observed her breath make small circles that floated up endlessly and then just vanished. Fall had finally made its entrance. Charlie took a sip of her hot chocolate, savoring the comforting flavor. The taste brought back memories of her childhood--how she wished she could turn back the clock and be a child again with no worries or responsibilities. But most importantly, with a trip back to that time, her father would still be alive. The pain of his loss still cut deeply into her heart, and until today, she had been unable to discuss him or how his passing had affected her. Even after all these years, it still seemed like just yesterday that he was taken away from her.

She gently placed her cup on the glass table that sat next to her chair, closed her eyes, and concentrated on the sounds of the waves as they came in and rolled out. Her mind wandered back to one particular day when she was in the hospital. Robert had gone to the office to conduct some business, one of the few instances during her recovery when he had left her alone.

CHAPTER 100

FATIGUE HAD OVERCOME HER, AND JUST when she felt herself dozing off, a soft rapping sounded on her door. Forcing herself to stay awake, her voice croaked out, "Come in."

Antonio Bellesto hesitantly stuck his head in and softly asked, "Is this a good time, Charlie?"

Strange, he thought, how her real name sounded on his lips. He had known her as Maria and couldn't seem to get used to such a masculine name for such a feminine woman--not that she wasn't tough, though. He now knew she was tough as stones. Despite everything she went through, she didn't break. He knew men who had endured far less than her and were broken and damaged goods after the fact. But no, not this incredible woman. Charlie, yes, he now believed the name suited her to a tee.

He didn't give her time to answer as he continued his spiel and stepped inside. "If not, I can come back another time."

She was, for the moment, in shock. She didn't think he would come to visit her, but then her mind quickly reasoned, why wouldn't he? Especially after everything he endured with her, Robert, and Fredrick. What a strange alliance the 4 had created, she thought. The question that remained was, how long would this tentative partnership last? Adjusting herself up against the comfort of her pillows, Charlie tried to sound reassuring when she countered, "No, please, Antonio, come in."

He took two steps into the chilled room and closed the door behind him. Striding to the bed where she lay, Antonio said nothing as he took Charlie's hands in his and placed a light kiss on top of both of them. His eyes bore deeply into hers, making her shudder inwardly. She wondered what was going through his mind at that exact moment, but fear of his answer kept her silent. She detected something in his eyes she had never seen before. Antonio gently placed Charlie's hands back onto her lap. He didn't know if now was the right time to tell her all he had found out. He did know he needed to tell her while she was alone so that she could digest everything he had learned. It was vitally important that she know everything. He just hoped to God she was strong enough to handle it all.

As if on cue, she shifted on the hard mattress. Sensing her discomfort, Antonio cleared his throat as he pondered how to broach the troublesome topic. His instincts told him to go slowly. "Do you mind if I pull a chair up to the side of the bed, Charlie?"

"No, no, not at all, make yourself comfortable, Antonio."

He turned and walked to the other side of the bed, picked up a straight back chair that was there, and in one swift movement, lifted it up over his head and gently placed it down as close to the side of the bed as possible. Gazing into her tired eyes, he asked the question he supposed was appropriate for him to begin with.

"How are you feeling, Charlie?" She didn't answer right away, because she was preoccupied. She lowered her head, her eyes riveted to the spots where he had just kissed her hands. She was surprised she could still feel the warmth of his breath on her skin.

"Charlie, are you okay?" Concern flowed through him and he considered leaving. She looked exhausted and haggard, but who the bloody hell could blame her?

Snapping her head up, she replied, "I'm sorry, Antonio. My brain is still a little fuzzy."

Breaking eye contact with her was difficult. Even though her eyes were somber, they still had a sensuality that took his breath away. He glanced down at the wing tip shoes he wore and studied the intricate detail of carvings that intertwined in the fine leather. Finally lifting his gaze back to her, he said, "I fully understand, Charlie. There is no need for you to explain."

Giving a small smile, Charlie said, "To finally answer your question, I'm doing well, the wounds are healing, and I am getting stronger every day."

Antonio nodded, saying nothing. He understood she was giving him a pat answer. He needed to know the deeper truth, though. He needed confirmation she could handle what he had come here to tell her.

"Charlie, I am glad to hear that, but do you mind if I ask how you are really doing?" Noticing her stunned expression, he hurried on before she could reply. "I know the physical wounds are healing, and that's wonderful news. I guess what I am asking is... how are you emotionally?"

Charlie sat dumbfounded. No one had asked her that yet, including Robert. Frankly, she didn't know how to reply. She was never one to discuss her demons, and God knows she was plagued by many. At this time, she was trying not to dwell on everything that had happened to her. Stumbling over words, she answered evasively, "I... ah... guess I'm doing fine, Antonio. All things heal with time." Even as the words flowed from her mouth, she didn't believe a word of it, and hoped Antonio didn't pick up on her lack of conviction.

His eyes bore into hers. He wasn't buying a word she had just said. Time was of the essence, though, and he made the judgement call to tell her everything right now. Leaning forward, Antonio again grasped both of Charlie's hands in his. He saw questions cloud her still swollen features. Taking a deep breath, he plunged ahead and prayed for the best.

"Charlie, I need to talk to you about some pressing information."

The fatigue that plagued her only moments ago vanished, and her curiosity got the better of her. She had a strange feeling ever since he entered her room; he was not here for a social call. There was something troubling him, and he was having a hard time getting to the point. When Charlie spoke, her voice took on an authoritative manner, surprising not only herself, but Antonio, also.

"Okay, Antonio, I hate bullshit talk. You obviously came here to tell me something. I can handle whatever it is, so before you pass out on me, spit it out. Oh, and no pussyfooting around, I'm not as fragile as I look!"

Now he was the stunned one. Charlie was a loaded pistol, and he liked that about her. He regrouped, fixing the lapel on his handmade silk jacket. After a deep inhale, he exhaled out through his mouth, and plunged ahead, "I have some information I know you will be interested in hearing."

She said nothing, just nodded, letting him know he should continue and he had her full attention. "I found out some things, although much too late, I might add. It seems your ex-husband Darrell is involved in much more than just stalking you."

When Antonio's said Darrell's name, Charlie recoiled.

Instinctively, she pulled her hands away from the warmth of Antonio's and crossed them in front of her defensively. Though he hesitated, and she urged him to continue. "Go on, Antonio, it's all right."

"My people have found out your ex-husband is heavily involved in an intricate plot to overthrow The Vatican." There, he had said it. Judging from the expression on her face, Antonio knew a slew of questions would soon follow, and she didn't disappoint .

"What do you mean, 'The Vatican'? As in 'The Vatican' in Rome, Italy? What do you mean 'overthrow,' and who wants to destroy it? How does Darrell fit into all of this?

Antonio raised his hand to silence her and inhaled sharply. Once again his eyes were riveted to hers as he explained, "Charlie, my men searched Darrell's home and found folders containing cryptic information. We had them translated, and it seems the Jihad extremist group that you're ex-husband is a part of, wants to overthrow the Vatican and destroy the Catholic Church."

"Oh, my God," was all Charlie could muster She couldn't believe what she was hearing!

"Charlie, I'm so sorry to have to tell you this, but Darrell married you so he could make the connection with your uncle, the Archbishop. That contact was a vital part of the plan, because your uncle helps control The Vatican's finances. I would like to add, I personally know your uncle and am quite fond of him."

She was dumbfounded. Her brain was also trying to comprehend how Antonio knew her uncle.

Bellesto recognized he would need to explain that part of the equation as well. But for now, his priority was to give her an overview of what his investigation had uncovered. One thing at a time, he told himself.

Out of all the words she had just heard, the revelation that rang loudest in her ears was the disclosure that her ex-husband had used her to make a connection with her uncle. Charlie was more confused than ever, and it showed as she struggled to process all of the information. For the next two hours, Antonio explained everything in detail to Charlie as best he could, including his own high position within the walls of The Vatican, and how he and his men had failed to pick up on Darrell's charade.

By the time Antonio finished, Charlie was breathless, and her head ached terribly. She had a decision to make, and needed to discuss it with Robert as soon as possible. Time was of the essence. She had to hurry and get better so she could fight the devil once again. This time, though, the battle was against so much more than just her demented ex-husband. It was a fight to save the most powerful state and religion in the world. Who would have ever believed The Vatican had so much evil lurking within its walls?

He needed to pace so he could think better. Rising from the hard chair, Antonio walked to the foot of the bed and began his ritual of pacing and scrutinizing the cracks in the worn linoleum floor. He determined the floor needed to be replaced, or since that probably would not happen, at the least could use a good cleaning and waxing. As he pondered these two options, he thought he heard a woman's voice call his name, then realized it was Charlie speaking to him.

"Antonio... Antonio, are you listening to me?"

He turned and faced her. "Sorry, my dear, but when I get into a thought pattern I seem to leave this plane of existence."

"Okay," she replied, as she bit back a small smile.

"Now where was I—oh, yes, your ex-husband."

Charlie noticed a dramatic change in Antonio's appearance.

His voice was lower now, and strangely, more articulate; his accent was more pronounced, and his facial features reminded her of Sherlock Holmes. She couldn't explain why, but she was definitely intrigued by this man of many faces. She listened intently as he proceeded.

"It seems your marriage to Darrell was part of the plot, so to speak. You see, for Darrell and many of his men, your uncle was the conduit into the inner realms of The Vatican's money management."

He looked deeply into her eyes, studying her features. Although the story seemed so surreal and unbelievable, something deep inside told her it was indeed the truth, and soon, even more would be revealed to her.

"The Jihad has infiltrated the walls of The Vatican, Charlie. They have loaned The Vatican an astronomical amount of money. The Jihad group also has knowledge of... how shall I put this?... Delicate matters, that if made public, would rock the core of the largest religion and most powerful state in the world."

He stood at the end of the bed, no longer pacing, but rooted to where he now stood. They needed to act now. The big problem was, would Charlie be up to the challenge?

CHAPTER 101

WHEN CHARLIE WOKE FROM HER NAP, she stretched her tired and aching limbs. Her body shuddered, from not only the cool breeze, but from the overload of information Antonio had relayed to her. She knew she needed to fill Robert in as soon as possible, as Antonio had stressed that time was critical. Not wanting to move just yet, Charlie stared into the darkness, listening to the waves lap against the rocks. She didn't feel refreshed in the least, and desperately needed to go to bed. Just as she was about to get up, she heard the French doors open behind her. She turned and smiled as Robert gracefully strode towards her. The smile that started to form not more than a second ago froze and morphed into a frown of concern.

"Charlie, what's wrong?"

Letting out a dejected sigh, Charlie conceded, "Am I that transparent?"

Chuckling, Robert said, "Only to the trained eye, my love. Now what gives? Are you uncomfortable or, in pain?"

She didn't know where to begin, and when Robert tried to help her up, she refused and instead pulled his massive frame down onto the chair next to her outstretched legs. All thoughts of going to sleep vanished. "Robert, we need to talk, and the eeriness of the night suits the mood of the conversation we're about to have, so please, let's just stay here."

Robert was thoroughly bewildered. Never had he seen her like this; so cryptic. The chalkiness of her face was in stark contrast to the darkening sky. Her body was rigid, and he knew something was up, big time...

Charlie filled Robert in on her discussion with Antonio. Disbelief, shock, and pure horror rocked him to the very core. He said not one word as she spoke. Her tone was hushed like she was afraid Darrell was lurking somewhere listening, and said as much. Personally, he couldn't blame her one damned bit for being paranoid, and a part of him wished Darrell really was nearby, so he could capture and torture him...show no mercy.

Charlie and Robert were in agreement that they must not only find Darrell, but also must help Antonio to rid The Vatican of the evil within its walls. It was up to them to save the largest religious institution in the world from collapse.

CHAPTER 102

BREATHING HARD, HE PULLED HIMSELF UP out of the frigid waters. Anger surged through him as he walked, half ran to the safety of the car he had hidden two days prior. Once inside his vehicle, he blasted the heat full force. The black cape that earlier had billowed out in the harsh winds was now soaked, sticking to him like plaster.

He reached around and lifted the small duffle bag that lay on the floor behind the passenger seat. With trembling fingers he forced the zipper open and pulled out the clean clothes that were packed inside. He took no notice of the pools of water dripping on his new leather seat or pooling on the freshly installed carpet. He changed right there, jockeying with the steering wheel for space. He had no time to lose and wished his fumbling hands would move more quickly. He thanked Allah he had finally learned how to swim. One more minute in that treacherous water and he would have been a goner.

Once changed, he started the car and drove to the hideout where his luggage was stashed, along with money and his passport. His contact would drive him to Logan airport, where he would board a flight to Italy. He felt a keen sense of victory for finally killing his ex-wife. He didn't want to dwell on what was going to happen to him once he went before the board of the almighty seven. He knew the punishment coming to him would be brutal. But he was fine with that; the physical pain would be fleeting.

As he drove along the deserted roads, the evening's events replayed in his mind. At last, the cause was fully underway, and no one, and nothing, could stop the series of events from unfolding now. Once the secrets of The Vatican were exposed, his superiors would be ready to move in and take over the largest and richest institution in the world. A sneer formed at the corners of his still shivering mouth as he mulled over the fact that The Vatican had killed their own Pope. The secret books, unknown to all those in the inner sanctums of the Holy Palace, were now in the hands of his superiors. At first, he could not believe what he had seen in those tombs. But all of it was true, and then some. As he pulled onto the cobblestone road, his sneer was replaced by a wide smile. Finally, all unsuspecting Catholics would learn the farce of their belief system. Never had he imagined the Catholic Church held so much evil within its precious walls. Soon those walls would crumble, and the result would be all he and his superiors had planned for, a one-world religion... the religion of Islam.

ABOUT THE AUTHOR

Elaina Colasante graduated from Salve Regina University in 1986 with a Bachelor's degree in Investigative Reporting that specialized in writing and minored in Communications.

Elaina then graduated from Weiss Barron in Boston, Ma.

Elaina was a writer for At Home in Rhode Island Magazine and has completed her second novel with two more in the developmental stage.

Elaina was a Private Investigator for many years and a native Rhode Islander who now shares her time between the South and North.

Elaina is also a professional chef who created and developed an Organic Skin Care Line, Elaina Marie Beauty, which ships worldwide.

www.elainamariebeauty.com

evilwithin77@hotmail.com